THE POSTOFFICE

JOHN ELLSWORTH

PROLOGUE

Herat Province, Afghanistan

THE SMOKE WAS THICK IN THE AIR, AND THE SOUNDS OF SIRENS bleating overwhelmed his senses. Johann Van Giersbergen covered his ears but realized he couldn't keep his balance like that as he waded through the rubble—cement, metal, and glass everywhere—looking for survivors. After uncovering his ears, the sirens penetrated his body, the sound thrumming through his veins. He coughed into his elbow, his eyes and nose watering.

Johann had been drinking tea with the other nurses at the hospital when the drone attack came out of nowhere. There'd been no warning, no rumors beforehand like there usually were before something big like this happened.

All the nurses had scattered to the village, doctors, too, to locate the victims, help anywhere they could.

"Save my baby!" a woman wailed in Arabic. The woman in a full burqa knelt next to a tiny figure, gray with dust and half covered in debris.

Johann almost didn't hear the woman over the sounds of war. The sirens and people shouting, the deafening thunder of buildings in collapse. The wails and moans of those dying.

He quickly moved next to the woman who was rocking back and forth, her hands fluttering about as if she didn't know where to place them. Johann cleared a large slab of cement from the child's legs and then dusted away smaller pieces of wreckage. It was a young boy, no older than four, Johann guessed. He lifted the body gently and shouted for the woman to follow. His Arabic was excellent and the reason he'd been posted in Afghanistan with Doctors Without Borders.

The older woman struggled behind Johann, who was only 21, strong, healthy, and at the prime of his life. The posting to Afghanistan was the first job he took upon graduation from nursing school. He had meant to somehow payback for the education he had received. He led the woman back to the hospital, which luckily had gone unscathed in the attack. Men and women ran in and out of the building, some carrying an adult body between two or three of them.

Out of the worst smoke, Johann was able to get a better visual of the small child in his arms. He wasn't moving, no breath, and without having to take his pulse, Johann knew he was dead. The boy's dark lashes sat like dark half-moons on the cheeks, his small mouth in a slight frown. Johann couldn't tell the mother, couldn't be the one to bear such news, so he led her to the emergency room.

Inside, it was chaos. All the examination rooms were already full, so people sat and lay everywhere in the hallways and waiting room. Johann looked for his boss, an English doctor from Manchester, Dr. William Blake, and finally spotted him across the room.

Johann took the boy to him. With a barely discernible shake of his head, Johann handed the boy over to Blake. It was enough. Blake would understand. With the boy still in his arms, Blake told Johann, "Go. Find as many as you can and bring them back here. Quickly!"

Johann didn't hesitate but turned on his heel and weaved his way around bodies until he was at the emergency room doors. On their way in were two of Nangyalay's men with a young man, maybe twelve or thirteen years old, strung between them. One of the teenager's arms was missing, and he was bleeding profusely from the hole. Johann knew the boy would not make it. Johann bit his lip. By thirteen, Johann had already surfed most of the beaches along the California coast, had traveled to Europe on a family vacation, skied in the Rocky Mountains. This boy would have never known a life like that. But now, this Afghani boy would know no life at all.

Johann let them pass, but two other men from the Taliban followed right behind, another two Johann recognized as part of Nangyalay's command. They each carried young girls on their backs, holding the girl's arms around their own necks.

"Who made the strike?" Johann couldn't help but ask. All this pain, blood, and death! Who had created this?

The last man through the door smirked at Johann. "Who do you think?"

Johann pushed through the door and stopped to take in a few deep breaths. The air was just as bad outside as in. He stepped aside as two men with a makeshift stretcher carried an old man with a long gray beard. His leg was twisted unnaturally, but the man was still conscious, murmuring prayers with his hands clasped to his stomach.

Johann took a long look around at the horror of the drone strike. Then he bent to his work, the nurse doing what he could to save lives.

But he would remember it forever. He would never forget what he saw and heard that day. He would never forget the death that screamed down from the pale blue sky and the cries of the innocent.

He would never forget.

1

Celena Murfee's birthday was Valentine's Day, and the party for the fifteen-year-old started at four o'clock. This allowed time for the partygoers to get home after school, change clothes, and pick up their presents for their friend.

Celena was Thaddeus and Christine Murfee's second eldest daughter after Turquoise who, like Celena, was adopted and held a special place in her parents' eyes. She was five-six and tall for her age, blue-eyed with flouncy blond hair that insisted on coming down across her forehead in a sweep no matter how hard she tried to keep it up. On the day of her birthday, her hair was pulled back in a ponytail to allow for the showing of her newly-pierced ears, four holes on the left, one on the right. Celena, a student of the clarinet, wore a turquoise and coral Southwestern Indian flute player figurine, the Kokopelli, in her right ear.

Thaddeus gave his daughter a Westphalian dressage horse for her birthday; his wife Christine gave her the gift of horse boarding and care at La Jolla Equestrian Center in the Tassajara Valley of the East Bay. Celena had already all but moved into her gelding's stable, spending hours with a curry brush and happy voice, getting to know her mount.

It was just after four when Celena's friends—mostly classmates—began arriving in carpools. It was an all-girls shindig, a sleepover since it was Friday night and no school the next day. Thaddeus was certain he'd be awake most of the night, lending a male referee's voice to Christine's pleas for less Jonas Brothers and more quiet time when some of the crowd wanted to actually sleep. Even if it was only just Christine and Thaddeus who did!

The west-facing family room opened onto the beach so there was a round of surfing to be followed by Thaddeus's charbroiled burgers on the grill and Christine's angel food chocolate cake, Celena's favorite. Thaddeus was one cut above a "poor" surfer, said Celena, who had picked up the sport very quickly, as had her brothers and sisters: Sarai 13, Parkus 12, Chad 12, and Missy 10. The surfing would be followed by a quick burger, then off to the stables for a twilight ride along the main trail. Then would come videos and music and late-night pizza.

Turquoise arrived home at five to help keep the peace. She shared a two-bedroom apartment with a young investigator from the San Diego District Attorney's Office, a woman about her own age. Turquoise and Dana had been spending a lot of time together outside of work, socializing with other colleagues and going to the pub or movies. Thaddeus was happy that she had friends outside of the family and had finally started living a little outside of work.

But Turquoise had given up one of her night's off to lend a youthful voice of authority to the melee and let Mom and Dad catch a few hours' sleep if possible.

Following the trail ride and snack, everyone gathered around the fire pit while Sarai led a sing-along with her guitar. Parkus and

Chad pulled out drums and a bass guitar, and soon the place was rocking.

Just after ten, when the local custom was for the outdoor music to shut down, Thaddeus was emptying his coffee cup and preparing to go inside when he was approached by Rebecca Sundstrom, or Becca as she liked to be called, Celena's best friend. There had been a sorrow wrapped around her family ever since her older sister's leukemia had come roaring back from a period of remission. Becca's sister was now wasting away.

"Mr. Murfee," said Becca, "can I ask you a question?"

"Sure, Becca," he said, settling back into his patio chair, "what's up?"

"Rachel doesn't want to go on living."

"I'm so, so sorry to hear that. Bless her heart."

The girl shook her head. "Her pain is so bad—" Tears streamed down her cheeks, and she could barely speak. She drew a deep breath and continued, "The medicine quit working. It used to make her sleep and took away the pain. Now she says it doesn't help at all."

"How sad. If there's anything Chris and I can do…"

Becca stared at the floor, worrying her fingers together. "Maybe there is."

"What's that?"

"Rachel wants a doctor to help her end her life."

"Well, how old is Rachel?"

Becca looked up at him. "She's seventeen."

"What do your mom and dad say?"

"They say absolutely not. They say they'll find a doctor with stronger medicine. So, Rachel cries herself to sleep every night and wakes up and cries some more. In the daytime, it's even worse." Now Becca's body was shaking with sorrow and sobs.

Tears came to Thaddeus's own eyes as he fought to remain a good listener. "How can I help?"

"Maybe if you talked to my parents. They talk about you and Christine with admiration. They love that Celena and I are best friends. They were so glad when you moved to La Jolla and when Christine helped my dad's medical practice with its new forms. They might listen to you if it's both of you. Please help my sister leave this world and stop the pain."

The girl was drying her face now on her beach towel. She was wearing cutoffs and tennies and a Fender T-shirt. She looked cold. Thaddeus offered her a dry towel, but she waved it off. "Could you call them and talk? Celena says you can talk the birds out of the trees. Well, maybe you could talk my mom and dad into listening to Rachel. She's seventeen, but pain is killing her. That's what her doctor says."

"Are your parents religious?"

"Yes. Our religion doesn't believe in assisted life termination. That's the big problem for Rachel."

"Well, Becca, let me talk to Chris and see if we can get together with your folks. Do I have your permission to tell them you approached me and asked me to talk to them?"

"Yes, sir."

Thaddeus pulled out a chair and gestured for Becca to sit. "Can you tell me a little more about Rachel?"

Becca sat, but on the edge of the chair, and dropped her hands between her knees, squeezing her wrists together. "She's almost three years older than me. She'll be eighteen in a few months. She's taller than me and gotten real thin, but before she got sick, she played on the line in volleyball. She was a spiker big time."

"What kind of music does she like?"

"She plays the violin. All kinds of classical and some bluegrass, believe it or not. She was just getting into Nickel Creek when she got sick. She loves Sara Watkins of Nickel and she'd marry Chris Thile. Big fan."

"What classes does she like in school?"

"Did like. She's not going this year. Loved history and English. Hated chemistry but she was straight *As* in chemistry and trig. She loves to read romance and spy novels. Her big hero is Joseph somebody, *Heart of Darkness*."

"Joseph Conrad?"

Becca pointed at Thaddeus. "That's the one. She loves him. Also belongs to Oprah's Book Club. About the only thing that helps her anymore is reading and listening to music. It gets her mind off her pain for a minute or two so it's really good for her."

"What about her own religious beliefs?"

Becca twisted her mouth in thought before she said, "I would say Rachel is probably someone who doesn't believe in anything. I know she doesn't pray, and when I try to talk about God and stuff, she just rolls her eyes and plays like she's about to vomit. So, we don't go there anymore. Mom and Dad still have their church, and their pastor comes once a week and gives her communion, which she takes because Mom and Dad are watching. She doesn't want to hurt their feelings. Rachel is a very sensitive girl and hates seeing anything in pain. She belongs to the Sea Shepherd and PETA, and when we were little, we always had a stray dog or cat or two hanging around. In fact, she wants to be a marine biologist when she grows up. *If* she grows up."

Thaddeus didn't know what to say about a girl with very little hope in life so shifted to Celena's best friend. "What about you, Becca? How are you holding up under all this?"

Becca began crying again. The tears rolled heavy and fast down her cheeks, faster than she could swipe them away with the towel. "I just want my sister to stop hurting. I would do anything to help her, Mr. Murfee. Just sit with her once and watch her pass out from the morphine, listen to her cry. It's horrible, and I hate her cancer. I hate all cancer. I wish they'd find a cure instead of making more bombers and bullshit tax breaks for the top one percent."

"You sound like someone who keeps up."

"Nowadays, we get so much information from the internet, whether we want it or not. Like Tik Tok, Instagram, Snapchat, Twitter, news alerts constantly pinging our phones. It's always there, the world and everything that is going on."

Thaddeus didn't envy their generation. "What else should I know?"

Her head tilted to the side in confusion. "What do you mean?"

"Like is there anything else about this situation I should know about before I meet with your parents?"

Becca stood from the chair, her fists clenched at her sides. "I'm about to buy my sister some heroin and let her OD, that's what. If somebody else doesn't do something, then I will. She shouldn't have to keep hurting like this. I say let's cure her or let her go. It's not fair, and I hate my parents for not helping her."

Thaddeus understood the emotion radiating off the young woman but needed to keep things calm, keep her calm. "Please sit back down with me, Becca." Thaddeus patted her vacant seat, and when she sat again, he continued, "What would you like to see your parents do?"

"Give her enough drugs to allow her to go asleep peacefully and not wake up. She doesn't want to be alive anymore. Why does she have to be?"

He shook his head. "I'm sure I don't have that answer for you," said Thaddeus. "Tell you what, though, how about I call your parents and try to talk to them about what's on your mind? I'm sure it would be extremely difficult for them to let go."

"Wow, I can't believe you said it that way."

"What, let go? It sounds to me like you've made your case for letting go. Why complicate a terrible situation?"

"You could sort of be my lawyer with them?"

"Something like that. But you have to promise me one thing. You have to promise me you won't buy heroin and give it to Rachel. That's definitely not the way to handle this. Okay?"

Becca squirmed in her patio chair. "I don't know. How can I promise something when I don't know what might happen? If it just turns into a bunch of adults talking but doing nothing to help my sister, I want my options open. I don't think I can make that promise, Mr. Murfee. Does that mean you won't talk to them for me? For Rachel?"

Thaddeus smiled. He appreciated her honesty. "No, it doesn't mean that. I'm still going to talk to them. At least give me a chance to do what I can do first, okay?"

"Okay. But I reserve the right to help if I have to."

"All right. I know you have to do that, and I respect that. I respect your judgment and your right as Rachel's sister to step up and help if nothing else works. I understand."

"All right, then." She clapped her knees and stood. "I'm going inside for pizza. I heard the doorbell and those guys won't leave me any. Thanks, Mr. Murfee!"

"You're welcome. I'll call them right away."

"Bye!" She waved as she left. "And thank you!"

2

Thaddeus and Christine took Jim and Louisa Sundstrom to dinner the next night. They knew each other well since their daughters were best friends and they could always be located at one house or the other. After drink orders were taken and the waiter returned with two wines and two coffees, Thaddeus took up the question.

"Let me begin by saying we were crushed to hear Rachel's problems had returned."

"Yes," said Jim Sundstrom. "It's really got a foothold this time." Jim Sundstrom was a family doctor in downtown La Jolla with a subspecialty in gerontology. The Sundstroms and the Murfees had spoken before; Jim didn't pretend to be a cancer specialist or have any oncological insights into his daughter's case. She was being managed by a team of oncologists out of La Jolla and her treating physician was one of Jim's classmates from UCSD med school.

"So sorry to hear that," said Christine. Like Thaddeus, she was a lawyer but practiced separate and apart from him. Their theory was the too-many-cooks one. So far, it seemed to be working to keep their respective distances.

"I know," said Jim. "We've been everywhere, talked to everyone, tried every medication and treatment modality. If it's approved or even experimental, we've done it all."

"Now all we can do is pray," said Louisa. "We're strong believers."

"What about Rachel?" asked Thaddeus. "Is she a strong believer, too?"

"She blows hot and cold," said Jim. "Near as her mother and I can tell. She's young, that's all."

"Well, if there's ever anything we can do to help, please let us know," Christine said.

"I really wanted to talk to you tonight," Thaddeus said, "partly because we've missed you guys and partly because Becca spent the night at our house last night. She posed a particular question to me, and I wound up promising her I would come to you and ask you myself. She's very persuasive, that one."

"Bless her heart, seeing her sister like this is killing her," Louisa said. "I don't even know where to begin with her anymore."

"Well, your Becca is very mature for fifteen," Thaddeus said. "Frankly, I was impressed. So, here it is, without beating around the bush. Becca tells me that Rachel is suffering terribly and there's no hope for her—"

"Prayer, Thaddeus," Louisa broke in. "The Divine Healer."

"I understand that. But in the meantime, Becca sounded pretty despairing of her sister's condition. She says the pain is unbearable and she cries the entire time she's conscious. She says the drugs have stopped working. Please forgive me for barging in like this, but the lawyer inside me promised your daughter I would come before you on her behalf and ask whether there'd been any thought given to allowing Rachel to terminate her own life? To ask for physician-assisted ending of her life? Is that something that's discussed or being considered?"

"Thaddeus," Louisa said, a deep frown on her face, "you've really crossed the line this time. This is a very private family matter, and I'm not comfortable discussing it with you. Can we change the subject, please? I hear there's a new horse in Celena's barn."

"Forgive me," Thaddeus said, "but I promised Becca I would act as her attorney and try to help her understand if there was any discussion of just letting Rachel go?"

"Thaddeus," said Jim, "our religion doesn't believe in physician-assisted suicide. We consider it a sin. A dreadful sin. And that's our answer and that's Becca's answer. We've been over it and over it with Becca. We've discussed it with Rachel, too. She asked, and it was the hardest thing I've had to do in my life to tell her we don't do that in our family, that our beliefs don't allow it."

Thaddeus cleared his throat. He shot a look at Christine.

Christine said, "What if your beliefs aren't Rachel's beliefs? Should she be consulted and listened to?"

"She's only seventeen. That isn't old enough to decide," said Jim. "You're both lawyers. I don't have to remind you she's still a minor."

"I know that," said Christine, "but it seems it isn't a legal question requiring someone to be an adult as much as it's an ethical question, a question that people of any age should be allowed to answer."

"We disagree," said Louisa. "She's too young to decide. Now, please, let's talk about something else. I'm getting very uncomfortable sitting here and discussing such private business."

"I appreciate that," said Thaddeus, "but I also know I feel an obligation to my client, Becca, to come back to her with an answer. Will it ever reach a point where you can let Rachel go, so she doesn't have to suffer anymore? Is that even a possibility?"

"Not a possibility, Thaddeus," said Jim. "That's a position that our God takes, and we cannot disagree. Her life cannot be taken from her by men."

"All right then, thank you," Thaddeus said. "With your kind permission, I'll report back to Becca that the matter is closed."

"Report away," said Jim. He dropped his empty coffee mug heavily onto the table.

"I hate the sound of that," said Louisa. "I cannot imagine in my wildest dreams one of our best friends stepping up to act as our daughter's lawyer against us."

Thaddeus shook his head. "I would say I'm acting more in the support of the family than I'm acting against you. I'm your friend and supporter. Always will be. I also know where I'm not wanted insofar as discussing a matter, and I respect that. I won't ask again. Please forgive me for crossing any lines."

"And me, too," Christine added. "We aren't those people."

Louisa reached and took Christine's hand. "We know you're not, sweetheart. We just know our little girl got to talking and lured you in. Becca's quite good at that."

"I wouldn't say lured us in, not at all," said Thaddeus. "I'd say she acted as a mature and responsible member of your family, and you should be proud of her for reaching out for help."

"Agree," said Jim, "but let's move on. Tell us about the Lakers game at the Staples Center you went to. Was it amazing?"

"It *was* amazing," said Thaddeus.

"Excellent. Next time, we're going. Sorry we had to miss out this time."

"No worries. We'll go again."

3

Johann Van Giersbergen arrived at the post office on Grayling Drive at 8:13 a.m. He pushed through the glass doors and made his way inside. The clerks were ahead and to the left through double doors, while directly in front of him was a long, wide table with pigeon slots holding mailing labels and envelopes of all sizes, as well as a dozen ballpoints secured by chains at the corners. When he pushed through the interior doors, his heart fell. There were already ten in line for the clerks. The line of patrons started at the far end of the table, wound back around the near end, and bodied up to Johann. He took a service ticket. It said he was number eleven. He inhaled a deep breath, holding the manila mailing envelope against his chest. He was in a hurry, yes, but he might as well not have been. It was time to dawdle.

Dawdle. It sounded like something a duck might do. Or maybe something a high school student would do in his trig class, behind a curled hand, with a ballpoint pen. "Let's play hooky and go dawdle in the pond," he whispered to himself, last in line where no one would see his mouth move soundlessly. Except for maybe the postal employees facing his direction. But they were all under-water with so many impatient patrons stamping and steaming at the molasses bureaucracy they had voted into office yet again. *Now how did that happen?* wondered Johann. He was twenty-two but had never voted in a presidential election. Next time he would vote non-molasses, he told himself. Which was the moment when —just then—the line moved ahead three people, placing him perpendicular to a corkboard and its 9 x 12 notices.

His gaze roamed to the row of faces on the FBI'S TEN MOST WANTED. The wanted poster was behind glass and under lock and key. Number One looked insane. No problem with him getting put behind bars. Number Two looked like a prostitute with a swastika tattoo on her forehead. Number Three was a bank robber who looked like he might have played piano in a church at one time. Number Four was... Johann looked closer. Number Four was—was—him!

He strained to see clearly. The picture wasn't fuzzy or faded. The photograph could've been made as recently as that morning, in fact, and it looked like no one but him, complete with the mole at the corner of his mouth. He sucked in his breath and shrugged his head down between his shoulders as far as it would go, a reflexive effort to hide himself away from the three people behind him who, thank God, hadn't yet drawn abreast of the bulletin board and caught a glimpse of him, too.

Thoughts tumbled through his mind. He couldn't breathe. He gasped hard, but his lungs wouldn't fill, and he felt paralyzed from the waist up. His mouth was fixed in a crazy smile expressed out of trauma and horror. Worse, his brain was racing and his thoughts receding, carrying away information that he desperately needed.

Needed or not, he was unable to access his mind. He felt the artery threatening to explode in his neck while his pulse galloped and called all blood home to his core. His hand left a sweaty palm print against his manila envelope when he turned, dropped his eyes to the floor, and passed back along the line of people waiting behind him, fleeing the post office and its rogues' gallery.

He stepped into the cool morning air of San Diego and came to a complete stop. One thought had come full-circle: he had no idea what crime the wanted poster said he had committed. His first impulse was to dive back inside, reclaim his place in line, and study the poster close-up. But he came back to his senses. Going back inside was an arrest waiting to happen should any of the citizens in line match the poster and his face. So, a trip back inside was definitely out.

Down the sidewalk he went, stepping off the curb at Gerry's new Yukon XL. He had tossed him the keys that morning and told him to make a special trip to the USPS to mail the manila envelope Johann still carried. Turning, he ducked his face and retraced back to the curbside slots and dropped his envelope into the red-white-and-blue receptacle. Then he turned and hurried back to the SUV. He climbed up and inside and punched the starter button. The V8 jumped to life, and the rear camera flashed on the second he dropped it into reverse. Two cars coming, slowing and searching for parking—nothing to do but wait.

Sweat had formed on his upper lip and brow. He ran his tongue along his lip and removed his right hand from the wheel momentarily to wipe his brow. Good God, this can't be happening. The man on the poster even had the same exact mole at the side of his mouth. It was him. It had to be him. He had to get to a computer and hit the FBI homepage.

Traffic cleared, and he was able to take his foot off the brake and let the SUV back up. He was inching away from the tight confines of his parking spot when a car suddenly came roaring out of nowhere—off to the right side—and clipped him in the right rear quarter panel. His Apple watch immediately asked if he had taken a fall. His first impulse was to leap from the car and tear some dumb driver a new asshole. Johann had a mouth and quick temper, and this was one of those moments made for his anger.

As he was about to leap out—opening the door to let himself slide to the ground—he realized there would be a cop here before it was all over. Someone with a badge was going to get a good look at him and probably match him up with the face plastered on the wall inside the post office. Hadn't he heard somewhere that all cops study the pictures of the Ten Most Wanted every day before they go out into the world? Hadn't he heard that on TV?

But Johann was sharper than your average criminal. He stepped around the Yukon, back around to the hapless woman driving the Ford that had just hit him. "Hey," he cried at the woman, "are you okay?"

The startled woman's mouth fell open. Then, "I should be asking you that. I hit you! I don't know what to say."

"Wait here," commanded Johann. "I saw a cop inside. Let me go grab him so we can answer some questions and be on our way. Is that okay?"

"I'll pull up and park at the end," said the Ford driver. "You can't miss me. I'm the one with the crumpled front end her husband is going to leave her over. It's my third accident this month."

"Don't move then. I'll be right back with a cop."

As the woman nodded then pulled ahead, moving down toward the end of the parking zone, Johann, instead of returning back inside, climbed up into the Yukon's driver's seat and restarted the engine. He continued backing into the slot behind and then immediately shot forward, making a right turn in the parking lot and heading for the entrance where the Ford driver had come from. He made it to the entrance despite being waved at and shouted at for going against traffic. He waited there while a car in the street was trying to turn in. He surrendered to the inevitable, backing away, but flipped the driver off before he made his escape and made a left turn onto the road.

He headed for Rady Children's Hospital. For the last two weeks, Johann had been working for Gerald M. Isherwood, M.D.—the city's top diagnostician and treating pediatric psychiatrist. Johann was one of many nurses who provided nursing care at the Chadwick Center of the hospital. He had, at Dr. Isherwood's suggestion, even undergone psychoanalysis as part of his training and had come away with a gold star for mental health.

His shifts now were dedicated to children of abuse, the kids who had been thrown against walls, burnt with cigarettes, and sexually used, photographed, and discarded. The toughest of all were the head-bangers, the three, four, and five-year-olds who threw themselves against the walls of the unit and slammed their heads against hard surfaces until they acquired their sweet comatose. In the short time he'd been at the hospital, they'd become his kids, each of them, and he knew they would be his life's work. The kids had his heart, his mind, and his soul. While he gave them their medicine, helped them bathe, held their hand while they cried, Johann vowed to protect them.

Johann studied his rearview. Good, it was clear. No one following. He felt himself gasping for air and realized he was all but anoxic with panic and fear. He shut his mouth, forcing himself to breathe only through his nose and slow down his oxygen exchange.

He made a left and headed up three blocks to the stoplight on Sandrock and Aero Drive. At the light, he covered the side of his face with his hand, pretending to be adjusting his sunglasses but actually shielding his face from the older man in the passenger's seat of the car beside him. So far, he hadn't looked his way even once, but that didn't matter.

He realized, with a drop of his stomach, that he couldn't be too careful now. Then another thought formed—he needed to get home to his laptop to try to figure this out. When the light changed, he gunned it, raced ahead of the car on his left, moved into the left-turn lane and spun a U-turn at the next intersection. Then he was heading eastbound, back toward his apartment complex. It came up on his right a mile later, and he was soothed to see the familiar sign Sunnyside Meadows, where he turned in and raced ahead for his parking spot beneath the carport.

He leaped from the Yukon and jogged toward his apartment. As he went along the walk, thoughts sailed through his head at lightspeed.

At the top of the first flight of stairs, he had just turned to his right to work his way three doors down to the safety of his own apartment when he came face-to-face with two clean-shaven, short-haired Caucasian men wearing dark suits, sunglasses, and carrying a walkie-talkie. He dropped his head and hurried past them, down to the end, where he made another right turn, this time out of their line of sight.

He was scared to death when he climbed back inside Gerry's Yukon and slammed the door shut. The motor caught instantly. He pulled the shift into reverse. He was stunned and panting for air, and he was gone before the men in the suits came looking. The suits had been about to knock.

On his door.

4

Johann had never been treated for mental illness. Never had a bout of forgetfulness, hadn't been in some kind of accident with amnesia or a head injury, none of the stuff you see in movies and read in books. There was no family history of mental illness, and he didn't take drugs. No blackouts from alcohol, no multiple personality scares. No, he was perfectly normal, Johann was, and he was scared to death.

The Yukon knew the way to Rady's. Johann, upon arrival, remembered none of the drive. But he did remember studying the rearview mirror block after block while holding his breath and praying the men in suits hadn't pulled their black car in behind him and followed. It turned out they hadn't.

He parked in the employees' lot and tried to act like everything was okay and it was just another day at work as he sauntered inside. He badged the first level of security, the bag checkers, and then went on down the hall to the locked door and entered the passcode. The door buzzed with a sharp eruption, and Johann passed inside and onto the ward.

Johann found Gerry inside his office, making toast in the Toast-R-Oven his wife had given him at Christmas. It was a half-joking gift, but the other half, the serious half, was for Gerry's low blood sugar. He snacked all day. Before it was ready for eating, his toast would be layered with cheese to deliver some high protein into his system. All part of the deal, Gerry said. "Hypoglycemics like me gotta eat," he proudly told Johann as he entered to find him taking his first bite out of a toast and cheese. "Did you mail my package?"

"I did." Johann shot a look back into the hallway. "Has anyone come around looking for me?"

Gerry was a long, thin man who dressed in jeans and turtlenecks every day. He was bearded and wore frameless eyeglasses beneath a close-cropped head of black hair. He shook his head at the question. "No one came looking for you. Did you shoot someone at the P.O.?"

"Funny man. No, nothing like that. At least I don't think so."

"Ha ha. Your life is pretty sheltered, dear Johann. Had you shot a member of our community, you would've noticed." He was joking with him, of course.

On the personal side, Johann lived to play lead guitar in a band, loved beach volleyball, and was dating a gal named Sally who dealt Blackjack at the Namatukee Casino. Sally was a fun-lover who never missed Johan's closing performance with his band at the casino on Friday and Saturday nights. She was reliable, always in the front row, dancing by herself and stomping in the pit while Johann lit up the air with his Steve Vai and Joe Satriani licks. He was all of that and more, according to Sally and according to his growing fanbase. But now he was wanted by the FBI and, he realized with a shudder, running from the law.

"Gerry, can I ask you something?"

Gerry smacked his lips. "Ask away. As long as it isn't to ask when you're getting out of here to go home. That's the one I hear the most and hate the most."

"Actually, it is about getting out of here."

"Oh, Lord."

"No, getting out of here without getting arrested. I saw my picture on a wanted poster at the post office."

"That's preposterous. Get your vision checked. Next case."

"Seriously, it was me. Down to the little mole beside my mouth. I'm not fooling around here, Gerry. I'm scared to death."

Gerry had been lounging in his chair behind his desk, but now sat up and wheeled the chair forward. "No, I can see you're not kidding. Let's see. Why don't we check my computer and see what we can find out? You got time right now?"

"I do. Where else am I going to go?"

After a few clicks, Gerry said, "Here we go. Let's start with the FBI home page."

Johann watched while the browser loaded the page. When it appeared, all the faces were identical to what Johann had seen at the post office. And there he was—Johann. There was no doubt.

Gerry's face went pale. He shuddered. "It says you work in mental health in Los Angeles. But we're in San Diego. What the hell? Do you have a second job, fellow?"

"No, I don't. When would I? We're doing tens and twelves every shift right here."

"It says you were born in Amsterdam, moved to the US when you were five, private school in La Jolla, and then University of

Wisconsin in Madison where you received a BSN. How we doing so far?"

"Perfect. They know everything about me. What am I wanted for?"

"You're been charged with participation in the bombing in Mexico where eighty-two people were killed, eleven of them FBI agents."

"Holy shit! I was there with my dad, but I didn't do anything! My dad died there!"

"This can't really be happening," said the psychiatrist. He was remaining somewhat calm, Johann saw. Probably his training at keeping cool in the face of threats. "I-I—I'm just not following. Tell you what, Johann. Why don't we call security and get ourselves calmed down here? You're about to explode, and I'm frightened. I need this sorted by smarter people than the two of us."

"You're calling security on me? I haven't done anything, Gerry!"

He sat forward in his chair and ran his palm over his cropped hairline. "We can't make decisions without more clarity here. I'm dialing now. You can stay and walk through this with me, or you can leave the premises, Johann. I'll give you a ten-minute head start, though I don't know why I should. I guess so you won't tarry and hurt anyone. I'm not sure what I'm thinking. I'm losing it here. Protocol, doctor, think! I have to call security. Your head start begins right—now!"

Johann didn't hesitate. He leaped from his chair and ran outside the office into the hallway, heading directly for the exit at the far end of the hall. There was no procedure for exiting the ward other than logging out, so he burst through the exit and ran for the hospital elevators. He was on the second floor; the elevator was on the seventh and stalled. He ran for the stairs and headed down as fast as his feet could move.

Outside he flew, his ears on the alert for the wail of sirens. Nothing heard, he ran for his own car parked in the second row in the hospital employees' parking lot. His smart key was sensed by the small BMW, and the doors unlocked. He dropped into the driver's seat and screeched out of the parking spot and headed for the exit. His ID card raised the security arm, and then Johann squealed the old BMW up a row and then left onto the freeway frontage road.

5

W as that really his picture? Why would he be wanted?

He had spent too much time wondering last night, holed up in a cheap motel off 395 in a small town called Randsburg. Was he himself going crazy?

Yesterday, when Johann had dashed away from the hospital, he had taken US-395 North. I-5 was definitely faster and the stops more reliable, but he couldn't chance that. South was Mexico, and he didn't want to cross any borders. The entire world would know where he was if he did that. 395 it was then.

He was now again driving north on 395 but still pulled up the FBI website on his phone. Yes. Definitely his picture. He kept looking at the picture, couldn't help himself, but he didn't know why. But what *did* he know? He was a nurse. He wasn't Gerry who could analyze and break down a person's actions. He was there to care for the patients. Why would the feds want a man who dedicated his life to helping others?

Cops were crazy. FBI agents were worse. You couldn't trust cops or agents. His dad taught him that. No matter if you reason with them and were telling the truth, they'd cuff you and haul you off.

He had only been driving for an hour and a half but really had to use the bathroom. The coffee from that morning had run its course.

He put his blinker on and merged right. *Rest stop in 10 miles* read the road sign. Free coffee, too? Better not chance any more caffeine. This trip was going to be long enough.

He had spent three months at a summer camp up in Oregon when he was little. Both of his parents were too busy to take time off during the summer when he was off school, so summer camps it was. For the most part, he'd been okay with that. At least there were other kids to play with, unlike during the school term. Then it was just him and whatever nanny his parents had hired. As soon as he was old enough to stay on his own, he went surfing after school, every day no matter the weather. That's where he'd met his real friends.

This particular camp was practically on the water and had a decent amount of surfing possibilities. Oregon beaches weren't California beaches by any means. But the surf was all right, as long as you had a wetsuit on. So, Johann was headed to that same area.

"Exit the highway for your destination," his phone's navigation told him.

"Finally," Johann said to no one.

The moment he turned his steering wheel to merge, he heard a loud horn blaring at him.

"Shit!" he yelled. Where the hell did that semi come from? It was a close call. He must have been daydreaming about that camp for too long. He pulled into the car side of the rest stop, and the semi-truck pulled into the haulers' side.

As he walked to the men's restroom so did the truck driver. The driver was an overweight, burly man about 6'3" with a bushy black beard and a bright red trucker hat with an American flag. They made eye contact.

"Hey kid, you betta' watch yourself. I was in that lane for five minutes before your stupid ass tried to exit." His teeth were spotty, and a bright gold canine stood out from the rest when he talked. He spit his chew on the sidewalk. "You ain't in charge of the road here. We are." His voice was deep but had a southern pull to it. You never knew what area truckers were from; they could be from anywhere. He shouldered past Johann, an average-sized twenty-two-year-old and knocked him toward the cement wall of the building.

"Ow!" Johann gasped. The trucker man didn't bother looking back as he went into the men's room.

Johann didn't want to be in the same bathroom as the asshole, regardless of how bad he had to go, so he decided to stand in line to get some free coffee. If he was lucky, the volunteers might have cookies, too. The woman in front of him was gabbing away with the older man behind the glass and finally stirred her sugar into her coffee and left. The old man had a dark blue hat on with a gold insignia, indicating his time in the war. He was a Vietnam veteran according to his hat.

"Hi, sir. Coffee please," Johann said briefly.

"Just one moment, son. Would you like cream and sugar?"

"A splash of cream, please."

The veteran pulled down the lever of the coffee pot to fill the

Styrofoam cup. He attempted to pull back the lid of the little miniature white cup of cream but couldn't get it open. His hands were shaking as he was pulling the lid, so Johann offered to help.

"Let me get that for you, sir." Johann reached for the little white cup.

"Oh, thank you. Those buggers get me every time. What's your name, son?"

"Joh—er..." He didn't exactly want to give out his name or have anyone else overhear. He cleared his throat. "Joe, sir."

"Well, thank you, Joe. Where ya heading?" the man asked in his shaky voice.

"I'm not quite sure yet myself. North, for now." Johann really needed to head to the bathroom.

When he turned to look, the trucker was just exiting the bathroom, readjusting his belt as he went.

"I'll be right back," Johann said to the man and darted toward the restroom.

Inside was the typical rest stop bathroom. Stained tiles on the floors and walls, clouded mirrors that no one could actually see themselves in.

He chose the first urinal and relieved himself.

Washing hands didn't really happen in these types of places. Johann made a metal note to use the hospital grade hand sanitizer he had thrown into his duffel bag this morning. He had been in such a frenzy that he himself wasn't quite sure what he had bought at the first Walmart he came to. He knew he had grabbed some changes of clothes, some toiletries, but the rest was a guess.

He should take a moment to account for what was there, but there was no time. No time!

Back outside, he returned to the metal counter where the old man was now helping another traveler. Johann grabbed his coffee that was waiting for him and took a second to look at the side-of-the-road directory. A green and white map showed him *You are here.* A red star marked where the rest stop was along the highway. To the right was a cork board with notices held up with push pins.

There he was. Bright as day.

Wanted: Johann Van Giersbergen

A phone number was listed below his picture.

"Shit!" He backed away, threw his coffee in the nearest trash, and half walked, half jogged back to his old BMW.

There were just too many posters to keep running.

Too damn many.

6

Monday after school, Becca arrived unexpectedly at Thaddeus's office. Would he see her? asked his secretary.

"Send her on in. She's a special client, Marie. We'll always see her and take her calls."

Becca came into the office, a bookbag suspended from one shoulder and sunglasses atop her head. She looked to be in disarray, her hair wild and she was breathing hard as though she'd been running.

"Mr. Murfee, my parents said you talked to them. They were ma-aaad."

"Doesn't surprise me, Becca. They were kind of caught in the headlights when I brought it up about Rachel. How is she, by the way?"

"Worse. I hate to leave her to go to school. I don't feel like it's fair, me getting to go off to school and have a normal life while my sister's trapped in her bed, dying every day. It's horrible. I feel trapped, too."

"Your parents were very clear about your question, Becca. They don't believe in helping your sister die before her time. They are very firm in their conviction."

Becca frowned. "But what about what Rachel wants? She, like, totally disagrees with them. She has her own beliefs."

"I know, I know. It's a shame your parents and your sister are so far apart on this. But there's really nothing I or Christine can do. Your parents have the say-so about Rachel, not you. I guess that's what it means to be a minor, for better or worse."

"Mr. Murfee, would you please come talk to my sister?"

"When?"

"Now. No one's at home but the nurse. My mom ran down to San Diego and my dad's doing rounds at the hospital. This is the perfect time."

"I don't know. Not without your parents' okay, I probably shouldn't."

"Rachel asked me to bring you to see her. It's her asking, not me."

Thaddeus studied his visitor's face. She was so young and so desperate, he was overcome with a need to reach out and help. A need to get outside his own comfort zone and risk a visit.

"All right. Do you have a bike outside?"

"No, I ran here after school."

"Let's go down to the garage. We'll take my car."

They drove down Seashore Drive and up Third Street and down

several blocks, then south. Finally, they came to a 1950-ish ranch with a modern addition on one side. No vehicles in the driveway but one.

"That's June's car. She's the day nurse."

"Let me just whip in here and we'll go right in."

Inside they went, Becca leading. Thaddeus stepped into the foyer and through to the living room/kitchen, which Thaddeus was familiar with, then farther back into the family room. Off of that was a den where they had set up a hospital bed and IV poles for Rachel. She was lying on her side, eyes closed, a grimace on her face.

"Hey, sister," said Becca. "Look who I brought to see you."

The patient opened her eyes. She wiped her mouth and made an effort to smile. "Hello, Mr. Murfee. I haven't seen you in a while."

"Chris and I haven't been over in a while, Rachel. How are you feeling?"

"Feeling like I want to die. I hurt, Mr. Murfee. I need help. I just want to leave this body behind and fly away. They can't offer any new treatment. The bone marrow transplant worked for a year, but now I'm sick again. This time was like a double whammy. It came roaring back, but I'm dying a slow, terrible death. Why won't they let me call a doctor who can help me die? Why, Mr. Murfee?"

Thaddeus sat in the bedside chair. The nurse, named June Cavanaugh, came in and straightened Rachel's pillows and helped her into a half-sitting position.

Rachel grimaced and cried out as she came upright in the bed. "It's in my spine," she said weakly. They want to do surgery to fuse some vertebrae or something. I won't let them. They've already done that twice. No more surgeries, thank you very much."

"All right, sweetheart," said Thaddeus. "Let me tell you about my talk with Mom and Dad. First, they totally love you and want only the best for you. Second—"

"Wait! If they want the best for me, why don't they listen to me? It hurts so much I just want to die. I'm crying all day and night until the exhaustion takes me under for a half hour. Morphine doesn't even touch it. If I breathe in too deep, it hurts. If I go to turn over, it hurts. God forbid if I cough or have to sneeze. I want to die!" Rachel was agitated, her hands flinging around, and Thaddeus could tell just the small motion was draining her. She pleaded with her eyes. "Please take my case, Mr. Murfee, and find a judge to tell them they have to let me go! Please help me!"

Thaddeus had to look away. He wasn't even able to maintain eye contact it hurt him so much. He took off his glasses and wiped the lenses on the hem of his shirt. He didn't want her to see him crying so he turned away in the chair and nodded, then continued nodding. "I know," he muttered, "I know, I know, I know."

"Please! For God's sake!"

He turned back around, unable to fight it off any longer. There was a more important principle here than his relationship with Jim and Louisa. There was a human need that had to be addressed. He couldn't just stay turned away.

"This goes against my friendship with your parents," he said slowly. "I'll lose their friendship if I do this. But I'm going to take your case in front of a judge and see if the court can help. How's that sound?"

She was crying now. "Oh, God, Mr. Murfee, thank you so much!

Thank you thank you thank you!" exclaimed Rachel through her flow of tears. "This means so much to me, you'll never know."

"I'm going to file a dependency petition seeking temporary guardianship of Rachel and see if I can get the court to specifically give that person the authority to hire an end-of-life doctor. I can't promise anything, but I'll try. Now I'm going to have my secretary call and get some names and numbers of treating doctors so I can get some subpoenas served on them. Are we good?"

The young woman was still crying. "Oh, it even hurts to cry!"

Becca put her hand on his shoulder. "Thank you, Mr. Murfee. Thank you from the bottom of my heart."

"All right. I'll duck out now, but I'll have Marie call right back. Nurse June, can you get the phone to Rachel?"

"Sure. She has her own cell phone right on the table."

"Let's get that number, and I'll get going."

After Becca typed Rachel's number into Thaddeus's cell phone, he was set to leave.

He drove slowly back to the office, alone with his thoughts. What had he done? What had he agreed to? But how could he be expected to just stand by and do nothing? She was obviously receiving no help from her parents, and the pain was unbearable. Maybe someone else could've resisted, but not Thaddeus. He regretted already going against her parents' wishes, but there wasn't a good alternative. It had to be done.

He went into his office and summoned Marie. "Here's Rachel Sundstrom's phone number. I'm going to help her die."

Marie looked up from her computer. "What?"

"She's slowly dying, and she's only seventeen. There's no medical hope left. We're going to take her to court and see if end-of-life arrangements can be made. Please call her and get her particulars and her treating physician's information. We'll need a dependency petition based on the parents refusing to provide necessary medical care. That's going to go over with everyone like a lead balloon. And we're going to need to subpoena her doctor. Set the hearing ASAP. Call the court for the earliest date possible. The child's in unremitting pain, and time is of the essence."

Marie scribbled furiously on her legal pad. "All right, what else?"

"Call her parents. Make them an appointment first thing tomorrow morning. We need to talk about what comes next."

7

J im and Louisa Sundstrom refused to have a seat in Thaddeus's waiting room. His receptionist crept into his office as he was finishing up with another call on another case. She whispered, "It's the Sundstroms. They won't sit down in our waiting room."

Thaddeus checked his watch. "They're thirty minutes early."

"I know. You have a call with the District Attorney on Malaren's case."

"I'll do that call, and then we'll take them early."

"What do I do with them until then?"

"Offer them a drink, put your headset back on, and ignore them."

He placed a call to the DA ten minutes later. They talked about a plea deal and trial preparation for another ten minutes, then hung up. He buzzed his receptionist. "Marie, send in the Sundstroms."

"Yessir." There was relief in her voice.

Seconds later, the door opened and in marched a steaming Jim and Louisa Sundstrom, all but purple in the face with rage.

"Hey," said Thaddeus, rising from his chair. "Jim and Louisa, thanks for coming."

"Thaddeus, how dare you—"

"Hold on, Jim. I have a little speech prepared. Please let me make my speech, and then I'll listen to you for the rest of the afternoon if you want. Here goes. When I first began practicing law, an older, very wise attorney asked me what I would do on such and such a case. He told me what the case was about and what the police said and what the judge said. He then asked me what I'd do. I said I'd do so and so. He told me I was wrong, and the first thing you must always do is consult the client. Ask the client what they want. It might not be the best thing the law will do for them, but they don't always want the best thing or the most money or the best deal. Sometimes they want much less to make them happy. And what they want is what you have to want, too. That's how you practice law."

"Very homespun, Murfee," said Jim. "Now, what the hell is this about taking our daughter's case? What case does she even have?"

"Your daughter wants out. She wants to die. Your religion forbids that. Big disagreement between parents and child. A judge needs to settle this because I can't, and you won't. All I'm doing is going to let a judge listen to her, listen to her doctor, and listen to the two of you. Then the judge will decide what's best for your daughter. It might not be what you want, it might not be what she wants, but at least the law provides a mechanism for getting everybody heard by a disinterested third party. As for me, I have no opinion which way it should go or what should happen. I'm not a judge and don't have that wisdom. All I have is a bookcase full of books and my law license that says I can represent someone. What would I expect you to do? I would expect you to get a lawyer and have them present your side of the case. That's the best thing for you."

Even though the Sundstroms wouldn't take a seat, Thaddeus did, if only to show them he was not a threat. "Or, if you want to avoid all of this, I would really like to have you and Rachel meet with an end-of-life doctor and talk about possibilities and reasons. That's all. But I don't think you'll do that because of your religion. I think you'll fight it, and I'm ready for that. I'm ready for a fight. You have been warned. Now, please. Do the right thing and let's find a doctor to call in and discuss how to end Rachel's life and help end her suffering. The call is yours to make."

Louisa was silent, just staring out into space. Jim was shuffling his feet. His jaw tightened and loosened several times, just like in the movies. Louisa's hands clenched and unclenched. She cleared her throat several times, obviously wanting to be heard, but full of the realization she had nothing new to say except a broken record. It was her church, actually, and her religion that forbade end-of-life solutions.

Finally, Jim managed to speak. "Thaddeus, I've known you for a long time now. You've been to our house, enjoyed our company, and we've enjoyed you and Christine. But this is way above your pay grade as a family friend what you're doing here. Rachel is a minor, we're her parents, and this matter is totally private."

"Jim, you say she's a minor like that means she has no right to choose. That's where you and I disagree. Actually, the law recognizes the rights of minor children to do and ask for certain things. Medical care under certain circumstances is one of those things. It's time to let her have her say. Hard as it may be to accept, her life is her life to end when she needs to. It's not your right to extend hers beyond what she can endure."

Jim stepped closer to Thaddeus's desk to stand between the two visiting chairs. "You make it sound like we're ghouls. We're not bad parents. Thaddeus, as a doctor, I can tell you there are breakthroughs in cancer medicine and oncology every day. Who's to say they won't have something more to offer Rachel before she dies? Who's to say that in six months they won't have a new medication to shrink her tumors and give her back her health? We're praying for that. You could do better for our family if you would join us in that prayer."

"Tell you what. I will join you in that prayer. And I'll take your daughter with me into court and allow her prayer to be heard, too. She deserves her own prayer, her own religion."

Louisa spoke up finally, "Thaddeus, I could—I could—I could shoot you!" Her face was a mask of anger and hatred at the moment. It was hard for Thaddeus to see this on his friend, such emotion directed his way. Where he would normally have stepped forward and hugged her, he remained silent behind his desk.

Louisa spat, "You have no idea how wrong you are. It's the way of the world that has you in its grip. Walk with us into the light and see the errors of your way. We promise you'll see things and hear things you never imagined possible."

"I'll do that with you, Louisa. But I'll also take your daughter with me into court so maybe she can hear the things she needs to hear, too. Her way of hearing might be totally different from yours. Does that make it any less valid? I don't think so. For her, it's even more valid than your view."

Jim turned on his heel and grabbed his wife's arm. "C'mon, Louisa, Thaddeus is speaking in circles. And we're no match for him. We need our own spokesman. Thaddeus, you'll be hearing from our lawyers," he said over his shoulder.

"I would expect no less. Be sure and pick up my card on the way out so you have my number to give them, Jim." Thaddeus stepped around his desk and folded his hands in front of him. "Louisa, I'm sorry this can't end in a way you like, but my client has told me what she wants and that's what I've promised for her."

At the door, Louisa whispered, "Goodbye, Thaddeus."

Thaddeus cleared the wedge in his throat. Like anyone that he cared for, their sadness became his own to bear, too. "Yes, goodbye."

8

Johann was now on Interstate 5 and heading south. Every few minutes, he checked his rearview and side mirrors. No red lights, no sound of sirens. After seeing the poster in the highway rest area, Johann had pulled into the nearest cheap motel and locked himself inside, even ordering pizza delivery so he wouldn't have to go out.

He was heading back to San Diego. There was nowhere to hide, and he couldn't stay in motels much longer. He'd been paying for everything in cash, but that had run out. If he used an ATM, wham! They'd catch him. If he called his parent and asked for money, they'd find him.

Johann finally reached Ocean Beach where he took the ramp and headed for the beach town. There was no plan, no evasive maneuver, nothing going except his fear and a looming sense of unreality, as if the world had distorted from a friendly, fairly happy place to a monster coming awake and preparing to squash him inside a system, one that had agents capable of extreme violence.

He thought about a contact he had. It was someone he could call, someone he knew only casually from his Friday night band performances but had been a police officer at one time. Her name was Safari Frye, and she'd been shot and paralyzed and now danced the slow dances in her wheelchair. In between songs, she crowded up near the bandstand, nursing a gin and tonic (Johann had bought her a drink or two during breaks). She was the one person Johann knew who was in any way involved with law enforcement. Safari now worked as a private detective so there must be a listed number. He Googled PIs in the La Jolla area, and minutes later, he had Safari's number. He couldn't dial it fast enough.

"Friday Investigations," said the female voice upon answering.

"Safari Frye? This is Johann Van Giersbergen. I'm the guy who plays guitar—"

"Sure, Johann, we know each other. I'm the fan in the wheelchair. Your wheelchair fan base is small, but we're dedicated. What's up?"

"Incredible what's just happened to me. I just saw my picture on an FBI Most Wanted poster at the post office. There's no mistake, it's me, because my boss looked it up on the FBI website, and it even has my name and location in La Jolla."

"What do they say you did?"

"It says I was involved in last year's terrorist bombing in Mexico City."

"I remember that. Didn't it turn out to be a local dissident acting alone?"

"Yes. Reason I know, my dad died in the attack. He was FBI."

"And now somehow your name is mixed up in it. Were you there?"

"I was there with my dad. It happened August ninth. I obviously wasn't at the restaurant where it happened. It was a huge explosion and even killed people across the street."

"You called me, and that's good. But now you need a lawyer. I'm going to give you the name and number of Thaddeus Murfee. He's a La Jolla lawyer I would trust with my life, and he's wonderful. Let me call him now, and we'll do a conference call. Hang loose."

The line could be heard ringing as if from a distance. Johann chewed his cheek, then kicked himself for his weakness, but at the same time reminded himself he was only human, that anyone would be doing fight or flight just then.

"Hello, this is Thaddeus."

"Thaddeus, this is Safari."

"Hey, girl, what's up?"

"I have Johann Van Giersbergen on the line. Johann is a local nurse. Maybe I'll let him explain what happened to him."

After Thaddeus was briefed, he considered how a simple trip to Mexico could have gone so wrong for Johann Van Giersbergen. Johann had had no idea he was even wanted by the FBI until the poster. That was unusual; ordinarily, they would hunt someone down way before the need would arise for wanted posters. Those were saved for the most successful runners and hiders, the fugitives who had an underground network capable of hiding them out indefinitely. Those networks almost always belonged to the *narcotraficantes* and the mafia. Never to a nurse in La Jolla, someone going to work and living right out in the open.

So, the first question was why? The second question was what to do about it? He knew there were all sorts of federal and state laws against harboring a fugitive and helping a fugitive remain hidden away. Any lawyer worth his salt would be considering those things before getting too up close and personal with such a case. The third question was the key one, and that was, how do you go from being a tourist in Mexico City to being a hunted terrorist accused of killing his own father with a bomb? The fourth thing, not a question, really, but a consideration, was, what if he'd really done something terrible in Mexico City? What if he were actually involved and toying with Thaddeus right now? He didn't for a minute believe that, but the lawyer side of him always examined all the angles and was doing so again this time.

He decided to call Jack Rasso at the FBI, an old friend. He told Safari and Johann to hold a minute and dialed a local number in La Jolla, California.

"Jack Rasso, please, Thaddeus Murfee calling."

The call was placed on hold momentarily. Then, "Thaddeus, my boy, what loser and threat to society are you turning loose today?"

"No one I'd tell you about," Thaddeus joked back. "You guys want to arrest the school crossing guards for wearing flannel."

"Your FBI at work, Thaddeus."

"Look, why I'm calling, I have a potential client. He's evidently plastered all over the post office on an FBI Most Wanted sign.

"What post office?"

"That doesn't matter. He's seen himself and looked himself up on the website. It's definitely him you're after."

"Are you helping him hide?" Jack was all about business now.

Casual friendships went only so far in the world of FBI and defense lawyers. Thaddeus felt his face twitch.

"Yeah, I've got him in the trunk of my car on the way to Mexico. No, Jack, of course I'm not helping him hide. That would be a crime, and I'm too chicken to do crimes. All right, here's the deal. His name is Johann Van Giersbergen. Does that ring a bell?"

"Thaddeus, you're not playing with me?"

"No, Jack. That's really his name."

"Yes, he's a wall banger."

"Wall banger?"

"That's what we call the head shots you see in the post office hanging from the walls. The wall bangers."

"Well, he's all of that," Thaddeus said. "You guys have somehow gotten him confused with the assholes who killed his father in Mexico City. What if you and I meet and talk about what you have, and you convince me to turn him in?"

"That, I can do. Tonight?"

"Sure, tonight. Where?"

"Noodle House in Ocean Beach."

"Be there in sixty."

"See you then."

The lawyer immediately reconnected with Safari. "I've got a meetup with the FBI. Is your friend going to hire me and who's going to pay me?"

"His mother is a surgeon in LA. She'll pay you. Yes, you're hired."

"Put him on, please."

A moment passed, then, "Mr. Murfee? This is Johann. My mom will be the one paying you. How much is it?"

"I won't know until I talk with the FBI and see what they have. But I want you to personally pay, not your parents. I want your buy-in to your case, not their buy-in. Understand me?"

"Yes."

"If the evidence is overwhelming against you, you might not need a trial lawyer. You might just need a lawyer to cut a deal and do your time. If the evidence isn't convincing, then you just might want me on the case."

"Okay."

"How much do you earn a year?"

"Around eighty-thousand."

"Then I need eight thousand from you for your retainer. Before we go to trial, if there's a trial, we adjust that. Maybe more, maybe less, if I think there'll be a plea after jury selection, which is often the case. Either way, you need eight-thousand dollars and you need to sign a promise to pay my retainer once it becomes known. Can do?"

"Yes, can do. It's my problem, not my mom's problem."

"What phone are you on?"

"My cell phone."

"All right, take your cell phone behind wherever you are and throw it in the trash. It's already being located. Don't use it again. If you don't get far away from it in the new few minutes, you'll be picked up and find yourself in jail. So, clear out of wherever you are and go somewhere else."

Safari came on the line. Johann was disconnected while they talked.

"Thaddeus, can Johann come to my place?"

"Sure, if you don't mind being an accomplice."

"What about a hotel?"

"Have him go there alone. You stay far away right now. He's just waiting to get his ticket punched, and you don't want to toss yours in there, too. Stay far away. Leave your office now."

"Where should I go?"

"Go home and go to your computer and login to your website. That way you'll establish you were home and what time you were there. He's in his own car?"

"He is."

"Leave now. Tell him to find a hotel and call me from his room phone. I'll give you another number."

"All right, shoot."

Thaddeus gave her the number of a burner cell phone. Johann could call him on that, and then Thaddeus could ditch the phone. Tomorrow they could begin using his office phone after he was contracted on the case.

Thirty minutes later, Johann called Thaddeus. Thaddeus was driving to the Noodle House to meet with Jack Rasso. Johann was at the Whispering Pines Motel on the east side of the freeway at La Jolla. He asked if they could meet.

Thaddeus continued driving. "Not tonight. I'm being watched now since I've called Jack Rasso at the FBI. You'd be on your way to jail as soon as I walked in and shook your hand. But we can talk. They don't have a tap on your room phone, and this cell phone's a burner. Give me the overview of Mexico. What was going on there, who was there and why, and what happened?"

"It was in August of last year. I went there with my dad while he was meeting with the Mexican government on a joint task force to interdict Medellin drugs. My purpose in going was to look for a language school. Believe it or not, I wanted to do a one-month immersion Spanish language program so I could do a Doctors Without Borders working holiday. I was there with my dad, but he was business and I was just window-shopping schools."

"Tell me about the bombing."

"Right. We were staying at the Mexico City Hilton. He said goodbye at about seven on our first morning and off he went to meet with the federal police, an undercover unit, he said. It was a breakfast meeting in the rear room of the Sonoran Restaurant, kitty-corner from the hotel." There was a pause and a deep breath then, "This is what I've learned since. A bomb was planted in the restaurant. The entire place went up maybe ten minutes into the meeting. It killed everyone in the back room, in the front of the restaurant, and even people across the street."

"How did your name get mixed up in all this?"

"The FBI seized my cell phone."

"Your cell phone? Why?"

"They were checking everyone and everything. All I know is I didn't get my cell phone back. Next thing I know, there's my picture in the post office. Mr. Murfee, I'm terrified. I didn't do anything. I'm afraid they're going to shoot me."

Thaddeus understood. The last people in the world anyone wanted after them was the FBI. He knew they were the best—and he knew they could also be the worst at hanging onto clues even when they were just plain wrong. He intended to get to the bottom of it when he talked to Rasso. For now, he could only try to put Johann's mind at ease. "I'll be talking to the FBI in about fifteen minutes. We'll talk after. Don't call me again. I'll contact you when I'm ready."

He disconnected the call.

It was time to talk to the FBI.

9

Thaddeus and Jack Rasso met at the Ocean Beach Noodle House, Jack Rasso's choice. Jack had just had a quick bowl with his daughter, he explained to Thaddeus.

"She's UCSD?" asked Thaddeus. When the server approached, Thaddeus ordered the beef Saigon fried rice and a coffee and water.

"SDSU," corrected Jack. "Majoring in police science, I'm sorry to say." Jack's head was completely shaven, his scalp pale and translucent over a full head of black hairs beneath the surface. He wasn't bald, just shaved. Thaddeus wondered why he would do that to himself, especially if he needed to just blend in, as Thaddeus knew was true of most FBI agents. But he let it go. For all he knew, the guy could be a desk jockey who hated to deal with hair, someone who didn't give a damn about blending in.

"Oh, well, it could be worse," Thaddeus mused.

"That's right. She could be pre-law."

"Touché. Jack, I called about Johann Van Giersbergen. He hasn't retained me yet but will. I'm very perplexed how a person could find their picture in the post office without knowing the FBI was after them."

"Simple, as you'll see when you talk to him. He's been in Brazil on a Doctors' Without Borders mission. We couldn't find him, and he didn't know we were looking. Now we're both onto each other at the same time. Seriously, he needs to surrender and let the judge set bail."

"He's indicted?"

"I can't give you particulars just now because I don't have the information, Thaddeus, but he's wanted."

"The poster says terrorist bombing. It doesn't get any more serious than that."

Jack sighed and stirred a cup of coffee he'd been nursing since Thaddeus arrived. "No, it doesn't get any more serious than that, which is why I wanted to meet with you. He needs to surrender before someone gets hurt. These arrests can be very dangerous if the agents feel threatened. I don't want to see him hurt for no reason. His dad was a very close friend of mine. I know the kid. For his own safety, Thaddeus, surrender your client."

"I tend to agree. I'll talk to him tonight. You want the collar?"

"Sure, why not? You have my cell. Call and I'll come get him and take him in for booking. You know the drill. I'll make sure he's safe after that."

"Can you comment on the particulars of the case against him yet? Can you generally let me know what you have?"

"No can do. I'm not sure we're even clear on that yet, Thaddeus. But I can say this. A chemical transfer was in his suitcase."

"Transfer? As in the marker from the explosive?"

"Bingo."

"So, Semtex?"

"Bingo. That's all you get."

He was telling Thaddeus that the Semtex explosive, which comes compounded with marking agents that tell investigators where the Semtex came from, left a trace of its marker in Johann's suitcase. Thaddeus knew that was huge.

"How did the investigation focus on him?" Thaddeus asked.

"The Mexico City police did a smart thing—they preserved the scene. No one was allowed in, and no one was allowed out of the perimeter they threw up. When we arrived, it was pristine. The entire area was searched, including the hotel. Luggage, room contents, clothing, electronics, we left nothing undone. There were other items found, but none as damning as your client's suitcase."

"He says he's innocent."

"Isn't that why we have trials?" There was a pause, then, "Says he's innocent? Thaddeus, you know better."

Thaddeus smiled. It really was no time to plead his case. Johann was in for a ride through hell before it was all said and done. The feds had him in their sights, and they were always very good at running their prey to the ground and finishing it off without a second's hesitation. A ride through hell, indeed. He sighed and pulled himself away from further argument for it would only fall on deaf ears and, worse, he might inadvertently tip a hand he didn't even know he held yet.

"All right. I'm speaking with him tonight. Either way, I'll call you after, Jack."

"Be careful. We're everywhere, you know. You don't want to be brought up on a concealing charge."

"Concealing a witness? Hell, Jack, I hardly know his name at this point. At least let me do some actual concealing before you jump me."

Jack laughed. "You talk to him and then call me. I'll freeze everything for one hour. After that, all bets are off."

"Make it two hours. I have to get back to the office."

The two men rose. Each left a twenty for bill and tip. Jack hiked his pants up and started walking out of the restaurant. "Two hours, then. It's seven-twenty now. If I don't hear from you by nine-twenty, we're moving in. It won't be pretty. If that happens, make yourself scarce, Thaddeus. Don't be close to him or you might get painted along with him."

Just outside the door, Thaddeus said to Jack before they went their separate ways, "I'll be in touch shortly."

Thaddeus left OB Noodles and went out to the street-side parking. He found his Mercedes sedan and climbed inside.

One hour later, Thaddeus was finishing up with Johann at his office. The decision had been made to do a voluntary surrender. Jack Rasso was expected in the next half hour. Voluntary surrender was the only way to keep him one-hundred percent safe against a take-down by FBI agents armed to the teeth, maybe even SWAT. Besides, if he gave himself up, it would prove to the judge he was no flight risk. He might even get bail, depending on what the charges against him turned out to be, if they weren't murder.

"Let me just ask, Johann. Your suitcase contained trace elements of Semtex. How did that get there? Any wild guesses?"

He shook his head. "My wildest guess would be someone planted it while I was out of the room. I was off that morning, exploring language school options. My room could've been accessed by any number of hotel workers."

"Okay, let's say the How is the easy one. Here's the hard one, the Why."

"Why would anyone choose to implicate me? That, I have no idea. What good does it do the real killers to have a slightly manic hospital nurse brought up on charges? That makes no sense, Thaddeus."

"I tend to agree. But from a legal standpoint, the problem with these cases is that we can't just sit back and make the FBI prove its case at trial. Instead, we have to become proactive. We have to come forward and prove your innocence at trial. Which really boils down to us being able to point the finger at the real killers. That means I've got some investigating to do. In Mexico, which isn't easy. I'm going to need help. I'm thinking I need an Interpol agent, someone with experience down there. That's just for openers. So, that's my first step, to find that certain someone and then proceed to the hotel and nail down who had access to your room and then investigate them one by one. It's going to be a painfully slow process. Painfully slow, because you're going to be locked up the whole time. You're going to have to steel yourself. You're going to jail for something you didn't do. Somehow you have to get through that jail time. Do you have the resources inside to help you now?"

Johann's eyes clouded over. His voice broke when he said, "I don't know. I've only heard stories about innocent people being in jail. I never thought—"

Johann was interrupted by Thaddeus's cell phone. Thaddeus held up one finger to Johann and answered when he saw the caller was Jack Rasso. Rasso told Thaddeus he was just outside the office, to please let him in.

Thaddeus left Johann in his office and went to the front door of his premises. When he pulled the door wide, Jack stepped in alone. "Where is he, Thaddeus?"

"My office. Follow me, please."

Down the hallway they went, then down another. At the end was Thaddeus's private office behind two stained-glass double doors. The doors stood open, and the two men went inside. Jack was introduced by Thaddeus, who then stood aside while the FBI agent searched Johann. He then cuffed Johann in front since he was voluntarily turning himself in and wasn't a suspect who might make a break for it.

"Jack, no statements, please, and no questions. That's part of our deal, remember?"

"I remember. No one will approach your client for a statement, Thaddeus."

"All right, then. Johann, are you feeling okay?"

"Scared. Really scared."

"I don't blame you for that," Thaddeus said. "Being placed in handcuffs and arrested for any crime is terribly frightening. Just remember, I'm here for you, and no one is going to try to further incriminate you by taking your statement or anything. Fingerprints will be part of the normal booking process, but they already have your fingerprints anyway from the nursing board. So, go along with it, don't resist, and you'll be held safely. I'll be in touch everyday with updates. You'll have that to look forward to."

Johann finally broke, and tears escaped down his face. His captor and his lawyer were sympathetic to his plight. However, Thaddeus knew the FBI agent was also pleased to have him in custody. Brother FBI agents had perished. And here was a suspect, a person whose luggage had once come into contact with the explosive that killed those brother agents. He was a hot commodity, and his arrest would be a huge coup at the field office in San Diego.

"Jack," Thaddeus said just before Jack took him away, "I'm going to need an international agent to help me investigate Mexico City. I'm wondering if you—"

"Say no more. I worked against a guy in Chicago two years ago. Name of Marcel Rainford. He's in with a lawyer named Michael Gresham out of Chicago. Suggest you call Michael and ask to borrow Marcel. You could do a hell of a lot worse and not much better out of everyone I know. He's absolutely the best and he's ex-Interpol. He'll have all the right contacts in Mexico City."

"R-A-I-N-F-O-R-D?"

"Yes, Marcel Rainford. Gifted investigator."

10

Having just been arrested a day earlier, it was Johann's time for his initial appearance. At such appearances in federal court, the court would consider bail and make sure the defendant had counsel and other pertinent housekeeping and constitutional matters. Sometimes, the initial appearance was combined with the taking of a plea or arraignment, which is what Thaddeus wished to accomplish this morning so that he could ask the court to rule on his motion for bail.

The motion was based on the fact that bail was available, generally, in all cases where homicide wasn't charged. He had acquired a copy of the indictment, filed under *49 U.S. Code §46505: Carrying a weapon or explosive on an aircraft.* That was the first charge. The allegations made clear the U.S. Attorney and FBI were confident they could prove beyond a reasonable doubt that Johann had knowingly taken the explosive onboard the aircraft in which he had flown to Mexico with his father. Thaddeus thought it was quite a stretch from a chemical marker inside the young man's suitcase to a full-blown case against him for knowingly trans-porting explosives.

The second charge was the much more serious charge, for in Count II, the government was charging Johann with conspiracy to commit murder. The allegations were that Johann had conspired with another unnamed person or persons to murder certain FBI agents with an explosive in Mexico City. Venue was going to be an issue, but at this point, it remained to be properly researched and argued in a separate motion.

"Is the defendant present in court and represented by counsel?" asked Judge Whittier once the case was called by the clerk.

Thaddeus approached the lectern, and Johann came forward. "Defendant is present in court and represented by me, Thaddeus Murfee, Your Honor."

The judge then went into a line of inquiry about the defendant's rights and whether he'd received a copy of the indictment, whether he read and understood English, whether he needed an interpreter, and the like. When these matters were concluded, Thaddeus addressed the court, inquiring whether he might enter the defendant's plea of not guilty, and the court agreed. Thaddeus then proceeded to the motion to set conditions of release.

"If it pleases the court, the defendant has filed his Motion to Set Conditions of Release. As you can see, Judge, we're seeking release on bail at a reduced amount based on the defendant's youthful age, his contacts with the community, the fact he's never been in trouble in his life, and the defendant's earning capability and assets. Defendant asks that bail be in the amount of ten-thousand dollars."

"Counsel?" the court said to the Assistant U.S. Attorney. "What is the government's position regarding bail?"

The AUSA for this trial, Abigail Shue, was known to be a determined woman, a feminist, and a bit of a pit bull when it came to cases. "Ten thousand dollars is a joke, Your Honor. The defendant is indicted for the crime of conspiracy to commit murder, which ordinarily is a non-bailable offense in this jurisdiction anyway. Minimally, the bail should be set, if it is to be set at all, in an amount of no less than ten-million dollars. Granted, the defendant is young and, granted, this might be his first offense, but still, the first offense he selected to commit is the most serious possible, the killing of another with premeditation and pre-planning. It is a crime punishable by death in some cases, and we're going to proceed as if that's the case here. Bail should be set at ten-million and not a dime less, Your Honor."

"Counsel," the judge said to Thaddeus, "while the court notes the youthfulness and lack of prior convictions of your client, still, the court is of the opinion that the case is devalued in the eyes of the public if bail is set below one million dollars. For that reason, bail is set at one million dollars with the usual proscriptions in the order of release. Anything further, Counsel?"

Thaddeus was first to speak. "No, Your Honor."

"No, Your Honor," echoed AUSA Shue.

Thaddeus and Johann moved away from the lectern, back to counsel table, where they had a moment to discuss the case until Johann was again taken away by the bailiff.

A panicked Johann whispered to Thaddeus, "My mother works and earns a great living, but we don't have money like this!"

Thaddeus shot a look at Johann's mother seated in the front row of the courtroom, her hands clenched and her knuckles white. The woman's eyes widened in question as Thaddeus made eye contact.

Thaddeus walked over to where she sat, squatted so they were eye level, and said in a low voice, "Can you come up with one million?"

"Not all at once. It would take weeks."

"But is it doable?"

"Yes, it will just take a while. There are stock funds to liquidate, that sort of thing. Plus, I'd have to borrow against my house."

"Got it." He turned back to Johann. "You're going to have to cool your jets in jail while your mother makes her arrangements."

"But I'm not guilty of anything."

"I know, I know," Thaddeus said. By now, they were receiving impatient looks from the judge for their impromptu conference in his courtroom. A minute or two might be allowed, but this was ongoing now. They were going to need to continue their talk back at the jail facility. "I have other clients this morning. I'll come see you in jail this afternoon. Please try to hang in there."

The bailiffs then took away Johann, and Thaddeus gathered his file and briefcase and left the courtroom. Dr. Van Giersbergen was waiting for him just outside in the hallway.

"Thaddeus, I spoke with FBI Agent Billy McCrory last night. He was my husband's best friend in the FBI. Billy says the FBI means to make a capital case out of Johann. He says the loss of FBI agents was too much for this to ever go away with a negotiated plea, or even life in prison. It sounded horrible what he said. I know I'm driving him crazy with all my calls and my begging him for help. In fact, he said I shouldn't call him again, that we couldn't talk again until after Johann's case concludes. Is this unusual for the FBI to just break off conversations like this?"

"You know, I've never had a case where the defendant's family is personally acquainted with the FBI, so I don't know how to answer that. But it doesn't surprise me that he feels unable to talk anymore. He can't be seen as giving care and comfort to one of the people indicted for the murder of other FBI agents."

"So, we're pretty much left in the cold with no one to talk to there, even after Ned served them for eighteen years?"

"Pretty much, yes."

"What did the U.S. Attorney give you when you were leaving? A file?"

"She handed me the government's discovery. It will contain file memoranda of interviews, descriptions of physical evidence, lab reports, intangible evidence, and a ton of other documents and statements. I'll go over it tonight and then present Johann with a summary that he can share with you if he wants."

"You can't just send me a copy of what you have?"

"If Johann wants me to do that, yes, I can. Also, I need to have some timeline for posting his bail."

"Cash is required?"

"You need to see a bail bondsman. Please call my office and speak to my paralegal Michael Knowles for a list of companies we work with. Bail is controlled by federal criminal rules and can be quite tricky, so you need the kind of help these people can offer."

"I know I'll be deluging you with questions and phone calls, but there's so much I don't understand and—and—since Ned was killed, I'm so damned alone! There's so much... I'm just lost without him."

"Hey," said Thaddeus, "I've got thirty minutes until my next arraignment. Would you like to drop down to the cafeteria and grab some coffee and chat? I have time, if you do."

"I'd absolutely love that, Thaddeus. Thank you, thank you, thank you."

"No problem. You'd do the same for me if I were having surgery, I'm sure."

"I...just...thank you."

The duo headed for the elevators at the end of the hall. Thaddeus would hand off the discovery packet to a paralegal to rush the documents back to the office and put them on Dropbox so that Thaddeus could read through the information in the next few hours. He also planned for Turquoise to take a look. It would be key to how they approached their investigation in Mexico.

They found the cafeteria downstairs and ordered coffee. It was an unusual public cafeteria in that it had table service. The waitress brought two house dark-roast coffees, and Thaddeus, with Dr. Van Giersbergen, sat back to talk. Just as they had decided first names would be best between them—Thaddeus and Gretta—his cell phone beeped. Christine was calling. Thaddeus took the call. The Sundstroms had hired a lawyer to help keep their daughter alive.

He wanted Thaddeus to call.

11

Wednesday afternoon—his afternoon off—Thaddeus sat wearing his headphones, enjoying the Joe Rogan podcast with Elon Musk. Anywhere Musk appeared, Thaddeus was a fan.

At four o'clock, his Apple Watch told him to stand, which he did, just in time to take a call from his daughter Celena. "Dad, we're taking Rachel to the Jonas Brothers concert at the Hollywood Bowl. We need someone to drive."

Thaddeus's jerked upright, startled. Wasn't the girl in so much pain she couldn't be moved? And as for who was doing the taking, was she referring to herself and Becca alone? Or were there others?

"Okay," he said, "who is taking Rachel to Hollywood?"

"Becca and I are taking her. We need you to drive."

"Seriously? I thought Rachel was bed-ridden, in so much pain—"

"She'll be bringing her morphine drip. She'll travel just fine if she's knocked out."

Seriously? Knocked out?

"Hold on. Do Rachel's mom and dad know you're taking her to the concert?"

"They've given their approval for anything Rachel feels up to. They tell her that every day, Dad. They encourage her to do things."

"Yes, but specifically, do they know I would be taking the three of you to Hollywood?"

He could hear Celena shouting to Becca a repeat of his question. Then he heard Becca answer back from afar, "I told them. They said they would love it if your dad could take us to see the Jonas Brothers."

"So, I'm basically taking the three of you to see the Jonas Brothers, and it's with the consent of the Sundstroms?"

"That's right, Dad. Please say you'll take us!"

"Let me call Jim Sundstrom. Better yet, have Becca ask a parent to call me. You have my number. I need to know there's parental approval for this."

His phone beeped five minutes later. "Thaddeus? Louisa Sundstrom calling," she said, barely above a whisper. "Sorry to bother you. I think the entire thing is wrong, wrong, wrong, but I'm not going to stand in the girls' way of seeing JB. They love JB, especially that Nick. It's all they ever used to talk about. Now they want to go see the band now they're reassembled."

"I'll be glad to help. If you're sure."

There was a pause, then, "Thaddeus, I'm talking where the girls cannot hear me. This might be—will be—the last chance our precious Rachel gets to see the Jonas Brothers. The idea terrifies me of her leaving her bed, much less leaving our house. But she asked. Her nurse, June, will go with you. She'll have the medication to make the trip painless for Rachel. She'll be in charge of all her medical needs."

"Then what am I there for?" Thaddeus asked.

"Your job will be to get them there and back safely. I understand you have the motorhome. That's what made the girls start thinking about this. Celena said you'd volunteer to do it. She said you'd love the idea. I even asked if I could come along. You would've thought I'd asked if I could spend the night with them on their wedding night. Obviously, they don't need me along, and I'm not hurt. I'm just in tears over the idea this really might work, and our precious girl might get to see JB. We would be thrilled if you would take them in your motorhome."

Thaddeus relaxed. "Can do. What night is it?"

"Tonight. The girls have their tickets at will-call."

"Tonight? Good grief. All right. I'll be by your place in about thirty minutes. We'll leave from there."

"I'll have them ready. You're a brave man, Thaddeus Murfee."

"I do what I can. Besides, I might learn something from all this. I'm in."

He disconnected the call and made a quick call downstairs to XFBI, the civilian security firm that made Thaddeus's life happen behind the scenes. Thaddeus told them to have his Newmar Ventana motorhome ready to roll in ten minutes. They were also to score concert tickets for Thaddeus and two other security. It wasn't his own safety he was concerned with, but that of the girls'. If an old resentment flared and someone took a shot at him over an old case or incident, XFBI would be there to take up the challenge. It was just how he lived and had for years now.

The RV was ready and waiting after he had changed from sweats into jeans and boots and a T-shirt. He folded his Ray-Bans into the pocket of his Tee and sat back while the driver, a young man by the name of Sandy, pulled the unit from the garage into the drive.

His house was built into a hill and opened below onto the beach. In front was a circular drive, which Sandy navigated on his way to the cross-street. He followed Thaddeus's directions to the Sundstroms', where they pulled in and parked. Thaddeus climbed out and went to the side door used by friends and family. He rang the bell.

Becca came to the door. "We're getting her in the wheelchair, Mr. Murfee."

Sandy came up behind Thaddeus. "Need help with this?" It had been already discussed. Sandy was there to lend muscle.

They followed Becca to Rachel's bedside and watched as nurse June lifted the patient into a sitting position. She was then assisted from the bed into the wheelchair by the nurse and Becca and Celena. Thaddeus and Sandy watched, learning what was to be done and how. During the procedure, the IV was never removed from the back of her hand and the IV bags were moved from the bedside pole to the IV pole sticking out of the wheelchair. All this time, Rachel was unconscious and held in place by a seatbelt and loving hands. Then Sandy went around behind and began wheeling the chair.

It was time to go see the Jonas Brothers.

Inside the RV, Rachel was moved from her wheelchair to a recliner and belted in. Again, her IV bags were nearby. Fifteen minutes down the road, she opened her eyes momentarily to cry out from the pain as her drip had been lessened in anticipation of the stage show. However, the lessening was too soon—too much pain—and the drip was increased again, allowing the young woman the comfort of unconsciousness. Thaddeus was taking all this in as they rolled down the road and the two fifteen-year-olds began discussing their excitement and the show they were going to see.

Thaddeus struck up a side conversation with June, learning as much as he could about his client's medications and daily routines and how unusual it was for her to have any time away from the house at all. Everything else in her young life came to the house to her, including doctors, treatment devices, food, of course, and all clothing, bathing, medical, and medicines she could possibly ever need. On those rare occasions when she had to return to the hospital for scans or X-rays, there was an ambulance for that, coupled with the bliss of unconsciousness, as it were. When June laid it all out before him, he had a huge appreciation for what a lucky man he was to be able to take the child on an outing like tonight's.

Ninety minutes later, they reached the beginnings of LA County and were engaging with their first real LA traffic. During the trip, the girls had chattered away, the patient had slept, and Thaddeus had ruminated about the upcoming hearing on Rachel's dependency petition and her desire to end it all. He felt, at moments, like he was living a dream, like life was skirting so close to death that it was almost impossible to tell them apart. He realized, then, that he was experiencing the journey as Rachel might be experiencing her daily life, death being the dearest old friend that offered the change she must have. Sitting there, he so admired the girl's courage and strength that tears came to his eyes, and it was all he could do not to jump up and give her a huge hug. He wiped away the tears with a tissue and looked at June and smiled with a shrug.

"I know," she said, tears in her own eyes, "she does that to all of us."

Up ahead, in the driver's and front-seat passenger's chairs, Sandy and his XFBI partner were on their phones, talking to Hollywood Bowl security and making plans for how to accommodate the RV and its special occupants. Obviously, there was a system in place for those guests who needed special accommodations as well as security provisions, and those things were hammered out before arrival.

At the gates to the Bowl, LAPD traffic officers were in the streets, directing traffic and seeing to it that parking lots filled properly, and special need vehicles, RV's and buses, got to where they needed to be as well. They finally parked and began unloading their passenger with her wheelchair. Then they were navigating the rolling walkways into the arena.

The upslope ended for them midway up the ramp, where they turned into the seating area and found themselves twenty rows from the stage. The wheelchaired patient was rolled into place at the end of row 20, and the others took their seats around her. Food was ordered, and soft drinks and coffee, then the lights dimmed, and the show got underway. Just as it did, the drip was cutoff, and soon Rachel was awake, sitting bowed in her wheelchair, her head and upper back resting against pillows, sipping Pepsi and nibbling popcorn.

Sitting beside her, Thaddeus felt the need to wait on her, but refrained from asking whether she needed anything so she could simply enjoy the show. But he could tell not all was well. As he stole looks at her face, he saw the grimace of pain and the stolid mask that said, even if it killed her, she was going to see the show start to finish.

And she did see the show, even weakly giving out with a shrill, two-fingered whistle at the end of a particularly wonderful love song about the type of boy-girl love Rachel would never experience. Thaddeus knew it, the others knew it, she knew it, and the moment was overwhelming with sadness yet joy that she'd gotten to experience the feelings expressed in the love song. The girl's face was tear-stained and yet gritty with determination as she sat through song after song and enjoyed the antics and sensuality of the young men onstage, whom she adored.

Then it happened. It was as simple as Rachel leaning to her left to June and whispering to the nurse. A small line switch was opened, and the drip-drip-drip resumed. Within minutes, the show was over for Rachel as she succumbed to the morphine flow and the blessed relief it gave her. The pain had just gotten to be too much for her, and she was no longer in the moment with them.

Which, try as they might to keep going, really meant the end of the show for the others as well. June motioned, and Sandy and the other XFBI began preparing the wheelchair for movement back to the RV. The others, without speaking, stood and began filing out.

The show was over and done.

On the drive home, the girls' talk was suppressed and almost without animation as they were careful to allow the patient to remain asleep. Seriously, from what Thaddeus could tell, no amount of noise would have awakened Rachel, a testament to the strength of the narcotic drip. But still, the RV interior was, for the most part, bathed in blue light and very quiet all the way home to La Jolla.

At the Sundstrom's, Sandy wheeled the patient inside, and June returned Rachel to her bed, the IV bags replaced on the bedside pole. Jim and Louisa watched the process while the girls excitedly retold the evening in detail, including humming and dancing parts of the songs they remembered well. When Thaddeus turned to leave, he was only aware that a tiny, 100-pound girl of seventeen years was being left behind in that bed to face the night and face her body and mind alone. Because he knew, deep down, that all people in the end, must, as the song said, do the final dance alone.

He wept openly in the back of the RV on the ride back home.

The XBI pretended not to notice, but Celena stayed beside him and held his hand. She wept, too.

The phone rang when he arrived home. It was Jim Sundstrom who said simply, "Thank you, friend," and then the line went dead.

Thaddeus kissed the sleeping Christine as he climbed into bed. He stared at the ceiling and saw the lawsuit spread out before his eyes. He saw the path it would inevitably take because he knew the law and knew the courts. Still, even knowing, it was more than he could do to think all the way to the end when Rachel finally won.

When she finally won the right to lose it all.

12

The next morning, Thaddeus placed a call to Chicago attorney Michael Gresham about his investigator, Marcel Rainford. Thaddeus was told Michael was in court, to call back in two hours, which he did. This time, he was put right through.

"This is Michael Gresham. How can I help you, Mr. Murfee?"

"Please call me Thaddeus. I'm calling from La Jolla, California, Michael. I have a client here who was arrested two days ago by the FBI. He's going to be charged with the murder of several FBI agents, a capital crime."

"Definitely looking at the death penalty then. How can I help?"

"The killing took place in Mexico City. The bombing of an FBI-Mexican joint task force."

"I remember. Wasn't that last August?" asked Michael Gresham.

"It was. My client is innocent. He's a very believable nurse in a local hospital who's never been in trouble and had zero motive to murder those agents. In fact, one of them was his own father.

However, in his suitcase, the FBI found trace markings of the explosive used."

"Semtex, I'm guessing?"

"Yes, Semtex. Johann, of course, has no idea how the markings got there. Plus, they've found his fingerprints at the crime scene. Again, he has no idea how. I'm left with a case where I believe my client is innocent but where we're totally clueless about where to begin. I need an investigator to help me, someone familiar with Mexico, in particular Mexico City and maybe Latin American and South America as well. Someone who knows the language and customs. Someone who, hopefully, is ex-Interpol. Now you know why I'm calling."

"You want to borrow Marcel Rainford. Got it. Tell me this, how did you get his name?"

"The FBI agent who arrested my client after he surrendered is a man named Jack Rasso. Jack recommended Marcel. He said he's just the man I need to help me dig in."

"Let me get Marcel on the line. He's in his office. Please hold, and we'll find out whether he can help."

Thaddeus waited a long minute on hold. He was hoping against hope that this was going to pan out and that Marcel would be willing and able to come to California without delay.

Then a voice came on the line. "Marcel Rainford here, Thaddeus. Michael has filled me in. You need help in California with the investigation, correct?"

"California and all points south. Maybe as far south as Brazil."

"I know the area and still have contacts in Mexico City. When do you need me?"

"ASAP. My client surrendered to FBI custody two nights ago."

"What if I'm at the airport in San Diego tomorrow morning? Does that work for you?"

"Works perfectly. I have a large home with guest rooms. I expect you to stay with me. You'll have privacy and everything you need."

"Perfect. I'll text you with flight info."

"I'll personally pick you up at the airport. We can brainstorm on the drive up to La Jolla."

"Yes, and I'd like to speak with Johann before we leave San Diego, too, if possible."

"Definitely. I can't thank you enough."

"Jack Rasso and I go way back. If he gave you my name, we're all good. That tells me everything I need to know."

"Sounds great. I'll look for your text."

THE NEXT MORNING, THADDEUS PULLED UP TO THE CURB AT THE airport terminal and waited. Marcel, wearing a black puffy vest over a long-sleeved T-shirt, stepped outside the terminal and approached Thaddeus's white Mercedes. He was a big man, taller and broader than Thaddeus, some serious muscle. He had short dark brown hair, wavy and a bit messy, and beard stubble, as if he hadn't shaved for a couple of days. When Thaddeus jumped out of the car and offered Marcel his hand, the man smiled and gave it a firm shake.

Thaddeus liked him already. Even with the small scar along his right cheek that made him look seriously intimidating.

They loaded Marcel's luggage and pulled away from the curb.

"Great to see you," said Thaddeus. "I can't thank you enough, Marcel."

Marcel dug an old faded blue Army baseball cap from his back pocket and placed it on his head. "Glad to be of service. I read through your notes on the flight out."

"Yes, I know I don't have much. We'll meet with Johann and get the rest of the story now. The jail is only about fifteen minutes away."

The men talked about investigation ideas while Thaddeus drove them to the federal facility on Union Street. They parked and went inside.

Thirty minutes later, the authorities had placed them in a conference room with no windows, a table, and four chairs. Thaddeus and Marcel both stood when Johann was led into the room by a burly female jailer. Johann wore an orange jumpsuit and looked like he'd been without sleep. Thaddeus gave him a sideways hug and helped him sit down. The jailer removed his handcuffs and left the room with the admonition that no articles were to be exchanged between visitors and prisoner. She said she'd be stationed outside the conference room, to knock if anything was needed.

"Johann," said Thaddeus when the door was closed and the three were alone, "how are you holding up?"

Johann sniffed, and his face tightened. "Not good. I didn't do anything wrong, and I hate being here. I've been praying for help. Thaddeus, you're my only hope."

"This is one of my investigators on the case. His name is Marcel

Rainford. He's come from Chicago to help me learn how you've been caught up in this mess."

"Hello, Johann," said Marcel. He reached and took Johann's hand and gave a squeeze. "We're going to do everything possible to make this go away. Thaddeus tells me you're innocent, and I believe him. I haven't had the benefit of hearing your story, however, so I'm hopeful we can start there. Why don't you just give me an overview?"

Johann dabbed his sleeve against his eyes and cleared his throat. "My dad and I checked into the Mexico City Hilton. Two separate rooms. His room was paid for by the government, mine was on his credit card. We split up, and he took a shower and changed while I went and laid down for a nap. The flight was long and uncomfortable, and I could hardly keep my eyes open. I must've been asleep an hour or more when I came awake with a start. Housekeeping had let herself into my room and was standing there with her cart just outside and her vacuum cleaner inside. She didn't speak English, and my Spanish was spotty, but I managed to figure out she'd been told my room hadn't been cleaned before I checked in and she was there to clean it. I don't know how long she'd been in my room. So, I asked her to come back later and tried to go back to sleep after she left. But I was too awake. So, I took a shower, dressed in shorts and a T-shirt, and went out onto my balcony to get oriented. It was bright and sunny, about three o'clock. My phone rang so I went inside to get the call. It was my dad. He told me we'd be going for dinner around five. I told him to come get me when he was ready. He had a place in mind, an Argentine steak house or something."

"When you were awakened by housekeeping, did you have any idea how long she'd been in your room?" Marcel asked.

"I didn't. I had the feeling it might have been more than just a few minutes because there was a stack of towels and wash cloths in the bathroom after she'd left. Evidently, I interrupted her. Why, do you think she might have been involved?"

Marcel sat back against the metal chair. "Could be. If you didn't hear her come in, there could've been others. Did you ever see her again after?"

"You know, I've thought about that. I don't really think I did, but to be honest, I can't say."

"And, of course, you didn't get her name?"

"No, sorry. She wasn't there but only about a minute or two after I woke up."

"It's a start," said Thaddeus. "We can get the work records from the Hilton and find out who was covering her floor."

"Exactly," said Marcel. "So, tell us what happened after your dad called."

"I sat down on the bed. I checked out the TV channels with the remote. Of course, everything was in Spanish. There might have been one English channel, but I remember it was an infomercial about a piece of workout equipment. Something weird, like a wheel with handles on each side. Then I ordered a Coke and a fruit and cheese plate from room service. My stomach was still upset from the airplane, and I needed to eat something. The plate came with the drink, and I munched and watched a soap opera in Spanish. It wasn't too bad because the subtitles were in English. I figured I was there to learn Spanish so watching Mexican soaps with English subtitles wasn't a bad start. After I finished eating, I got up and washed my hands then pulled out the local phone directory. I was going to look for a Spanish immersion school. I already had two names from a nurse in La Jolla I worked with. She'd gone to school in Mexico City and had two names of language schools there. So, I thumbed through the Yellow Pages after I put the TV channel on a music channel playing Dixieland music. I love Dixieland."

"If you didn't know Spanish, how could you read their Yellow Pages?" Marcel asked.

Good question. Thaddeus waited for Johann's answer.

"Well, I tried but wasn't really successful."

Marcel nodded, not showing what he thought of that one way or the other. "Okay, what did you do next?"

"I ordered a pot of coffee from room service and was kind of deciding I wanted to stay in that night and maybe eat in my room. But that didn't happen. My dad came over from his room and started telling me about the Argentine food, and I didn't want to let him down. So, I changed clothes, and we went downstairs together."

"This was about what time?" Marcel asked.

"About five, five-thirty. We were going to eat early and get to bed early because his meeting the next day was an early-morning one, and he always hit the gym to start his day."

"How long were you out of your rooms then at dinner?"

"We found the restaurant, went inside, and each had a beer, then we ordered, ate, settled the bill, and walked a few blocks outside. We stopped at a cafe and had our after-dinner coffee. Then we caught a cab back to the Hilton. We went upstairs to his room, hung out watching a soccer game, and then after about a half hour, I went back to my room. I changed into sweats and began reading on my Kindle. All told, we were gone about two hours, maybe a bit more."

"So, what time was it when you got back to your room?" asked Marcel.

Thaddeus was glad for him to take the lead so he could watch Johann's reactions. He wasn't a profiler like an FBI agent, but he'd learned some signs along the way when someone was lying or not.

"I'm just guessing now, but maybe seven-thirty or eight. It was after the soccer game on TV."

"What did your dad do that night, if you know?"

"I don't know. He got up the next morning and went to work out and then went across the street to his meeting at the back room in the restaurant. This was probably before I even woke up. I was tired and jet-lagged and slept in. Next thing I knew, there was this huge explosion. It sounded like it was downstairs in our hotel. The whole room shook, so I lunged out of bed and looked out my window. It was like looking through clouds on an airplane. Except the clouds were an ugly brown color and they were swirling and twisting all through the streets and climbing higher and higher. There were sirens going off and people running every which way. All traffic had come to a complete stop, like no one knew where to go to get away so they just pulled over."

"What did you do?"

"I immediately turned and called my dad's room on the phone. No answer, so I called his cell phone. Again, no answer. I was horrified and more scared than I'd ever been. My hands were shaking, and my room was filling up with the smoke from outside. Turns out, I'd left my sliding door open about a foot for fresh air overnight, and now the smoke was pouring in. So, I slammed it shut and went out into the hallway. People were standing in the hall, asking each other what happened in Spanish and basically looking as bewildered as I was. So, I went back inside and found a Mexican news channel. I watched and read the subtitles. There was no news—at first—about where the explosion had taken place. Then, after about fifteen minutes, word started coming in. About a half hour after that, they said the explosion had occurred at a restaurant across from the Hilton where I was staying. Then it came to me—it was the restaurant where my dad was having his meeting. I immediately ran down the stairway to the first-floor lobby and tore out into the street. There were fire trucks and police vans and cars everywhere. Men and women in uniform had taken over the intersection, and some of them were manning fire hoses. I was lost and didn't even know what I was looking for. A policeman told me in English to return to my room, which I did."

"What did you do there?"

"There was nothing to do. So, I called Dad's office in San Diego. I knew his SAIC and finally got through. His name is Special Agent Billy McCrory. I've known him basically all my life. He came on the line, and his voice sounded very calm and steady. He told me my dad had been at the restaurant that exploded. He didn't try to make me feel better or hopeful or anything. He just took my number and promised to call me as soon as he had news. So, we hung up, and I called my mom. She's a surgeon and was in surgery the first time I called her earlier. She does orthopedics, and her office told me the surgery was a spine something that would take about five hours. Of all mornings to have a long one. Anyway, there was nothing I could get done there, so I gave her office my hotel number and asked her to call immediately. Then I pulled a chair over next to the sliding door and began watching what was going on down below."

"How were you handling it by then?" asked Thaddeus.

"I was alternating between cursing a blue streak and just sitting there in terror. But I tried to stay calm. As a nurse, I'm pretty used to trauma and bad things happening unexpectedly. I also know about hospitals and ERs. I called up several in the area and left word I was looking for my dad. I gave everyone his name and my phone number. Then I waited."

"Who did you hear from first?"

"About an hour later, my mom called me. They were just finishing up and she was returning a page with my number. When we talked, she came unglued and said she was calling Billy McCrory and hung up."

"Johann, I don't want to ask you this, but I have to. How did you get along with your dad? Any problems there?" Marcel asked.

Johann re-settled in his metal chair. "We got along wonderfully. I adored my dad. I mean, there were some high school things that I'm not proud of when he came down hard on me and grounded me and stuff like that. There was one girlfriend he ran off my junior year. She was twenty-five. Stuff like that. But after I got into college and started studying nursing, there were never any problems between us."

"What about your mom? How do you get along with her?"

"Tell the truth? I knew my dad much better than I knew my mom growing up. She was always at the hospital doing surgery, rounds, or being on call. My dad was gone a lot, too, with the FBI, but when he was home, he was there for me, ya know? Even when my mom was home, half the time she ignored us. She had a home office she worked in."

"Us? There are siblings?"

"Two sisters, both younger. They aren't doing so good now with Dad gone."

"So, what happened after you spoke with your mom that morning?"

"I guess she called Uncle Billy because he called me about fifteen minutes later. They had preliminary confirmation that the FBI meeting and the task force was underway at the restaurant when the bomb exploded. He didn't have any other information, but he warned me it wasn't looking good. Then he said there was already an FBI task force en route and they'd probably contact me. I should cooperate with them and stuff. But he still said he'd be my main contact at the FBI since he'd know everything as soon as the FBI did."

"Interesting," said Marcel.

"What's that?" asked Thaddeus.

"The FBI has a field office in Mexico City. Interesting they'd send another team there. Or maybe not. I guess not. They probably sent a terrorism team to take over the investigation. We'll find out as we dig in."

"What difference does it make?" Johann asked. "It's all the same FBI, right?"

"Perhaps so," said Marcel. "I'll find out. I'm making my notes. So... when did you definitively find out something about your dad?"

"Late that first night, Uncle Billy called me. They had identified my dad, dead at the scene. No particulars or anything, just Uncle Billy telling me he had some bad news."

Thaddeus hadn't said much up to that point but wanted Johann to know he was sorry for his loss. It was almost a year later, but

Thaddeus knew from his own experience that pain lingered from the memories of a loved one.

"Thank you, Thaddeus," said Johann, who was then quiet for a moment before, "Oh, one other thing. The police came around to all the rooms and searched them. They told everyone not to leave. Not to remove luggage or other articles. The next day, FBI response teams were everywhere on the entire block. You could see a dozen FBI windbreakers just by looking out my balcony window. Then they started coming around to the rooms and pulling suitcases and travel cases and taking off with them. It was a massive logistical job since they had to load trucks down on the street with every conceivable thing they seized from all the guests. That's just from my hotel, let alone all the shops and restaurants and apartments around the area. By the time they were done with me, I was allowed to keep my toothbrush, my hairbrush, and clean socks and clean T-shirts. Everything else was seized. They didn't care that my dad was FBI, either. My stuff got seized just like everyone else's. Including my suitcase and carry-on bag. My mom made travel arrangements for me the next morning. I was going home."

"I thought the FBI told everyone to stay for statements."

"Uncle Billy got around that for me. I was allowed to leave the perimeter they'd set up the next morning. The taxi took me to the airport, and I was airborne before seven a.m. That's the last I saw of Mexico. I haven't been back there since."

"How many times has the FBI talked to you since then?"

"Maybe three."

"Where has Billy McCrory been? How come he didn't let you know you were wanted by the FBI?"

"I went on a Doctors Without Borders trip a week after the bombing. Billy had no idea where I'd gone. Not even my own mother knew because I didn't know for sure where we were going until after we left Rio by bus. But I was hurting real bad for my dad and I needed to get busy. Deep into the Amazon we went. That's all I know to this day. I have no idea where we were except it was jungle and it was the most ancient medical facilities. Most of their equipment had gone out at the turn of the Twentieth Century. They were still treating people without even the most minimum of techniques and medications and instruments. It was almost stone-age where we were."

"Could the FBI have called you there?"

He smiled. "It was jungle. No phones, definitely no cell service."

"But it was in Brazil?" asked Marcel.

He shrugged. "I landed in Rio, but then it was three days of travel by bus and a day by boat. I can't swear where we were."

"Name of the place?"

"Ixotl. That's all I know. Ixotl. It's pronounced Iz-Tell."

"All right. What else haven't we asked about, Johann?" asked Marcel.

"You haven't asked about the investigation. But you can get all that from the FBI."

"Tell me what you know."

"Nothing, really. The morning I went to the post office and saw my picture, I'd only gotten back to the States a week before. I just started a new job at Rady Children's Hospital, working with abused children. I hadn't even had a chance to call my mom or sisters. Uncle Billy had warned her they wanted to talk to me, but she hadn't been able to get hold of me either. So, it's been a mess."

"So, the FBI was hot on your trail, but your known trail actually ended in Rio de Janeiro?"

"Pretty much, that's it. Otherwise I would've come right in and tried to straighten this mess out. Now look where I am." Tears clouded his eyes. "I'm sorry. I loved my dad."

Marcel asked, "Johann, if I asked you how in the world an explosive marker found its way into your suitcase, what would be your best guess?"

"That I unwittingly smuggled the explosive for someone. That's all I can think of."

"Really? And how did that piece of luggage make it through TSA?"

"That's the hard part. I don't know."

Marcel said, "Johann, TSA's Analogic scanner works like a CT machine in a hospital, seeing through a cluttered bag and giving screeners the ability to zoom in and rotate the bag for a three-hundred-sixty-degree view. Even so, it's not fool-proof. But if an object is dense enough, as explosives are, either the scanners will find it or the dogs will. Still, you could've been one of the one-in-ten-million who makes it through with Semtex on board. Scary to think of, but possible. So, let me rephrase. Who might see you as a possible mule for explosives? Were you having trouble with anyone at work or elsewhere?"

"As a nurse, I've worked with people with lots of problems, from physical to mental. God only knows what's happening inside some of those brains."

"I get that," said Marcel, "but think hard. Is there any one of them who stands out as someone who might want to hurt you?"

"Not offhand. I can't think of anyone. On the great stage of life, Mr. Rainford, I'm a nobody."

Marcel nodded and continued making notes. "Now let's jump to the other end. The suitcase at the hotel. Who might want to sneak into your room and mark your suitcase with the explosive that was going to be planted to kill your dad? Who might want to do that to you?"

"Someone who might want to throw the FBI off the real killers' trail," said Thaddeus. "Someone who used Johann as a red herring."

"Exactly," said Marcel. "And I think that's our starting point. Johann, like any investigator, I want to simply believe your story because you're obviously a good person. However, taking that approach would be an injustice to you. Taking that approach might cause us to lose track of real evidence that might be there just waiting to lead us to the real killers. So, I'm going to remain neutral on your story going in. I mean, I'm going to try to keep a completely open mind."

Marcel tapped his pen on the notebook in front of him. His handwriting was so neat Thaddeus could read Marcel's notes from his adjacent seat. Most likely his military training and correspondence before everything went digital. "Having done that, I have no signposts pointing toward you as a smuggler. Now I'm going to look at you as a victim of someone who was using your suitcase and your position as an agent's son to throw the FBI off the track. Someone who wanted to make them expend resources going after you rather than after the real bad guys. Okay?"

"I think I follow."

"That puts me in your camp. I see no reason not to believe you at this time, and that is how I'm going to proceed. But keep in mind, I'm also watching for any sign, any jot or tittle or penumbra of a clue, that you might have done something to help the bombers. You might even have helped without knowing it, without intending to. So, I'm keeping that possibility in mind and, if it floats to the surface, I'm going to be the first to make the FBI aware. Ordinarily, in criminal cases, if I find out bad stuff about the defendant, I don't tell the cops. This time I would because there might be other lives at risk. Do you follow me?"

"I-I think so. Right now, I'm innocent until you think I did something. And if you change your mind and find something bad, you're going to go straight to the FBI with it. Am I right?"

"Pretty much that's it. Counsel?" This last was directed at Thaddeus.

Thaddeus shook his head. "I don't like the idea of you taking inculpatory evidence to the feds, Marcel. That would seem to violate my oath as an attorney."

"Ah," said Marcel, holding up with one finger and smiling, "don't forget. I said that would happen only if I believed more lives were at risk."

"Then, in that case, it would be my obligation to go to the FBI too," said Thaddeus. "So, I think we're on the same page."

"We're on the same page," Marcel said. "I always tell Michael Gresham the same thing. Even if a client has to go to jail in order to save other innocents, the other innocents will be protected. That is the only way I can work."

"Then that's how it has to be," Thaddeus said. "I think we're both saying the same thing, that inculpatory evidence will be disclosed to the FBI if lives are risk. But only if lives are at risk."

"Yes," said Marcel, "only if lives are at risk. If we learn that Johann, in fact, planted the bomb himself, or smuggled the bomb himself, and there's no threat of his one bad act harming anyone else, then we don't disclose. But if there's a chance it might happen again, we disclose. Johann, are you following?"

"I think so. I just want out of here."

"Of course," Marcel said, "and we want you out. I'm leaving for Mexico City tomorrow morning."

"And I'm sending my own investigator, Turquoise Murfee, with Marcel. So, we'll have two sets of eyes and ears on everything down there. We'll get it done."

Thaddeus knew he'd caught Marcel off-guard on that little tidbit of information he had refrained from telling him thus far. But as much as he trusted Jack Rasso's recommendation, he trusted Turquoise with his life. She just didn't have the Spanish and connections that Marcel had.

Even if Thaddeus's announcement bothered Marcel, he didn't show it. Marcel mollified the client with, "Thaddeus will do every-thing in his power to shorten your stay in jail."

Johann nodded. "I believe that. All right, please call me every day. I need to hear something."

"I will," Thaddeus promised. "Even if it's just to say, 'nothing new,' I'll call you."

"Promise?" he said.

"I promise to do everything that can be done."

13

The plane's wheels hit the hot tarmac at Mexico City International Airport just after two p.m. Turquoise let out a deep breath through pursed lips. She didn't mind traveling. She actually enjoyed it. But it had felt like a long flight with Marcel next to her.

He was a big man, and even with the first-class seating and extra space, he seemed uncomfortable, shifting often in his seat. During the flight, they had talked only briefly about the case, their strategy once they hit the ground running, and what were their hopeful results. But after that, Marcel put on Bose wireless headphones and closed his eyes. But before he did, he'd actually excused himself, stating that he wanted to rest up.

Wow, a gentleman of caliber. That was rare in today's world, she thought.

Turquoise was too wired to relax. She tried leafing through the inflight magazines and watching a movie but spent most of the flight juggling thoughts in her head. About Johann Van Giersbergen, about terrorism, about her family and work, but mostly about the man next to her.

So,she was thankful when the wheels finally touched down and they started taxiing to the terminal. Marcel had remained silent, his eyes closed, even at touchdown. But when the flight attendant announced their arrival, his eyes flew open and he was wide awake. Turquoise knew because her eyes seemed to be as often on him as they were out the window as the plane coasted through the clouds before landing.

Marcel insisted on carrying her carry-on luggage, the only bag Turquoise had brought. She didn't believe in checked baggage. And it seemed that Marcel didn't either. The big man pulled both of their cases, a leather briefcase over one shoulder. For the first time in a long while, Turquoise had nothing to do. So, she followed behind him, trying not to stare at his butt in his jeans.

Luckily, Marcel was all business, and Turquoise quickly shifted into her professional gear. After leaving the airport by taxi, they were quickly jetted away to the Mexico City Hilton, the same place Johann and his father had stayed while they were visiting last August. Her dad thought it was the most convenient and easiest place to start.

Turquoise agreed, but first they needed to meet up with one of Marcel's contacts. So, after they checked in—separate rooms of course—and dumped their luggage, freshened up with some deodorant and a brush of teeth, they were off and running. Turquoise didn't expect anything less. Her father was the epitome of professionalism, her mother, too. Both represented what it meant to work hard, be kind, and keep life's priorities straight. Meaning family, health, creativity, music, nature. Everything they'd taught her since she'd been adopted when she was sixteen.

Marcel made a couple of calls, and the next thing Turquoise knew, one of his "friends" had come around to the hotel with a car.

Surrounded by Mexico City taxis, the black and silver Range Rover stood out like a sore thumb. A man, younger than Marcel but older than Turquoise, with dirty-blond hair and a goatee, rose out the driver's side and came around the front of the car to the curb where they stood. He shook Marcel's hand heartily and then turned to Turquoise. He smiled and waited for Marcel to introduce her before he held out his hand for her to shake.

"This is an old colleague of mine with Interpol, Kevin Thatcher. Kevin, this is another investigator, Turquoise Murfee."

They all got into the car, Marcel in the front seat with Kevin, Turquoise in the back.

"We going to see Juan?" Marcel asked Kevin.

"Yeah, I thought we could start there."

"Good idea."

They traveled for about a half hour, out of the downtown and the *Centro Histórico* and into a suburb Marcel referred to as Le Merced. Off the main street on pedestrian avenues was row after row of markets, selling everything from shoes to traditional Mexican blankets, produce and cigarettes and T-shirts to Adidas and Nike knock-off gym bags.

Kevin told her to roll down her window. "Smell."

Not the safest area of town, but Turquoise still *felt* safe with Marcel, for some reason. After rolling down her window, Turquoise drew a deep breath. A couple of the spices she recognized, also used in traditional Native American food, like cumin and oregano. But there was also an unusual smell, just lying underneath the pungent smell of garlic and onion. Altogether, they combined to make her mouth water.

"Good, right?" asked Kevin.

Turquoise had to agree, and her stomach rumbled in response. Luckily, Kevin was playing Latin rock music so loud on the radio it hid the sound. He honked and yelled at a man on a scooter who was driving the wrong way up a one-way street that Kevin was trying to get down.

Finally, they parked across from Café Equis, a building painted in bright yellow with blue trim. Across the top read *La Casa Del Café*. The small tables outside on the sidewalk had yellow tablecloths and mismatched chairs of all types.

Kevin motioned for them to follow him and Turquoise was surprised when Marcel laid a hand at the small of her back and moved her forward, like a man would do for his date.

When she looked at him, he whispered, "Pardon, *señorita*, I forget myself." He gave her a cocky smile. "I know you can take care of yourself."

Before she could respond, Kevin told them to sit at one of the tables and said he would be right back. It was the middle of the afternoon, just after siesta, so there weren't many out and about yet. Kevin returned shortly with a Mexican gentleman in black jeans and a gray and white checkered shirt.

"Hola," said the man with a smile. He sat down and continued in English, "Nice to meet you."

Kevin introduced them, and minutes later, Marcel had dipped into business. He asked about the bombing last year, what the word on the street was who did it, how the Americans were involved. They spoke in English in hushed voices about what Juan knew. He'd been part of the Policía Federal Preventiva back then before he'd been shot in the leg and had retired to run a coffee house.

Mostly, the conversation kept coming back around to an American agent, Angelo Andrus. Juan kept repeating to Marcel that they needed to start with him.

After two cups of strong Mexican coffee, Turquoise was wired. Marcel's leg was also jumping underneath the table, and she was glad when Kevin finally said their goodbyes to Juan.

It was getting late, near to six p.m., but Marcel still wanted to talk to the housekeeper at the Hilton before they stopped for the day and got dinner.

Kevin dropped them off in front of the hotel, and he and Marcel embraced in a man hug before Kevin gave Turquoise a kiss on the cheek. "*Hermosa*," he said in Spanish to her, but when she looked to Marcel for the meaning behind the word, he only shrugged and smiled.

They made their way to reception where Marcel had already made arrangements to talk to the housekeeper who had cleaned Johann's room last year. They were lucky in that she still worked at the hotel. When Marcel asked for her, the clerk requested they wait a minute in the lobby area while she was fetched.

Turquoise dropped onto one of the brown suede couches, decorated with bright red and yellow throw pillows. There was a long coffee table separating the couches that sported wooden bowls filled with potpourri and decorative rocks.

Surprisingly, Marcel sat right next to her. He stretched his arm out behind her on the couch back.

A little nervous, and a little happy for his arm there, Turquoise asked him, "So, what does that mean? Hermosa?"

But just then the clerk, whose name tag read Alejandro, approached and asked them to follow him to a private room.

They walked inside a small conference room, void of any personal touches with only a long table and office chairs. There was one Frida Kahlo painting, or a print of her work, on the far wall. It was the one with the watermelons. Turquoise couldn't remember the name, but it was one of her more positive paintings, not as...dark as some of the others. There were no windows in the room. At the end of the table sat an older woman with gray hair pulled back in a bun at the nape of her neck. She seemed nervous, and so very small in her chair.

"Hola," said Turquoise and smiled, trying to alleviate some of the woman's anxiety.

Marcel greeted her, too, and then turned to wait for the clerk to leave. When he didn't, Marcel asked him to.

"Do you not need an interpreter?" Alejandro asked.

Marcel shook his head. "We're good, thank you."

The man nodded and left, eyeing the housekeeper quickly before he shut the door.

Marcel spoke to the woman in Spanish, of which Turquoise could only follow a little bit. When the woman finished speaking, Marcel translated for Turquoise. "Basically, I asked her why she'd gone into Johann's room that day. She said she'd been told to clean the room, that's all. When I asked her if anyone else had gone in with her, she was adamant there hadn't been."

"Why would she try to clean a room when there was a guest already there?"

Marcel turned back to the woman and said something in Spanish. Turquoise assumed it was what she had wondered a moment ago.

The woman then became agitated, repeating over and over, "*No quiero perder mi trabajo.*"

Marcel told Turquoise, "The woman was behind schedule cleaning the rooms. She was meant to clean it before the guest arrived. She didn't tell her manager this at the time because she didn't want to lose her job."

Marcel and Turquoise thanked the woman, whose name Marcel finally asked for at the end of the interview. Maria Gonzalez, she said. Mother of five and grandmother of thirteen.

As they were walking back to the lobby, Turquoise said, "Your Spanish is excellent."

Marcel smiled at her. "*Gracias, mujer hermosa.*"

Turquoise playfully punched him in the arm. "There's that word again. *Hermosa.* What does it mean?"

Marcel punched the up button on the elevator. He didn't look at her when he said, "Beautiful. It means beautiful."

14

Thaddeus had told Rachel what to say. The time came to say it during her weekly visit with her psychologist. The visit was a house call made by Dr. Indira Kapur to the Sundstrom home. Rachel would be awake long enough to participate for one-half of the thirty-minute visit. She struggled even to do that, adjusting the flow of morphine into her line with the self-dosing.

So, far, the psychologist had asked about her level of depression on a scale of one to ten, and Rachel had said her depression was a ten. She said she couldn't imagine feeling any more depressed and that her life had never felt this sad before. She talked about her loss of appetite and about how she even set aside her Air Pods and couldn't listen to her music anymore.

"You don't like music?" asked Dr. Kapur, a polite, quiet woman of twenty-nine who wore saris and a dot on her forehead.

"Music doesn't appeal to me right now. It's all about love and relationships. I'm never going to have a relationship, so how can I listen?"

"What else is going on? How is the pain for you?"

"Seriously? Do you not see this morphine bag?" Rachel cringed at her affront and apologized to the woman who was only trying to help her. "I'm sorry. It hurts right now."

"That's all right. It was not a perfect question."

Rachel thought, *here goes,* and said, "Doctor, I want to end my life. Will you be my psychological witness for that?"

Dr. Kapur put a hand to her chest. "I'm sorry, what are you asking of me?"

Rachel toyed with the IV line, sliding her fingers up and down the tube, a piece of plastic that had become so much a part of her life. "I'm going to court with Mr. Murfee, my lawyer. He says I need a psychologist to tell the court I'm able to think clearly and decide things for myself. Will you do that for me?"

There was a moment of silence when Rachel couldn't look at the doctor, but then the woman said, "I will. I don't necessarily agree with that decision, but I'm your doctor. You deserve my help, and I can't withhold it from you."

Rachel looked up then and smiled. "That's so cool. Thank you, thank you. I'll tell Mr. Murfee. If you go to court, what will you say about it?"

"I'll say your thinking and understanding are that of a typical late teen, and there's no reason you can't be relied on for clear thinking. I'll say I've watched you suffer. I'll say I disagree with your goal, but that my disagreement doesn't make it wrong. I've never been where you are, so how can I disagree with what you know is best for you?"

She self-dosed. Seconds later, her eyelids were closing. She was very still in her bed, and her head sagged sideways on the pillow. Dr. Kapur knew to wait, that it would be a matter of five or ten minutes until she came back from the slight dose. The doctor pulled out her iPad and began filling out insurance forms and making notes in Rachel's chart. She reasoned that the patient was living in pain and a situation that was far beyond her years in terms of how to deal with it. But wasn't that the patient's point? Hadn't she been given a situation that most adults would find impossible? It was no wonder she wanted to die.

The doctor could professionally take no issue with that. Plus, she was Hindi and a believer in reincarnation. She'd seen others like this in her hometown of Bangalore. She decided just then she would become an advocate for the girl. She would take her side in this. She could do that and still be able to tell the judge she disagreed personally with the patient's decision but that professionally she was able to pronounce the patient capable of making those judgments about her own life.

She had charted Rachel's visit and two more cases when the girl returned from her sleep twenty minutes later. "Oh," she said, stretching and yawning. "We were talking. I'm sorry."

"I was about to tell you that yes, I will be your witness, and I will tell the court you're mature enough and clear-minded enough to make up your own mind about your life. While I will also tell the judge I don't agree with your decision, should he ask me, I'll also tell him I won't stand in your way. I will encourage him or her to allow you to make your own decision. I think it's the right of a seventeen-year-old girl who's terminally ill to say what comes next for her. I'll be there for you, Rachel."

"Thank you. I'm really hurting now because it's getting later in the day. I'm going to dose again and sleep."

"Goodbye, Rachel. Sweet dreams."

"Thank you."

The doctor gathered her bag and slipped her iPad inside and headed for the family room where she'd tell nurse June she was leaving. June would be in there enjoying a cold frappe while Rachel was occupied. She'd be right back on duty when Indira went on her way.

"How is she?" asked June from Dr. Sundstrom's recliner.

"She's hurting. She just now dosed again and said goodbye."

"Did she ask about being her witness?"

"She did."

"What did you tell her?"

"I said I'd be her witness. I said her thoughts are organized and logical and her mind's clear. She has the ability to make life decisions about her disease and her life. It's all true."

"I know. I told her I'd say pretty much the same thing, without all the doctor curlicues, you know."

"She's a fantastic girl with a great mind and a huge amount of creativity whose energy has been zeroed out. As we sometimes say, it isn't a life worth living once that happens, especially to a teenager. With older people, that's not so unusual. But teenagers, they're on fire with life, soaring, creative, all-consuming of everything around them. To see that at zero in Rachel's life is tragic and actionable. She should be empowered to end it."

"I'll tell Doctor and Mrs. Sundstrom."

"Really? I'm under the impression her health care providers

discuss visits only with Rachel. That was her wish going in. Her waiver doesn't say anything about her parents. Let's leave them out of this, shall we?"

Chastened, June agreed. "Yes, you're right. I won't say anything to them."

15

While the criminal case was pending against Johann, Thaddeus decided it was best to go over the discovery documents with Turquoise and Marcel face to face in Mexico City. Time was of the essence, and he could work with them directly without interfering too much with their investigation on the ground. Thaddeus took a late flight out of San Diego and arrived after midnight where he booked himself into a suite at the Hilton where they were staying.

First thing the next morning, Thaddeus requested Turquoise and Marcel come to his suite where he had coffee, croissants, fruit, and yoghurt brought in for their meeting.

Surprisingly, they both arrived at the same time, and when Thaddeus joked about their timeliness, both seemed uncomfortable. Turquoise took a seat at the table and poured coffee for the three of them, then shoveled some fruit and yoghurt into a bowl. Marcel sat next to her and dropped a pad of paper on the table. "Shall we get started?"

Thaddeus looked back and forth between them, but neither caught his eye. Something was going on, but now obviously wasn't the time to approach whatever it was. Turquoise was a professional, and what he knew of Marcel, he was, too, so he had to assume they could conduct business as usual.

"The discovery is online. I suggest we go over it first thing today," Thaddeus began. He had placed his laptop on the table and began reading out loud.

First up was Johann's oral statement, taken from him by the FBI. *Defendant's Oral Statement* was the document. Upon reading, they had learned Johann had answered questions posed by the FBI and FBI crime scene techs on two occasions. The gist of his statement was what he'd told Thaddeus and Marcel when they visited him in jail. He made the point several times that he hadn't knowingly carried anyone else's bag or article onboard the aircraft out of San Diego, that he didn't know how the Semtex marker chemical came to be inside of his suitcase, that no one had approached him about helping with an explosive or package.

No, his father had never severely punished him, never hit or beat him, never denied him any financial assistance that he'd requested, and he'd never sexually assaulted him. No, he wasn't angry with him, didn't have a score to settle, and knew of no other person who might have a grudge or pent-up anger or want to do harm to Ned Van Giersbergen.

Johann didn't feel overly close to his father but didn't think that was unusual. This was the main difference in what he'd told Marcel and Thaddeus at the jail. At the time, Johann had said he was closer to his father than mother.

While at the hotel in Mexico City, Johann had voluntarily given fingerprints, hair samples, and allowed the computer techs to download a copy of his hard drive.

"What do you think?" Thaddeus asked when they'd finished reading that portion of the discovery document together.

"About what I'd expect," Marcel said. "Except the part where he said he never felt very close to his father."

"Yes, but honestly, I imagine Ned was away from home constantly, and Johann probably felt cheated or ignored. Most kids would feel that way," Thaddeus said.

"But different than what he told us at the jail."

"True," agreed Thaddeus, "but we change our minds about how we feel about people."

Marcel nodded. "He also was totally cooperative, as if he didn't have anything to hide."

Thaddeus smiled. "Playing devil's advocate—he has nothing to hide or he's so good at acting he has us thinking that."

Marcel smiled back at him. "I like you, Thaddeus. We think a lot alike. Okay, what else we got?"

"Uh-oh, jumping down here, look at this. Guy named Angelo Andrus. He's FBI counter-intelligence. Why in the world would they have counter-intelligence listed as a witness, I wonder?"

"That's strange," Turquoise pointed out. "That's the same name Juan gave us a couple of days ago."

"In what context?" Thaddeus asked.

Turquoise shrugged. "Basically, Juan said the word on the street is that he's the key to this whole thing. If we start with him, we'll find our answers."

"Counter-intelligence could be any number of things," Marcel said. "In the context of the FBI investigation into Johann Van Giersbergen and the bomb explosion, it might be they're looking into the possibility one of their agents was a double agent, *or* it could be as simple as Andrus was in charge of the terrorist investigation, the team the US sent here at the time."

"Are you saying they might be looking into an FBI agent who's gone over to the other side? Say, he's working with the Russians?" Thaddeus asked.

"Yes, or the Chinese or the Iranians. It's been known to happen."

Thaddeus moved the mouse and scrolled back up to the top of the witness list. "Let's see who else we've got besides Angelo Andrus and see whether we can derive more context about him. Under federal law and the rules of discovery, the government must permit the defendant to inspect and copy photograph books, papers, documents, data, photographs, tangible objects, buildings, or places. Which would explain the two-hundred-twenty-nine photographs attached. What in the world are they?"

All three crowded around to study the computer screen as Thaddeus slowly scrolled screen after screen of photographs. They depicted photographs of men and women sitting in open cafes, strolling past Mexican churches, making purchases in Mexican stores, studying a newspaper on a streetcar, waiting in lines at museums and art galleries, standing on street corners. The exposure ranged from early morning sunshine in the background to high noon to evening and night.

The more they studied the photographs, the more aware they became that the human subject was the same man: Johann Van Giersbergen. There were over a dozen of Johann with the same man, unknown to any of them.

"The FBI was surveilling one of its children," Marcel commented. "Which leads to me to believe they thought he was up to no good. I think we've got a situation where the FBI thought one of its sons was a foreign agent. This really skews this case around."

"Not only that," said Turquoise, "but I got the impression from Marcel that Johann said he wasn't in Mexico City very long. At least not with his father. So, when were these pictures taken?"

"Good question." Thaddeus dragged his hand down his face. It looked like he'd bitten off possibly more than he could chew. "Johann is charged with facilitating the explosion by acting in concert with another. The conspiracy. And he's being followed by the FBI and photographed before his father was blown up in an explosion they're saying Johann facilitated. What in the world?"

"I know," Marcel said. "When the government starts thinking foreign agent of an FBI agent's child, you can get all kinds of crazy. This appears to be one of those cases."

"Still, how easy is it going to be for them to prove this loving son blew up his own father? They'll never make that case."

Marcel stood up and stretched. "Tell me, Thaddeus. How well do you know Johann?"

"Not well at all. Just like any other new client."

"What caused you to jump in one-hundred percent, going out of the way to hire me and finance a fact-finding trip to Mexico?"

Thaddeus nodded. "I get it. You don't know me, Mr. Rainford. When I take on a case, those items you mention are of no concern to me. I'm in for a dime, in for a dollar. I'm a hundred-percent guy."

Turquoise said, "I can vouch for that."

"I defend my clients the same way I'd want to be defended."

Marcel scratched his jaw. He checked his watch. "Mind if I order up some lunch? We've got a long afternoon."

"Sounds good," said Turquoise at the same time as her father.

16

A fter lunch, they reestablished their place with the discovery documents and resumed reading. They turned their attention to that part of the report entitled *Reports of Examinations and Tests.*

In a federal criminal case, if a defendant requests, the government must permit inspection and copying of the results or reports of any physical or mental examination and of any scientific test or experiment. In this case, there had been no physical or mental examination, but there were 200+ pages of reports and studies from the scientific testing and analysis of the bomb fragments and chemicals recovered from the crime scene. Testing, according to the FBI crime lab, included a determination that the explosive was, in fact, Semtex.

The FBI report stated about Semtex:

Semtex is the best plastic explosive in the world. It feels like Play-Doh, has no smell, and was designed in 1966 to clear land-mines and improve industrial safety. It is also undetectable by dogs and airport security devices, and after it left Mr. Brebera's laboratory in 1968, Semtex became the favored weapon of international terrorists from Libya to Northern Ireland.

Since Sept. II, the Czech Republic and its new NATO allies have become increasingly nervous about the continued production and sale of Brebera's fatal concoction.

Over the past two decades, terrorists have employed Semtex in several deadly attacks, including the 1988 explosion of Pan Am flight 103 over Lockerbie, Scotland, and the 1998 bombing of the US Embassy in Nairobi, Kenya. And no one has found a reliable way to combat it. Named after Semtin, the village in East Bohemia where Brebera invented it, this extraordinarily stable compound of RDX (Cyclonite) and PETN (Penaerythrite Tetranitrate) slips through airport security scans as easily as a pair of nylons.

At this point, Turquoise interrupted Thaddeus's reading. "Could've it been possible for Johann to have gotten it through TSA?"

Marcel must have filled her in. She was right. Thaddeus said as much and asked for Marcel's opinion since he'd been there at the jail.

Marcel nodded. "Looks like it's very possible. Like I told Johann, my mind is totally open."

Thaddeus continued reading. *According to the FBI, Semtex has an indefinite half-life and is far stronger than traditional explosives such as TNT. It is also easily available on the black market.*

Semtex became infamous when just 12 ounces of the substance, molded inside a Toshiba cassette recorder, blasted Pan Am flight 103 out of the sky above Lockerbie, Scotland, in December 1988, killing 270 people. A year later, after the Czech Communist regime was toppled, the new

*president, Vaclav Havel, revealed that the Czechs had exported 900
tons of Semtex to Col. Moammar Qaddafi's Libya and another 1,000
tons to other unstable states such as Syria, North Korea, Iraq, and
Iran. Some experts now put worldwide stockpiles of Semtex at 40,000
tons.*

*Brebera says that with so much Semtex already in the hands of terror-
ists, and similar explosives being produced in other countries, the Czech
Republic can no longer control it. "Semtex is no worse an explosive than
any other," he says, defensive at the sight of accusatory headlines in
Western newspapers. "The American explosive C4 is just as invisible to
airport X-rays, but they don't like to mention that."*

*After the Lockerbie tragedy, Brebera added metal components and a
distinct odor to make Semtex easier to detect. But that did not stop
terrorists from using it to bomb the US Embassy in Nairobi, Kenya, in
1998, or prevent the IRA, which received about 10 tons of Semtex from
Libya, from continuing its attacks.*

The report then went on to describe how, after several days of
sifting through the Mexico City evidence, the FBI identified and
marked 85 questionable specimens, including fragments of wire,
metal, magnets, cable, circuit boards, batteries, and other items.
The FBI noted that, in selecting items for examination, they
looked for debris that showed the effects of the explosion.

Several weeks later, they sent approximately half of the specimens, specimens Q41 through Q85, for examination to the FBI
Laboratory in Washington, D.C. After receiving the specimens,
criminalist Ian Whitehurst conducted examinations using gas
chromatograph/mass spectrometry.

Whitehurst reported that he found a residue of the explosive
compound RDX on three of the specimens, Q46, Q69, and Q72.
Whitehurst stated that the FBI had collected vials of acetone

extracts from swabbings at the scene and analyzed the vials using the Ion Mobility Spectrometer.

When asked if the FBI found any traces of explosives, Whitehurst stated to counsel that specimens Q41 through Q72, in particular, gave indications on the mass spectrometer of RDX. He added that after a second analysis, specimens Q46, Q69 and Q72 gave confirmation of RDX.

"What we have, in a nutshell," said Marcel, "is Semtex. Good old Czech Semtex. Bastards would blow up the world if left to their own greed."

"Twelve ounces took down the Lockerbie plane?" whispered Turquoise in awe. "Good God, what is this stuff they say Johann had in his suitcase? It's difficult, if not impossible, to identify at airports either with cat scanners or dogs, and it has no odor?"

Marcel smiled. "At first, I was very skeptical that Johann would've smuggled a load of Semtex. Now I'm thinking differently, given the residue report. This stuff moves around easily enough that anyone can smuggle it. Much less a young man traveling with a known FBI agent. I wonder if that might have served to make San Diego TSA even less cautious with their bags and carry-ons? Just how much did our boy know?"

Thaddeus tapped his pen on the table. "What we're now left with is ease of transport, coupled with the fact his bag was shown to have traces of Semtex. That's on the next page where they talk about external findings—findings external to the crime scene itself. His bag is the only other connection to the Semtex in the entire six square block area of the blast site. One suitcase."

"The noose has tightened around our client's neck," mused Marcel. "I hate to say it, but it's true, Thaddeus. This report is very scientific and is going to pull a jury's chain."

"Yes, a jury will be impressed. Very impressed. As am I. It's really got my mind racing, Marcel. I'm really wondering how innocent my client is right now. Forgive me, but I'm only human."

"We all have those moments of second-guessing ourselves. Michael Gresham does it every time he gets ready for trial. You're no different."

"Thanks for that," said Thaddeus with a broad smile.

"But you have to believe he is innocent, Dad. That is your job."

"Let's just say I have to make the jury believe that." He squeezed Turquoise's hand on the table.

"So, who do you depose first?" asked Marcel.

"I want Angelo Andrus first. I'll begin with counter-intelligence. He'll give up names that will lead me to my next deposition and my next. At the same time, I'll be passing names to you to investigate from the dark side."

"Please, not the dark side."

"Well, the deep side, then."

"How about, just the other side?"

"The other side. I'll be passing you names to investigate from the other side."

"Let me ask this," Turquoise interjected. "Are we going to talk about the FBI's counter-intelligence agents and what they might be doing right now?"

"Such as?" Thaddeus asked.

"Such as what kind of security precautions they take. How do we know while you're watching them, they aren't watching you back? And me?"

"I've got my methods," Marcel said to Turquoise, his gaze steady on her own. "I won't let anything happen to you. I was fourteen years with Interpol, and you're with me now."

17

Thaddeus was in court in La Jolla on the dependency petition for Rachel Sundstrom two days later.

The judge was a woman with nineteen years in the juvenile courts who had gone to law school after receiving her nursing degree from UCSD. Her name was Sylvia Rinker. She was in her mid-forties, a mother of two healthy teenage boys, and a woman who loved to cycle and watch the Padres from the right field line with Bud in her cup. She wasn't given to following the letter of the law but practiced from the standpoint of one sworn to apply the spirit of the law. For these reasons—that she wasn't a stickler—Thaddeus felt good about her assignment to the case. She asked for the spelling of Dr. Herzensky's name when Thaddeus called the oncologist to the witness stand.

The doctor was Dr. Grigory Herzensky, oncologist.

After the customary preliminaries, Thaddeus asked, "Doctor, as Rachel's treating cancer doctor, what is her life expectancy?"

"At least twelve months."

"Basing that on...?"

"Physical examination, scans and tests, experience in a thousand cases. She has a good year ahead of her."

"When you say, 'a good year,' you're not telling the court it's going to be a great year for Rachel, are you?"

"No, of course not."

"And neither are you saying it's going to be a good year either, are you?"

"Definitely not. It's going to be painful and mind-numbing to be in bed that long."

"Doctor, Rachel has filed this petition because she wants to die. Do you object to her wanting to end her life?"

"I do. First of all, the California end-of-life law only applies when there's less than six months of life left. Second of all, new drugs are being released to us almost daily in our fight against Rachel's disease and tumors. It would be heartbreaking to let her go and then find out there's a cure two weeks later. Plus, she's too young to make that decision."

"Too young, based on what?"

"Based on talking to her."

"Did you know her before the disease?"

"No, only since."

"So, you don't know what she's usually like?"

"No."

"But you do know enough from talking to her as a patient that she should not be allowed to chart her own course of treatment and end of treatment?"

"Yes."

"Tell us what words she's said that made you believe she's too young."

"Mr. Murfee, she's only seventeen. The California law only applies to adults, anyway."

"You've seen the law allowed in other's lives?"

"Yes."

"All adults?"

"Yes."

"Ever any children?"

"Never."

"Because children can't choose to end their lives like adults can?"

"That's correct."

"Because you said so."

"Because the legislature said so. Adults only, Mr. Murfee. It might not always be fair, but it's the law. I'm sorry."

The doctor then went on to give the particulars about Rachel's case, filling the judge in on the medical aspects of her diagnosis, treatment, and prognosis. One thing became very clear: he sided with the parents in pulling the rug out from under Rachel in her quest for the freedom to choose.

At the end of his testimony, Judge Rinker said she wasn't ready to enter any permanent findings and continued the hearing for another eight weeks. In the meantime, the attorneys were to keep the court apprised of any changes in both the patient's condition and the new medications and treatment modalities developing on her condition.

Then they were finished. The court addressed Rachel by TV uplink, making sure she understood what was happening. She feebly asked whether she would be allowed to end her life now, and Judge Rinker referred her to her attorney for details and explanations. Then the screen went black and the court began clearing.

Across town in her quiet room, Rachel turned onto her back and started crying. June handed her a cup of ice chips, but she brushed it away. And knowingly, June left the room and closed the door quietly behind her.

After a couple deep breaths, Rachel felt better, more determined, so she wiped her tears away on her sleeve and pushed herself up in her bed. She moved her legs over the edge, as if she would run away. But then her body's reality exploded over her, driving her back onto the mattress, her face turned into her pillow.

The dependency petition hadn't worked. For weeks, she had hoped, and that hope had energized her in a way she hadn't felt in a long time. But with that hope now gone, she'd become only a physical shell of a human. And like this, she would have to wait.

18

———

At fifteen, Becca already knew all the bad boys in La Jolla. In a glance, she knew who was holding and who was pretending at the beach. One guy, in particular, was on her mind the next morning after Rachel's hearing. His name was Judd Franklin, and he rode a crotch rocket and drank wine on the beach, illegal or not. The cops turned their heads; they'd just as soon ignore Judd as tangle with him. It just wasn't worth it because, while they'd eventually win out, at least one of them would wind up in the emergency room and have to explain to his wife, again, why he didn't get into a different line of work.

Becca watched him wheel his bike into the lot and back it into a no-parking slot. He shut it off and kicked the stand to take its weight, then removed his boots and stuffed them inside his saddle bags. Barefoot, he took to the sand still wearing his leather jacket and waded deep into the surf, his jeans getting wet to the knees. He kicked along in the water, stopping to watch the little kids with the buckets and shovels, the young guys with the kites, and the girls with eyes on him.

From several feet up-sand of the water, Becca began pacing the man. Maybe, she thought, she was actually stalking. Wouldn't that be a twist?

"Hey, Judd," she called softly. "I need some stuff."

He came out of the water and approached Becca. She was wearing a two-piece. No recording wires. "What are you looking for?"

"Brown."

"*¿Cuánto necesitas?*"

"Enough to kill my sister."

"That bad?"

"It's bad."

"What about the doctors?"

"Nothing."

"Go to my bag on my bike. Leave a hundred. I'm gonna hook you up."

"When can you get me the stuff?"

"Walk to school tomorrow. I'll find you."

She left her driveway at 7:11 the very next morning. She was wearing a school uniform of plaid skirt with knee socks, white shirt, and navy necktie. Her backpack was carelessly slung over her shoulder and held her lunch, her Air Pods, her iPad, and a few books and folders. In her hand was her phone. She would text as she walked to school and exchange selfies with her friends, mostly Celena, of the day's hairstyle.

Up Center Street and across to Pasadena then east four blocks. She strolled along, waiting for the thrum of the straight pipes and the whine of the 1100 that was running up behind her, slowing and then drawing alongside.

Judd said, "Hop on," which she did.

As they rocketed down the road, he shouted back, "Front pocket, right side!" Becca slipped her hand into the pocket of his black leather jacket and came away with five baggies. "Enough to bring an elephant to its knees." He laughed back into the stream of air curling past her ear.

Then he dropped her at her school and shot off down the street. Becca had already transferred the baggies into her backpack, now slung across her shoulders and back.

At lunchtime, Becca found Celena, and they took their lunches out to the picnic tables. They sat on the tabletops, feet flat on the concrete bench below, testing their sandwiches and trading halves. Two chocolate milks, Fritos, chocolate chip cookies that cost $1.29 at the 7-Eleven, and Dubble Bubble gum per girl. Celena had a roast beef sandwich while Becca had her usual cheese and turkey on whole wheat.

Becca leaned forward onto her knees and said low to her friend, "Like, I got the brown."

Celena gasped. "You've got to be shitting me."

"I shit you not."

"From who?"

"Judd Franklin."

"No way!"

"Yep, way."

"Judd hooked you up?"

"Uh-huh."

"What are you gonna do with it?"

"Inject it."

"Into your sister?"

Becca rolled her eyes. "No, dummy, into her line. I'm not, like, injecting *her* her."

Celena stuck out her tongue at Becca. It was immature, but then it was also funny, and they did it often to each other, only as BFFs could. "Well, it's not like I do drugs. How would I know?" Celena took a sip of her milk. "When are you going to do it?"

Becca crumpled her empty Frito package and set it aside. "I don't know. Whenever Rachel says, I guess."

"What about your parents?"

"What they don't know and all that... They just want her to suffer so they all go to heaven."

"That church stuff again?"

"Isn't it? Forever and ever amen and amen and amen. I hate it."

"Yeah," said Celena, "I don't think I'd be into it either. My mom and dad don't do church."

"But do they talk about it all the time?"

"No way." Celena mimicked vomiting. "I'd stick my finger down my throat."

"See," Becca said, "that's what's great about your mom and dad.

They're keeping hands off and letting you decide your life. My mom and dad could learn something if they'd get their heads outta their Bibles long enough."

"Will you tell them... I mean, like, they'll know what happened and everything, won't they?"

"After Rachel is gone? Duh, I guess. My dad's a doctor. He's going to figure it out pretty effing quick, you know."

Celena took a huge mouthful of roast beef sandwich, which she washed down with a double swallow of chocolate milk. Then she looked off into the distance. "How do you feel about doing it?"

"How do I feel? Like, how would you feel? Bummed, that's how I feel. No one should have to help her sister die. But I can't just stand there like some useless shithead and let her suffer, ya know? I mean, she'd help me if it was the other way around and me in the bed. She'd probably have it over and done with by now. That's how good a sister Rachel is. I'm sad I've taken this long. I'll give it to her tonight if she wants."

Celena reached around and scratched her shoulder, then examined her nails. "What about the police?"

"Oh, there's gonna be police. I have no doubt I'm going to juvie. That's the only part I hate. Like, I love my room and my stuff, and I love my friends and the beach and all. I don't even know where juvie is or what they do with you, but one thing's for sure, I won't be going back to Kansas anymore."

"It ain't Kansas, Dorothy," said Celena. "I wish we could talk to my dad about it. Criminal law is his specialty. I know he could help."

"Are you blind and stupid or just blind? Like, they went to court yesterday, and he lost."

"Didn't lose."

"She didn't get to have a doctor end her life, did she?"

"No."

"Well, I'd call that losing, duh."

"But they'll review it again in eight weeks," Celena said, as much in defense of her dad as anything by now. "My dad doesn't lose."

"I don't mean he *lost* lost. But the judge said come back in eight weeks. Eight weeks! Do you know how long eight weeks is for Rachel? That's like four lifetimes! She can't even wait two more days."

"So, you're gonna give it to her tonight?"

"Or tomorrow. She'll say."

"You're strong, Becca. I couldn't do it."

Becca stiffened, "You could if it was Sarai or Turquoise. Yes, you could."

Celena took it in. "Well, if it was my own sister... God, it makes me want to cry. The whole thing makes me want to just cry. I'm sorry." Celena wiped her shirt sleeve across her eyes. "Sorry."

"Don't get me crying, or I won't be able to do it." Becca gathered up her wrappers and tossed them and her half-eaten sandwich into the shop bag. She looked Celena right in the eyes. "I can do this. I don't have any choice. I'm Rachel's last hope."

"I know you will, Becca. You're so strong."

"This time, I have to be. I have to be for my sister."

"There's first bell. Let's head back."

19

"**R**ight now, I'm just waiting to die. That's my life," Rachel said to Becca that night. "I don't read, watch TV, have visitors, go for walks, go shopping, none of that. Just waiting to die. Give me the heroin."

"It's brown, so it's stepped on."

Rachel cracked a small smile. "You know the lingo, weirdo."

Becca shrugged and smiled back. "Rap music."

"Anyway, thanks, sister girl. You're doing me a huge. Did you get it from Judd?"

"I did."

"Did he know what it's for?"

"Yes. He asked if you're still going through with it."

"So, he knows. Okay. Well, let's load up the needle and shoot it in my line and get me out of here."

"Right…but it's powder."

"Okay, so you'll have to melt it. I think you heat it until it melts."

"In the movies they use a spoon and a lighter."

"Use Dad's fireplace lighter."

"Good idea. And a big spoon."

"Maybe use a small saucepan lid instead. You can hold the knob upside-down and heat it up. When it melts, I'll draw it up into the syringe and then put it in my line. I know how to do that. I've seen it, like, a million times."

"Yeah, me, too."

"So, go get the fireplace starter and a saucepan lid. Something like a saucepan lid. Look under the cabinets."

"Uh, shouldn't we have a ceremony or something? You don't just heat it up and then die, do you?"

"Becca, right now my head is pounding like a huge drum. My back is burning up with pain and my shoulders are shaking it hurts so much. Please don't make me wait on words. There's nothing to say. I love you, you love me. That's all we need to know."

"I'm going to be in trouble."

"You won't actually do anything then. Hmmm…" Rachel tapped her finger to her lips as she thought about it. "Actually, I'll need you to heat it up. I don't think I can do that."

Becca patted her sister's knee. "Okay. Be right back."

Becca went into the family room from the den and approached the fireplace. It was a wood burner so her dad kept a fireplace lighter on the mantle for those rare nights in La Jolla when a fire might be nice inside. She located it easily and tried the trigger. She clicked it several times before discovering it was necessary to throw a small safety switch to make it work. Then she went into the kitchen.

Rattling around under the cabinets brought June into the kitchen. "Can I help with something, Becca? Does Rachel want some soup?"

"I do. I'm just looking for the smallest saucepan."

"That's it on the second shelf on the right. Be careful. It heats up quite fast on high."

"Got it, thanks."

June remained standing behind her, idly watching, as if she was out of ideas for things to occupy herself. Then, "I just checked on Rachel. She's sleeping peacefully. She's so beautiful when the pain lines are gone from her face."

"She won all sorts of beauty contests when she was a freshman. Mom told her she could be a model."

"Your mom's right. She definitely could've. But not—"

"Not now. I know. You don't have to stand here while I make my soup. Don't you have something...?"

"Am I bothering you? I'm turning into a helicopter cop with you kids. It's either very busy or very slow at this assignment. When Rachel's crying and the meds aren't working, I don't have enough hands. But when she's sleeping, it gets so quiet. I'm not complaining. It's a blessing to know you girls."

"Aw, that's a nice thing to say. We're blessed, too. I know Rachel loves you so much. Plus, it takes the load off Mom."

"I know she's up most nights. I don't know how she does it."

"That's when it's the worst and she wants to be there for my sister. Our mom is really brave."

"She is. She's amazing."

When June still didn't move, Becca prompted, "Okay, I'm going to heat up some tomato soup now and take it to my room. I've got to study."

"Oh! Of course. I'll leave you alone and let you get on with it."

June left the kitchen—finally. Becca ran the can opener as the next sound June should hear. She set the opened can of soup aside, stuck the saucepan lid in her baggy sweatpants, the fire lighter up her hoodie sleeve, and headed for the den where Rachel was bedded down.

Except she found June had beat her there and was going through the process of changing Rachel's bedsheets with Rachel still in the bed. Becca stood back but watched closely while the nurse did what the best nurses know how to pull off and make look simple. Five minutes later, Rachel, still asleep through the whole ordeal, was now resting comfortably on clean white sheets.

"This happens twice a day," said June. "She sweats so much."

"It knocks me out every time you do that," Becca said with no small admiration in her voice. "Awesome."

"Part of the job. Hey, you should become a nurse. You could work for your dad."

"I think I might want to go into law, but I'm still young so that might change."

"I see where you're coming from on that one. Okay, I'm gonna make myself some coffee and put my feet up before rush hour. You get on in your room and crack those books you brought home."

"Will do. I'm just going to watch Rachel sleep for a few minutes first. I'm memorizing her face."

"Aw, how precious." June gave her a big hug.

"I just love her." Becca had tears in her eyes as she hugged the woman back.

Finally, June left the room to give her some space with her sister. Becca would have to hurry. But Rachel was unconscious. She needed her to be awake and she needed Rachel's encouragement. So…Becca had to wait.

She changed the face on her Apple Watch to a sweep second hand and began timing Rachel's breaths per minute, counting them for ten seconds then multiplying by six. Then she did the same thing with her own respiration rate. She knew it was a useless exercise, but it made her feel better, knowing she could hear her sister actually breathing. She was going to miss coming in here and seeing her sister. Would they just clean out the room and pretend Rachel was never here? Would her dad ever use the room again? She was sure she didn't have the answers. She'd never had a sister die before.

Which was when it occurred to her: Rachel didn't have to be awake for this at all. Becca could go ahead and heat the heroin, liquefy it, draw it up in a syringe—they were everywhere in boxes —and inject it into her line. She knew every step. Should she?

Rachel could always change her mind at the last minute, but Becca also knew her sister; there wouldn't be any last-minute objections. She was going to go through with it. If it were her, thought Becca, she wouldn't want to be awake when it was put in her line. She'd want to be asleep for the whole thing. Becca decided that's what Rachel would want, too.

She pulled the saucepan lid out of her pants. She looked at the closed door. June could come in any second so Becca had to be fast. She dragged the fireplace lighter out of her sleeve. It was a silver tube with a handle and trigger. She pulled the five baggies of heroin out of her right front pocket. She carefully opened them one by one and sprinkled their crystalline contents into the saucepan lid. She carefully placed the lid on the floor and went around Rachel's bed to the table where her supplies were. A box of open syringes was waiting. She selected one and returned to her seat. She uncapped it and held it in her teeth. Then she snapped the lighter, and a tongue of blue flame leapt forth. She placed the flame beneath the lid and started heating. The powder was smoking in ten seconds and was liquefying at twenty. In under a minute, she was drawing the syringe full of the brown liquid while balancing the lid on her thighs. There, she had a full barrel of the deadly drug.

Just before she stood to go around and introduce the heroine into Rachel's line, she said her name. "Rachel? It's Becca. Can you hear me?"

Rachel's eyes popped open like blue butterflies settling down on white gauze.

"Huh?" said the patient.

Becca waved the syringe at her. "I've got the stuff in the needle. Should I inject you?"

Rachel took a few seconds to process. Then, "Yes, please. I'm so ready. Goodbye, Becca. Tell Mom and Dad I love them. And I love you."

She closed her eyes again.

Becca circled the bed and located the line junction where she'd watched the nurses insert their needles. She did the same. She was crying as she pushed the plunger all the way down. Becca watched in astonishment as the brown liquid swirled into the upstream drops as they passed through the Y junction and then began snaking their way into Rachel's hand.

Becca dropped the used syringe into a Sharp's medical waste box and re-took her seat at the bedside. Then she watched and waited.

Again, she counted respirations for ten seconds and multiplied. "Baseline," she muttered as she confirmed the earlier number she had established for Rachel's breathing. She timed the seconds to one full minute, then counted out the next ten breaths. Slower this time. She marveled. It was already working.

She waited another full minute then counted and timed yet again. Half as many breaths. She was amazed at how fast the drug was working. She watched her sister's face, watched for eye movement under her eyelids, but there was no hint she was awake or even aware. She was gone, Becca suddenly realized, and she, Becca, had killed her.

"June!" Becca suddenly screamed. "June! June! June!"

The nurse ran into the room. "Look!" Becca cried, pointing at the brown line.

"Oh, sweet Jesus! What happened here? Did you do something?"

"It's heroin. I put it in the line."

June flew into action, tearing the line from Rachel's hand and pressing the panic button on the wall, the button installed to dial

9-1-1 and then Dr. Sundstrom's pager. EMT's and Dr. Sundstrom would come running.

Then Becca felt herself slipping away. Her eyes closed. Her head rocked to the side, and she lost consciousness. She slumped forward and down onto the floor, looking like a marionette whose strings had snapped.

"Becca!" cried June. "Becca!"

20

"The one in the bed is dying. The one on the floor only fainted!" June cried to the EMT's as they streamed into Rachel's room.

The first responders were providing rescue breaths with a bag-valve mask when Dr. Sundstrom arrived. "Bounding carotid pulse," said an EMT, removing his fingers from Rachel's throat. A nasopharyngeal airway was placed in her mouth. "Bilateral lung sounds," said the second EMT with the stethoscope. "Heart rate of one-twenty-three BPM, blood pressure is one-twenty-two over eighty-six, Ox Sat of ninety-eight percent with assisted ventilation." The EMT spoke these values into his shoulder mic. A staticky voice responded. Then, "Skin pale, dry, cold to the touch. IV access, normal saline bolus, zero-point-four of naloxone."

Then they transported Rachel with Dr. Sundstrom riding in the rear of the ambulance with her. When she was placed on high-flow oxygen via a non-rebreather mask, she became agitated. He held her arms. After five minutes, her spontaneous respiratory effort had improved as they arrived at the hospital. "Respiratory effort of thirty," said the EMT into his mic as the rear doors flew open and they began pulling the gurney free of the unit.

Dr. Sundstrom followed his daughter into the ER and stood by while the ER staff went through their work. Thirty minutes later, the room relaxed as normal beats, pressures, and respiratory efforts returned. Dr. Sundstrom stood by until his daughter opened her eyes.

"Where am I? Is this heaven?" were her first words.

Jim Sundstrom choked up at her words and was about to pacify her when Rachel slipped back into unconsciousness.

But Rachel was now stable, so Dr. Sundstrom went to check on Becca, who had arrived by the second ambulance on the scene. She was sitting up in her curtain area, sipping orange juice and crying. He walked up to her, threw his arms around her, and drew her head to his chest. "There, there," he said, "it's going to be all right. Rachel's going to be fine now."

Becca's crying increased in volume, "No—no—no she's not! She wants to die, and you won't let her!"

"There, there," said the doctor, holding his youngest close. He patted her back and whispered to her. He said he was sorry for everything. He said they would all have a long talk. Then he asked what had happened.

"I—I put brown in her line."

"You put heroin in Rachel's IV?"

"Y-Y-Yes. I'm sorry!" More crying. He continued to hold her close, whispering and patting her back. Then he said they should go check on Rachel. She held his arm for support while they went to Rachel's curtained area. The sisters cried together when they saw each other, and the crying only got louder. Staff looked on help-lessly. Nobody had words. It was a small town. Everyone in the medical community knew the history. They gave way to the tears, allowing the sisters space and time to cry it out.

Ten minutes into the reconnection of the sisters, a police officer in a blue uniform parted the curtains and stuck his head in. "Becca?" he said. "Are your parents around?"

"I'm her dad," said Dr. Sundstrom. "How can I help?"

"Sir, on these OD cases, we always look at procurement. How did your daughter procure the drug? That kind of thing. Her urine came back with heroin in it. June the nurse said I should speak to Becca. May I speak with your daughter?"

The doctor sighed. "I suppose so. But I want to be present. Let's go back to her curtain."

They returned to Becca's curtain area where there was some privacy, no neighbors on either side.

"Becca, I'm Officer McCluskey. Did you give your sister drugs?"

"Yes."

"What did you give her?"

"Brown."

"Heroin?" asked the officer.

"Yes."

"Where did you get the heroin?"

"From a guy. I don't know his name."

"Where was this?"

"At the beach."

"You bought heroin from a guy at the beach, and you don't know his name?"

"That's right."

"All right, why did you buy the heroin?"

"So—so—so my sister could end her life."

The officer looked at Dr. Sundstrom, who answered, "My other daughter has a terminal illness with terrible pain. Becca was trying to—"

"I've got the picture. Unfortunately, I'm going to have to take her to jail." To Becca, the policeman directed, "Do you have shoes here?"

Becca and her father found her shoes. She slipped them on.

"Wait," said Dr. Sundstrom. "How do I get her back?"

"The judge will set conditions of release tomorrow. I'm sure she'll be turned over to juvenile caseworkers and detention."

"Where will she be tonight?"

"Kearny Mesa Juvenile Detention Facility. At the jail."

"Oh, my God," said Jim Sundstrom. "This is going to kill her mother."

"Here's my card," said the officer. "I'll call you when she's turned over to the jailers. I have my partner waiting outside. She won't be alone."

He helped Becca off the examination table and began escorting her outside. Dr. Sundstrom stood helplessly by as his youngest daughter went to jail. Then he reached for his cell phone.

"Thaddeus? Jim Sundstrom. Can you meet me at the hospital ER?"

No further explanation was needed. Thaddeus said, "I'm on my way."

21

Thaddeus had been working late at his office, but he immediately shut down his computer and left his office after taking Dr. Sundstrom's call. He went downstairs and loaded into his Mercedes, then headed for Genesee Avenue and Barbey Family Emergency and Trauma Center. Passing over the five freeway, he felt his heart jump as he realized he might be driving to learn about Rachel's death after a terrible, painful conclusion. He blinked hard several times, fighting off the worry that that might be the case. But what else could it be? As a lawyer with years of experience, his mind automatically dredged up a myriad of unhappy possibilities.

Dr. Sundstrom had left instructions with the admissions clerk to page him when Thaddeus arrived. After a very few minutes, Jim wended his way through the ER crowd and came to Thaddeus at Admitting. "Let's step outside, Thaddeus. There's a bench."

It was cool outside, the sun was going down, and the parrot community was screaming in the eucalyptus trees on-campus. Traffic could be seen from a distance as it streamed in from the five freeway as they came off at Genesee, one of the main roads spanning La Jolla.

Dr. Sundstrom sat wearily.

Thaddeus turned to face him on the bench. "Jim, what gives?"

"Not good. Rachel OD'd on heroin. It was supplied by Becca. The police are taking her to jail as we speak."

"Oh, hell," Thaddeus said. "I was afraid something—"

"I know. Louisa and I have been way rigid. Something had to give. The kids went ahead without us. I feel like a goddamn fool and have been tearing my hair out. Louisa's in there with Rachel now and wants to throttle someone. She just can't decide who."

"And, of course, Becca talked to the police when they came?"

"Yes, they came to the hospital. There's nothing to hide."

"No, there isn't, and I wasn't going to suggest that. It's just something we'll have to handle as a juvenile matter. Then you'll be left with a counseling matter on your hands. The judge on her case will consider this a very serious violation of the law. She could be removed from the home over this, Jim. I'll do everything I can to stop that, but just so you know."

"I was afraid that might be it."

"You know," Thaddeus went on, "the other side of it is the tremendous pressure Becca's been under. No kid should ever have to go through this. And, of course, I'm not even mentioning your precious Rachel. She's the one who's ultimately hurting the most from this for encouraging her sister. Assuming that's what happened, and I'm fairly confident that's how it will turn out."

"Can you see her tonight? The officer said Kearny Mesa."

"Juvenile facility. Ages ten to twenty. I'm on my way."

Thirty minutes later, he was at the reception window at the juvenile detention center in Kearny Mesa, San Diego County. She was still being processed in, and it would be another hour until she could have an attorney visit. Thaddeus said he'd go grab a bite to eat and return.

He found Maggie's Cafe on Grayling and ordered Maggie's bourbon salmon dinner with mashed potatoes—comfort food, given that he was exhausted after a two-day preliminary hearing and he had all but skipped food for those two days. The waitress brought coffee and cream, ice water, and his meal ten minutes later. He inhaled the main course then had caramel cheesecake, two slices. He called Christine—he had already called on the way down—and talked to her about the potential conflict of interest he might have.

"Let me get this straight," she said. "You're representing Rachel on a dependency petition for end of life orders."

"Right."

"And now Becca's been arrested for possession of heroin and possibly for attempted manslaughter."

"Right."

"And you're asking me if there might be a conflict of interest? Are you smoking weed, Murfee?"

"No, no, I'm just—I'm just tired, and Jim wanted me to talk to her. How about I refer her case over to you? Then you can defend her while I keep Rachel's case separate."

"That sounds much more appropriate. And manageable. Do this then, see her tonight just as a family friend. In juvie jail you don't have to be a family member to visit. See her, get her settled down and feeling better, then I'll be there with her in the morning when she goes to court. The deputies can give you her court time."

"Sounds smart. And thanks for not letting me walk into a spinning propeller."

"My, but we do have to be careful of our conflicts of interest, don't we?"

Thaddeus chuckled. He was looking forward to seeing his wife. "Okay, I'll be home around nine."

"I'll keep Sarai up. She needs help with her science project."

"All right. See you all then."

When he returned to juvie, Thaddeus was led into a large room of metal picnic tables. A female officer brought in Becca a short time later. She was wearing the tan shirt and trousers of the juvenile population at Kearny Mesa. She had been crying; her mascara was streaking her face and she needed a handkerchief, which Thaddeus offered. She blew her nose mightily and kept the cloth.

"So," he said, "I expect your feelings are just running away with you?"

"Mr. Murfee"—more tears streaked down her face—"what did I do? What was I even thinking? My precious sister, and I was going to help kill her!"

"I'm sure you felt it was the right thing to do. The only thing I have to say is this. That decision isn't yours to make, Becca. That decision belongs to adults. You're not in the picture when it comes to deciding about Rachel's end of life. Okay?"

Crying weakly now, she mumbled, "O-o-okay."

"Sometimes when we're young, we try to make decisions that don't belong to us. That's when young people get in trouble. Now, your mom and dad asked me to come here and see you. Right now, they're with Rachel. I just called your dad before I came in here. Your sister's vitals are normal, and she's doing just fine. She's asleep now and resting. You'll see your mom and dad tomorrow. Also, Christine is going to come and go to court with you instead of me. She's going to be your lawyer."

"I need a lawyer?"

"Yes, Becca. You do need a lawyer. What you've done is very serious."

"Am I going to have to stay in jail for a long time?"

"I don't want to lie to you. It's possible you could be here for a very long time. Sometimes people stay until they're twenty-one. That won't be you, I don't think, but it happens in murder cases. Thank heavens yours isn't a murder case."

Crying harder, she cried out, "Damn me!"

Thaddeus tried to calm her by redirecting, "Have they fed you?"

"No."

"Has a doctor examined you?"

"A nurse."

"Do they have you in with other girls?"

"No, they put me in a cell alone. They told me they do that with all the new people."

"How are you feeling physically? I know you fainted."

"Much better. I'm not hyperventilating. I was before."

"Glad you are doing okay, Becca. Hang in there, and Christine and I will do everything we can for you. Before I leave, do you have any questions for me?"

She sniffed. "Just one."

"What's that?"

"When does my sister get to die?"

Thaddeus jerked fully upright. Out of right field.

"When we—when we—I don't know. But we'll make it happen. That much I can promise you, Becca."

"Good. My sister deserves to get to die."

"She does."

22

Christine Murfee began working with a young Thaddeus in Orbit, Illinois as a paralegal. She had previously served two years at a Black Ops detention center in Baghdad during the Iraq war and came home with the Silver Star for gallantry in combat. She was 5-5" and Miss Hickam County of 2007 but was no stranger to hard, disciplined work alongside the men of the U.S. Army. Now, her law practice was separate and distinct from Thaddeus's law practice, though they worked out of the same building they owned in La Jolla.

After she received Thaddeus's call about defending Becca Sundstrom, she hung up and immediately began researching on her computer the ins and outs of the juvenile justice system in California. She was trying to pinpoint criminal conspiracies and attempted manslaughter, the two areas of prosecution she expected Becca to be facing the next day in court.

SHE DRESSED THE NEXT MORNING IN A TRIM, BLACK SUIT, NO JEWELRY and just a touch of mascara and lip gloss. Then she headed for Kearny Mesa and the juvenile court. She decided to meet up with Becca in the courtroom since they already knew each other from the many days and nights Becca had spent in the Murfee home as Celena's best friend. Introductions were unnecessary.

She watched as Becca was brought into the courtroom with twelve other teenagers. They were all dressed in the tan shirts and pants of the juvenile detention center and looked terrified to be there. Court began with the entrance of Judge Masinelli into the large courtroom at exactly 8:30 a.m. Everyone stood, and then the judge told them thank you and to please sit. There was a shuffle and exhalations as the thirty spectators and dozen lawyers sat and steeled themselves for the coming pronouncements of placement of the dozen teens. Most of the spectators were parents and fosters, but a few were investigators. There were no reporters since juvenile court was closed to the press.

Becca's case was up first. She shuffled forward from the defendants' holding area and visibly relaxed when Christine touched her arm and guided her to the lectern. The process was underway.

Said Judge Masinelli, "Young woman, you're here on a three-count complaint arising from your role yesterday in your sister's attempt to end her life. Are you aware of those facts?"

"I know about it," whispered Becca.

"Louder, please. The court reporter is taking all this down."

"I—I know why I'm here."

"Very well. You have counsel, and that's a good thing. Our purpose here today is to make sure you have a copy of the petition filed in your case and make sure you have an attorney. I see you do have a copy, and Attorney Christine Murfee is appearing with you. At this time, I am going to set a hearing on your petition and remand you to the custody of the juvenile division. Do you understand these things?"

"I do."

"Judge, can we talk about the conditions of release?" Christine asked.

"Counsel, the probation officer has committed the respondent to the custody of juvenile hall. She will remain in custody pending her delinquency hearing."

"Thank you."

"Very well, that is all for now."

With that, they were finished.

Christine took Becca into a conference room just off the court-room. They closed the door and took seats at a small table with four chairs.

"That was all?" said Becca. "I have to stay here?"

"At this point, the District Attorney will proceed with your case, and the probation officer will make some important decisions as we go along. One bright note, it looks like your case is staying in juvenile court rather than being remanded to adult court, where more serious offenses by juveniles can sometimes end up being prosecuted."

"So, I'm staying in this court?"

"Yes."

"Oh, hell," said Becca, her eyes clouding with tears. "I just want to go home. I miss everyone and I miss Rachel. How is she doing?"

"I called on the way here. Your sister is resting as well as she did before the incident. Your parents are both at the hospital or one of them would've been here this morning. I told them it was more important they stay with Rachel this morning, that your time here would be very brief, and I'd be with you since I know you so well."

"Thank you, Mrs. Murfee. Does Celena know about all this?"

"Not yet. I won't tell her, either, unless you want me to."

"I want you to tell her. She's my BFF. She has to know."

"All right. I'll be sure and bring her up to speed. Now, here's my card. Keep this with you. And if you need me, call me. I'm always just a call away. Both my office phone and cell are on there. Your parents will probably be here later today for a visit."

"Good. I want my mom to know I'm sorry. I already told my dad. Are they going to kill me?"

"No one's going to kill you, Becca. You were in a very difficult situation you didn't create. I think you'll find there are going to be changes around all that. Your parents want to talk to you about Rachel and some of the things they're deciding to do."

"Like what?"

"Well, when I spoke with your mom last night, they're asking Thaddeus and me to look around for other legal help for Rachel. I think they want to help her carry out her choices now."

"That's awesome. So, they're going to let her end her life if she wants?"

"That's what it sounds like. You'll know more this afternoon."

She was crying openly now. "Oh, God, what a relief."

"But for now, I've got an appointment with your probation officer so I can find out how they plan to proceed on your case. Once I know more, I'll call you or drop by and we'll discuss what might happen. Is that sounding better?"

"Yes, it would always help to know. Please tell her I'm sorry and what I did won't ever happen again."

"That's a good starting point. I'll make sure to tell her, Becca."

"Thank you." She hiccuped a few deep breaths, exhausted from her crying.

"That's all we can do for now. I'll be back to you after I've spoken to your probation officer. Please don't worry."

"Okay. Thank you, Mrs. Murfee."

"You're welcome. Sit tight and do what they tell you around here, okay?"

"I will."

"All right, we're going back out to the courtroom, and you'll rejoin the group now. So, goodbye until later." Christine gave Becca a long hug, trying to pass through her arms as much love and kindness as she could for the young girl. Not only was she Celena's best friend, but Christine's heart ached at what Becca must be feeling right now. Scared. Anxious.

One so young to have to deal with this hell.

23

J im and Louisa Sundstrom had the Murfees over the next
night to talk.

As the foursome sat around the kitchen table, Thaddeus said, "I've
done my research. Oregon, I wasn't surprised to learn, provides
end of life support for eighteen-year-old residents. California is
twenty-one. California is a lost cause."

"What's that mean?" Jim. "We have to move her there?"

Louisa poured them a cup of coffee and placed sugar and half and
half in the middle of the table. "She's eighteen in six weeks, so
there's that."

Christine offered, "Thaddeus, she needs to have residency by her
eighteenth birthday. I suppose it's proven with a driver's license
like most places?"

Thaddeus answered, "It is. Driver's license equals residency. As
for the six weeks, I'm happy to loan my RV to your family to take
her there and wait the six weeks while citizenship establishes. It

has two bedrooms and sleeps eight. There's a full kitchen, cable TV, Internet, outdoor TV and outdoor kitchen. I went a little overboard when I thought I was taking off a year to roam America."

"We moved to California instead," said Christine. "It's a long story for another day. Anyway, we can loan the bus to your family to make the trip."

"What do I do with Becca?" asked Louisa. "I can't just leave her here locked up. I think I have to stay here with her."

"What about our church's aversion to end of life?" asked Jim. "Do we just forget about that?"

"That's the last thing on my mind," said Louisa, "after this suicide attempt. We have to take action, and that's that, church or not."

"Agree," said Jim, "so we're over one hurdle."

"What about establishing residency?" asked Louisa. "Thaddeus, would you accompany Jim to Oregon for six weeks? You can be Rachel's lawyer in case that comes up."

"I don't see how—"

"Thaddeus would love to help out," Christine interrupted. "He's due for a break from work, and six weeks is perfect. My lawyers will handle his law practice. Isn't that right, Thaddeus?"

He was stuck, as it were. There was nothing he wouldn't do for the dying girl, but this was a bit beyond the pale, he thought. But Christine was giving off some heavy-duty signals that he should do this. So...his mind was made up...by his wife. "It sounds like something I want to do for Rachel and for the family. I'm in," said Thaddeus. "I think it's the only viable plan."

"Oh, dear." Louisa had broken down and was crying softly. "Oh, dear. She could be dead in six weeks." Her husband took her hand and kissed it without speaking. There were no words.

"Can she even drive a car—you know, to get a driver's license?" Christine asked, ever the pragmatist.

"Good question," Thaddeus said. "Jim?"

"We'll take along a supply of morphine capsules. Obviously, she can't drive under the influence, though. For that part, the actual driving test, she's just going to have to gut it out."

"Wow," Christine said. "This is one strong girl."

"Oh, she's all of that," agreed Jim about his daughter. "She's one strong girl and then some. Thaddeus, what are the life expectancy requirements of the Oregon law?"

"Well, Oregon law allows end-of-life medical help where the person is eighteen, a resident of Oregon, and has a terminal illness with a life expectancy of six months or less. Where are we with the last part?"

Jim lowered his head and closed his eyes. Then he said slowly and solemnly, "I can testify to six months. Yes, I'll do that."

"But is it true?" asked Louisa. "I don't see how—"

"I said I'll do it, Lou!" he snapped. "Let's just leave it at that." He took a sip of coffee. "Sorry, everyone. Outburst."

Thaddeus waved his words away. "Don't worry about it. It's an extremely difficult conversation to have for anyone," Thaddeus said. "The real tragedy is that if we're successful, your precious daughter gets to die. That's more than I can even think about, tell the truth. I'm going to do this with you, but you have to know it will be the saddest win of my life if it works. I know it's necessary for her suffering, I understand that. But still, the whole thing is just tragic."

"It—it—is." Now Jim was in tears.

Christine said to Thaddeus, "So, I'll stay here in La Jolla with your law practice and mine, and the kids. Who else will be going with you?"

Thaddeus said, "Obviously Rachel and Jim, me...June? Does June go?"

"I think June goes," Jim said. "I'll need someone for the night watch."

"Good point. We should also take a companion," Thaddeus said. "I'm going to volunteer Celena. I know she's younger, but she's always totally looked up to Rachel. And school's out when we leave, so she won't be missing school. What do you think, Chris?"

"Go for it," Christine said. "It would be good for both girls. I know Celena's heartbroken. It would be good for her to be there for Becca's sister when Becca can't be there for her. That's what friends do."

"Makes sense," Jim agreed. "What about living areas in the bus?"

Thaddeus took a sip of coffee. "You take the master bedroom with Rachel. You can walk on both sides of the queen-size bed, so she'll be accessible. You can sleep on one of the extra bunks in the bus. I'll take the second bedroom. Becca and June can grab bunks. I'll need a little time each day on a linkup to my office by laptop. That's why I'm choosing a bedroom for myself."

"Who will be driving?" asked Jim.

Thaddeus said, "Same fellow who drove us to the Hollywood

Bowl. His name is Sandy and he's ex-FBI. An employee. Also security. And I'll take turns, too. I have a CDL license already."

Jim tapped his mug with a finger as if deep in thought. "We'll need a car…"

"We can pull my Mercedes," Thaddeus said. "I use it for road trips, and this definitely qualifies."

"So," said Jim, "this sounds very doable, thanks to Chris and Thaddeus."

"It definitely is," said Christine. "As long as you don't all kill each other from being cramped up that long. Six weeks is a long time."

"We'll probably find a hotel or resort every few days," Thaddeus said. "Somewhere the kids might like to see. Well, Celena, anyway."

"We'll need a main campground once we get there, kinda to set up home base," Jim said.

"I've got a place in mind already, was thinking of it earlier," Thaddeus told him. "But we'll see once we get there."

"All right, then it's done," Louisa said. She started to weep. "There I am with the tears again, but I don't care. She's my firstborn, and I'll never be able to let her go. I'll be there for the week or two leading up to the—to the—"

"We know," said Jim. "We know you'll come up."

"It's settled then," said Thaddeus.

"Yes, it's settled," replied Jim.

"Leaving when?" asked Christine.

"Day after tomorrow?" asked Jim. "That work for you, Thaddeus?"

"I'll get the RV gassed and cleaned and be here early."

Louisa blew her nose into a tissue. Her eyes were swollen and red. "We'll have Rachel all set and her supplies ready."

Christine rose and so did Thaddeus. He placed a hand on Jim's shoulder. "We'll see you then."

24

———

Thaddeus and Christine were packing the RV motorhome the next day when Marcel and Turquoise drove up in her Mustang. Thaddeus hadn't expected them home so soon, so stepped down from the motorhome and met them as they walked up the driveway.

"Hello, you two," Thaddeus said and stepped in to hug Turquoise. "What brings you guys back Stateside so soon?"

"Thaddeus, do you have a minute to talk?" Marcel said. His tone was serious and alerted Thaddeus immediately.

Christine arrived just then and gave Turquoise a tight hug. "Sweetheart, you are absolutely glowing," she said. Turquoise snuck a peek at Marcel before she turned back to her mother. "Must be the Mexican sun, ya know..."

Thaddeus wasn't sure about that, and her words didn't seem to convince Christine either. "How about we go inside? We are just about to leave to head north to Oregon with the Sundstroms, so big news for us here, too."

Turquoise fell in with Thaddeus and Marcel followed with Christine. "Wow," said Turquoise. "What's going on?"

Thaddeus huffed out a loud sigh. "Long story, but we're taking Rachel up to Oregon to establish residency so she can end her life."

Thaddeus opened the back door to the house so Turquoise could walk through. The house looked dark after the bright midday sun outside. Turquoise sat at the table while Thaddeus turned on the electric kettle.

Marcel came inside a few moments later. "Christine is going to keep working on the RV. Said she'd catch up with everything later, Thaddeus."

Thaddeus plopped chai tea bags into three mugs. "Sounds good. Now, do you want to tell me what's going on in Mexico City?"

Turquoise and Marcel exchanged a look, and then Marcel started in. "Not sure if what we are going to tell you is good news or bad news, Thaddeus."

"Let me decide that. Keep going," Thaddeus said as he poured the hot water to steep the tea.

"While we were there, my connection at Interpol informed me that the FBI just arrested a Mexican man, Daniel Ortiz. Turns out Ortiz was on the run from a group in Europe. He was the one that supposedly marked Johann's suitcase with traces of Semtex and then backed out when the FBI came knocking. Admitted to it all. Said he acted on his own."

"That doesn't seem believable from what we know," said Thaddeus. He placed the tea bag on a saucer and took a sip. "Ahhh... that's better."

"I agree, Dad. It just doesn't sit right with me either. Something is up."

"So, what does that really mean for Johann and the case? That's my question," said Thaddeus.

Marcel blew across the rim of his mug. "You should be getting a call from Jack Rasso any minute now. I'm sure they're going to drop charges against Johann."

"Really? I'm going to call Jack." He dialed and put his cell on speaker in the center of the table.

"Thaddeus!" cried the voice at the other end. "You must have heard from Marcel. It's great news, and I'm so relieved to see Ned's son innocent. The US Attorney will be filing today to drop charges on my instructions. I'm going to call Gretta as soon as I'm off here and give her the news."

"How about we call her right now? Hang tight, Jack, and I'll dial her in." Thaddeus conferenced in Gretta Van Giersbergen, and when she answered, he introduced who was on the call, including Marcel and Turquoise."

Jack took only minutes to let Gretta know what had happened. Gretta was ecstatic and asked when Johann would be released. When Jack said the order was going through now, Gretta said she'd go and pick Johann up immediately. After many thank yous from Gretta, Jack excused himself, saying he had a lot of paper-work yet to do.

When he was off the call, Gretta said, "Thaddeus, can I buy you lunch this week? I owe you big time."

"Not this week. We're headed for Oregon. You might understand why. I've got a seventeen-year-old girl with a fatal disease and terrible pain. She wants to end her life and California won't let her until she's twenty-one. We're off to Oregon to establish residency there so she can get her help."

"Where are you staying?"

"She doesn't want hospice or a hotel. So, we're taking my bus. We'll find some cabins and check in at some point."

"What about nursing care?"

"There's one nurse. She's going to be busy."

"Take Johann. He owes me, and now he owes you. He can help. And after the way he was treated at work, he won't be going back there. They tried to turn him in to the FBI!"

"I know. Are you serious about him coming along? I know we could really use a second nurse. That would be incredible."

"Sure. I'll have him call you when we get home. I'm going to leave now for the correctional facility."

"That would be so great to have him. If you're sure he'll be up to it."

"Thaddeus, Johann is only twenty-two. All he really wants to do is surf and think about med school anyway. He'd love to come help you out. He owes, and I do, too. Consider it a done deal."

"All right, you have my numbers. We're leaving tomorrow."

"He'll be ready. Just say where and when."

"I'll pick him up at my office. Eight a.m."

"Done. He'll be there, Thaddeus."

25

They pulled out of La Jolla just after noon and made north Los Angeles by five when they had to stop for Rachel's car sickness. She had been sick several times along the way, and now she just couldn't go on and asked for the "rocking and rolling" of the bus to stop. They found a campground on the northern outskirts of LA in Santa Clarita that rented them a campsite for $85.00.

They pulled into their spot, and Sandy climbed down from the driver's seat and began hooking up sewer, potable water, and the electric line. Everyone on board admitted they were ravenous with hunger—all except Rachel, who rarely ate anymore, Thaddeus was saddened to learn.

He grabbed some refrigerator items, went to the bus's exterior kitchen, and started frying bacon and slicing tomatoes for BLT's. Just after six-thirty, they all ate at the picnic table beneath the roll-out awning. The sandwiches were hot, the iced tea was cold, and the passengers and Sandy wolfed down their food.

Back inside, Thaddeus listened through the open bedroom door as Jim Sundstrom tried to coax Rachel into eating something. It really mattered less than the others because she was receiving nutrition through her IV, but it was just that healthy people are instinctively pleased when a sick person takes real food. It was a sign of good health.

But it wasn't to be. She refused any and all offers. Thaddeus could hear her balking at June's advances with solid food. That seemed to end what he guessed was a nightly ritual, her father and June trying to feed her and the patient refusing all nourishment by mouth. So be it, thought Thaddeus. Maybe tomorrow.

He stuck his head in to check on Rachel. Her eyes were closed, but he took a chance she was actually awake.

"Hey, pumpkin," he whispered, "how's our girl?"

Her eyes fluttered open. "Hello, Mr. Murfee. Thank you for bringing me to Oregon."

"Not at all. I'd do anything to help you. I figure this is one way. Was the bus swaying and bumping too much today?"

"I got sick, but I don't know why." She was being polite. She knew exactly what had made her throw up along the way when they'd had to pull over and wait for the nausea to subside.

"Hey," he said, "I hear you love to play chess. How about a tournament?"

"Sure, I'd like that a lot." Her face brightened, and he knew it was the right thing to do. So, he said, "All right, I'll set it up. Ten bucks to enter, winner takes all."

"I don't have ten bucks."

"Never mind. I'll loan you ten bucks."

"Yeah, but then you're betting against yourself."

"Don't worry about it. I'm a big boy."

"And I'm a big girl. Big enough I can win this thing."

"Fine, we'll begin tonight, round one. Who would you like to play first?"

"My dad. I can get him eliminated right out of the gate."

"Fair enough. Sundstrom versus Sundstrom, coming up."

Thaddeus called Jim into the bedroom, and he gladly wanted in on the chess tournament. He sat in the bedside chair with the chess board and pieces on Rachel's bed. Just five minutes later, she was lying on her side, playing with one arm.

Thaddeus went into the family room where, he would later swear, he heard the girl laugh out loud three or four times while she destroyed her father in chess. Or had she? Maybe her father was so good he was no good? Either way, he lost and was eventually eliminated after losing two out of three matches over the next little while.

Twice, the game had to be interrupted while Rachel received a dosing from her IV and went to sleep peacefully when the pain was too bad. Then she'd come to, and the game would pick up right where they'd left off. It became apparent to anyone paying attention that she was accustomed to working around the interruptions, that they had become a part of her life, and she took them in stride.

After a half-hour of play, a defeated Jim Sundstrom came out of her room, announcing it was someone else's turn because Rachel felt up to taking on another contestant.

Not so surprisingly, Johann offered to play with her next. Thaddeus had always thought the kid was super smart. Even though he tried to come across as this laid-back surfer dude, Thaddeus could tell there was something more there, some driving force. With an FBI agent father and a surgeon mother, the genetics almost wouldn't seem to allow anything else.

"Thaddeus, how about we walk up to the campground store and score some ice cream?" Jim interrupted Thaddeus's thoughts as he watched the two young people through the open cabin door.

"Definitely," said Thaddeus. At the door, he slipped his Skechers back on his feet. "Let's go."

Off they went, the two men. Thaddeus was more than relieved to be out of the bus and moving around.

The sun was still high in the sky at seven o'clock, and the campground was bursting with kids of all ages out playing and squealing with delight on the jungle gym and merry-go-round and swings. Thaddeus felt a tug at his heartstrings as he thought of Rachel, relegated to her room but doing the best she could to put on a good front for her companions.

They walked along an asphalt path from their campsite up to the store, then went inside. The place smelled like a grocery store, and bored campers were everywhere, carefully examining and reading boxes and containers that ordinarily they would ignore. They finally tossed them into their carts and ran through checkout. There was a sense of everyone being in on some great adventure together, and serious study needed to be given to the replenishment of the ship's stores.

Jim and Thaddeus found the ice cream cooler. At least it was full, small containers and big buckets of all types of ice cream.

"Name your poison," said Jim who, upon realizing what he'd said, turned red-faced and obviously wished he'd chosen his words more carefully given his daughter's coming proximity to the poison that would end her life. "I mean, let's find some flavors everyone will like."

Thaddeus stepped up and chose a quart of vanilla and a quart of butter pecan, two innocuous enough flavors he doubted anyone would find objectionable.

They headed back to the RV and got out the bowls. Even Rachel was happy with the ice cream and actually ate two large table-spoonfuls.

She then fell asleep as it was getting dark outside.

The other folks went to the outside TV, turned it on, and found a video.

It had been a fairly good day, and Thaddeus was glad she'd had fun with the chess tournament and ice cream.

Not once during the night did she cry out. If nothing else, Thaddeus was determined to make her last weeks, her last days, as happy and enjoyable as he could.

26

On the second day of the trip, Thaddeus told Sandy he would take the wheel for the morning stint. At the same time, Rachel let it be known that she wanted to ride up front in the passenger's chair. This was a big deal, so her dad did a bit of scrambling to set her up. He gave her a dose of morphine and found a therapy gait belt to wrap around her torso and back around her seat to help hold her in place. Thus, she was sitting upright with a full view out the front window, supported by the therapy belt and the morphine capsule, and ready to enjoy the open road.

Thaddeus dropped the RV into drive and off they went. They were leaving Santa Clarita with a destination of San Francisco, or at least the south county.

Once underway, Rachel was brought a steaming cup of green tea —her choice. Thaddeus was passed a cup of coffee.

He blew across his coffee and said, "So...tell me about Rachel Sundstrom. What are your likes and dislikes?"

She squinted her eyes at the road, unused to the bright light. He passed her his Ray-Bans, which she put on.

"Likes? I like strong people. I like journaling. I love, not like, animals, and they are by far better than the human race. *Don't make fun of me, but* I like old classic eighties movies, like *The Breakfast Club* and *St. Elmo's Fire*. I like the sunset reflected off the ocean. I like it when I catch a wave while surfing that I can ride all the way to shore. I like 'The Love Song of J. Alfred Prufrock' by T.S. Eliot, which might seem odd, but I've always wanted to..." She didn't finish, but Thaddeus could fill in the blanks. Who didn't want to find love? She continued, "And I like...quirky. Different things. What are your likes, Mr. Murfee?"

"Well, like you, I like 'Prufrock.' I like woody wines. I like Klee and Van Gogh and *A Moveable Feast*. I do not like school zones and no passing lanes. I also like *The Sun Also Rises*. Obviously, I'm a Hemingway fan. I regret that I never did my year in Paris, sitting alone in cafes with a cup of espresso, writing my feelings in a spiral tablet. Maybe someday yet. Hah!" He gave a sharp laugh at his "someday."

She reclined her seat two inches. "What do you think of a girl client who wants to die? Is this a first time for you?"

"Actually, it is. What do I think? I think she's very brave, and I also think she's in more pain than I would ever be able to bear. I think she's beautiful and smart and able to see a future the rest of us can only guess about. That makes me want to ask more questions, but I also don't want to invade your privacy."

"My privacy?" she asked. "Go ahead, ask your questions. At this point, I have nothing left to hide. No cover-ups."

"Tell me about what happens when you die then."

"I've watched a lot of YouTube videos about that. I think when a human makes its transition, we are able to leave our bodies in a conscious state and go into the realm that's our real home, the place where we've existed for all eternity. I think we're welcomed there by family and friends from this life and by family and friends from prior lives. I think we're introduced into a great white light that's unlike any light in this dimension. It's a light that is composed of love and forgiveness and acceptance and wonderful things to come." Her face was aglow with her hope and belief in this afterlife.

Thaddeus couldn't help but be enticed by her words. "Wow. Go on, please."

"I think when we transition over, we immediately remember what we've forgotten in this realm, that we have all the world's and the universe's answers already in mind, but we've forgotten them on this side of the curtain. I believe we immediately know all of these things when we transition and all of the other souls there have knowledge of them, too."

Thaddeus had to wonder if being on the knife edge between life and death automatically matured a person. She sounded much older than her years. No seventeen-year-old he'd ever known, including himself, could look at life, and death, so objectively, with emotion...yet no emotion.

"What about sin? That's a huge question among theologians."

"Sin doesn't exist in the afterlife. As soon as we cross over, we have a life review, and we're able to evaluate all our transactions with all the people in our life. Those we've hurt and those who've hurt us. We're able to experience both sides of the equation as we meet these people and we forgive, and they forgive us. But I don't think there's any judgment, *ever*, not in the sense of judgment for sins. I do think we're judged on whether we completed our life plan on earth. Whether we did what we came to do. Sometimes people die and get sent back—their heart gets restarted or the cancer abates, and they return to earth to complete their work. But people like me, I think we came back to do one thing, and we did it at a young age, so now we get to return home."

"Wow." What else was there to say?

She sounded like someone who had done a study on the notions of consciousness and how consciousness persists even after death of the body. He was so impressed with her just then that it brought tears to his eyes. He plucked a tissue from the console and wiped them.

"What's the matter, Mr. Murfee, something get caught in your eye?" she whispered.

"No, I just—I—"

She rolled her head on the headrest of the seat until she could look at him. She smiled, and in that smile was a hundred years. "You heard stuff from me that even my parents don't hear. They have church beliefs, and they're close-minded to my beliefs. I think kids start having some pretty damn lofty ideas before their parents are ready for that. I think that's what causes a lot of friction between parents and kids."

Thaddeus was comfortable at the wheel of the beast of a bus he was driving, surprisingly enough. And Rachel was loquacious, which was unusual, but he was glad for it. There was something complete about their small group on their road trip. In the back was her dad, Jim, who was reading, most likely a professional text, Celena, who was texting with her friends, June, who was counting pills, Johann, who was on his laptop, and Sandy, the XFBI agent, who was grabbing forty winks on a spare bunk. The interior was now quiet as the RV ate up the miles and traffic whizzed by on the other side of the freeway.

Rachel broke the silence, speaking to Thaddeus. "Know what Steve Jobs' last six words were when he died?"

"What?" he asked, curious.

"OH WOW, OH WOW, OH WOW!"

Thaddeus chuckled. "No, I didn't know that. It sounds hopeful, though."

"I'm hanging onto that," she said. "I expect to have the same kind of gladdening, mind-blowing experience that I can leave my family with. I expect to take the drugs and give them a clue. A wisp of smoke. A snippet of a poem to remember me by. Even 'OH WOW' would be great."

"You are amazing." And she truly was. Thaddeus asked, "How are you doing for pain?"

"I'm okay. Surprisingly, it's low pain sitting up. Normally, it hurts like hell, but I think it's this chair and the therapy belt holding me upright. I don't think I could sit like this without the belt."

"Then I'm glad whoever brought it."

"June brought it. She helps me to the bathroom with it tied around my waist and holding onto the back of it as I walk. She's an amazingly capable nurse. I just love my June."

"Rachel, how far did you get in school?"

"I was taking AP Math and Literature. I've been accepted to Honors Math at Stanford, where my dad went to school. But I won't be messing with all that, Mr. Murfee. I'm going straight for the Ph.D. they offer star walkers when they die."

27

A half hour later, Rachel was tired and hurting and she was taken back to bed by June—with the use of the therapy belt to make it down the center aisle of the RV. Thaddeus called back that he needed someone else to come forward and talk to him and entertain him—his try at humor just then. Surprisingly, Jim prodded June to go forward. "It's your turn to keep our driver awake and in good spirits," he kidded her. "Give it a whirl, June."

June came forward and sat in shotgun. She was wearing blue jeans, a yellow scrubs top, and sunglasses perched on her forehead. She was nibbling a chicken wing she was holding with a paper towel. She stuck the chicken in her mouth and held it there while she used both hands to attach the seat belt.

"Oh, I hate having to do seatbelts while I'm holding chicken." She laughed. "Not that I ever thought I'd say those words in one sentence. Do you have any hates, Thaddeus?"

"Yes, I hate having accidents without a seat belt on."

"There you go. I knew there was something about it."

He called back, "Celena, put your phone down and bring Daddy a cup of coffee, please."

Celena set her phone aside on the dinner table and filled a travel mug for her dad. She added just the right amount of half and half and took it forward. He thanked her and watched her walk away in the rearview mirror. "She's fifteen, heaven help us all."

"That's about the age it starts," said June.

"Oh, it started long ago. Girlfriends, boyfriends, very little interest in STEM."

"Maybe she'll be a lawyer like her dad."

"Oh," he said softly, "I wouldn't wish that on any of them. Mom and Dad are both lawyers. That's enough for one family. No, Celena is going to do something with animals. She just got a new horse for her birthday. She might be a large animal vet. That wouldn't surprise me. Or an exotics vet. She loves guinea pigs and cockatoos."

"What about her dad? What does he want for her?" asked June.

"Happiness. What every parent wants. And for her to make her own way like her mom and I did. These kids won't ever hurt for anything, but I don't want them to miss out on the fun of being themselves either. There's no happier man or woman than the one who finds their true self. But tell me, what should I know about my friend June?"

"I'm a forty-year-old lesbian and Melissa Etheridge fan who raises orchids on her kitchen ledge and refuses to have pets until her old age when her running days are over. Sure, I'd like a little dog or a big cat, but not yet."

"Married or single?"

"Looking. I always put *looking* down on the forms when they ask marital status. How about you, Thaddeus?"

"Status? Happily married. Very."

"How do two lawyers keep from killing each other with words."

"We have a special arrangement. We agree that we both have fighting skills we learned in school and learned in the trenches of the courtrooms. But at home we don't allow those skills in the front door. So, there's no hair-splitting when we argue. It's that simple. No hair-splitting, no defining of terms, none of the crap that lawyers put in contracts to make themselves rich. Just plain talk. Lawyer skills in personal relationships are a fool's way out. But tell me, are you currently in a relationship?"

"Off and on. She's a high school guidance counselor who wants to come out and be an artist and give up the school gig. Except she's afraid, too. She's also afraid her husband will kill her."

They both laughed. "You mean he might not find it so funny that she's found someone else, a woman?" said Thaddeus.

"Exactly. So, she's afraid to tell him. Seriously, we love each other, but he's a scary man with guns and Victorian morals. Not a safe place to let our love bloom."

"Why doesn't she just leave him?"

"Honestly? She's afraid of him."

"Tell her to leave him and get a tough lawyer to handle him. That's not that hard to find."

"What about you, Thaddeus? Would you take her case?"

"Me? I don't do family law. I've never understood it."

"What's to understand? You've got two people who want to kill each other. Keep them alive and split the sheets. Isn't that about it?"

"I guess. I don't know."

"Seriously, would you take her case? Her name is Nina."

"Sorry, I don't do domestic."

"What if I begged?"

Thaddeus became thoughtful. He didn't say anything for the next ten miles. Then, slowly, he said, "Tell you what. I will take Nina's case if you'll do something for me."

"You bet. I'll do anything."

"When Rachel dies, I want to hear her say 'OH WOW!' Can you help her do that?"

"I—I don't know. Steve Jobs? I don't know what he was seeing."

"I don't either. But in case it's not there, you figure out some other way to help our girl leave peacefully. Fair enough?"

"I'm a pretty damn good nurse. Yes, that's fair. You've got yourself a deal, Thaddeus."

"Good, then."

They drove on another hundred miles. Sandwiches were made and passed around. Then came iced tea and yet more coffee. Soon they were passing the first of several Bakersfield turnoffs and then, another thirty minutes on, they were coming to the Buttonwillow Highway 58 turnoff, where they pulled in and everyone stretched their legs at a truck stop. More provisions were taken on in the way of Cokes and soft drinks and Fritos and peanuts and magazines and bottled water, then they were on the road again.

"June," Thaddeus said after a few miles, "where did you go to school?"

"I went to Caldwell in Idaho where I got my BSN. My first job was doing oncology at a large hospital in Los Angeles. I learned how to use every pump made in the medical profession and learned how to handle controlled substances and do my counts and all that. Then I started nursing for a group of surgeons and spent much of my days in pre-op and post-op with the patients in the hospital before and just after surgery. I then got tired of punching a clock and started working home health. That's how I came to be working with Rachel. Plus, Dr. Sundstrom knew me and recruited me personally for daytime caregiving. I love that man and love his family, and I'll be around as long as I'm needed."

"What did you think about Becca's heroin fiasco?"

"I thought it was very brave of Becca. She was trying to do for her sister what no one else would do. Sometimes—no, I shouldn't say that."

"No, go ahead and say it."

"Sometimes I wish Becca would've been successful. Except that wouldn't have let the parents say goodbye and would've landed Becca in much hotter water than she's already in. But the nurse part of me wishes she'd pulled it off. Rachel would've been much better off."

"No comment," said Thaddeus. "Except to say, I think we're doing the right thing here, don't you?"

"I do, Thaddeus. I think we're doing the exact right thing at just the right time. I'm going back for a nap. Good talking, sir."

"Thanks. I'll be helping your friend when we get back home."

"Thank you."

28

Johann volunteered to come forward next. He had been at the kitchen counter, making himself a ham sandwich. June walked past and gave him a playful punch in the kidneys. "You're wanted up front."

He went forward and took the passenger's seat, offering half of his sandwich to Thaddeus. Thaddeus asked what was on it.

"Mustard and mayonnaise. No lettuce."

"My God, how can you eat a ham sandwich without lettuce?" asked Thaddeus. "I'll pass, thank you very much. So...I finally get a chance to chat with my most recent ex-client. Tell me about yourself."

"As in?" Johann chomped on his sandwich, working down a mighty mouthful.

"As in what makes you tick."

"Let's see. I was raised by two white parents, which worked well enough since I'm white, too. I'm twenty-two, so I can vote and drink. The one I do often and too much; the other I haven't gotten to try yet. I studied history my first two years in college then switched to the nursing program when I found that eighty-five percent of history majors were working at something other than history. Kind of a waste of time, eh? But I love history. It's still my love for personal, late-at-night reading. I also like Sirius late-night talk radio. I know all the conspiracy theories and know how their proponents will vote next year. I love girls but can't afford one as I'm still paying student debts. So, that probably answers your next question—no, my parents did not pay my way through school. After high school, I was on my own like they were. Family rules, Mr. Murfee."

"Thaddeus."

"Thaddeus. I'm also a member of the Islamic Student Union and got a minor in Arabic."

"You studied Arabic?"

"I did, and the CIA tried to recruit me. I told them I wasn't a patriot, so they went after someone else."

"You're not a patriot, why?"

"Because I don't believe the U.S. has a corner on the righteousness market. I happen to think many Arabic countries, and factions, are righteous, too. There, I've said too much."

Thaddeus studied his passenger out of the corner of his eye. Given that the speaker's father was FBI, Thaddeus was almost without words. But he tried by saying, "What if the FBI finds out it was some jihadist faction that blew up your father? How's that sit with you?"

"There are always struggles, and struggles often get the wrong people killed." Johann wiped his hands on a napkin. He was overly nonchalant, and Thaddeus wondered if that was a youth thing or if it was something more. Johann crumpled the napkin and held it in his hand. "My father knew what he was doing, and he knew who he was working for. He knew about Hellfire missiles and incinerated civilians in Yemen. He kept working for the FBI anyway. He was a soldier, Mr. Murfee."

At that, Thaddeus was speechless. Never in a million years would he have expected these words from a twenty-two-year-old surfer who, his mother said, would rather surf than hold down a real job. Or words to that effect. A twenty-two-year-old who, his mother said, might be considering going to medical school. He collected himself and coolly asked, "But you won't forgive those who killed your father. I know you—"

"It isn't up to me to forgive. God forgives. It's war, Mr. Murfee. I think that's about all I want to talk about that. Can we change the subject? Ask me about surfing and let me tell you about the surf spots in Oregon I've been looking up online."

"How about that surfing in Oregon?" Thaddeus gamely asked.

"Do you know what? I need some milk. Be right back."

Five minutes later, he returned. This time he brought with him a ham sandwich with lettuce. He passed it to Thaddeus on a small paper plate with a square of paper towel. "For you."

"Thank you." Thaddeus took a bite and looked down. He still had some root beer left. It would do.

"Tell me about Rachel, Thaddeus."

"She's very sick. She's dying—wants to die."

"No, I mean tell me about her. Who is she?"

Thaddeus munched a bite. "I think you'll find she's just like any other seventeen-year-old American girl. She wants to live. She wants to go on dates. She wants to get married and have a family. Oh, yes, she's also a surfer. So, you guys should get along. Something about Surfrider."

"She belongs to Surfrider? Gnarly, Thaddeus. That's just way cool. I belong, too. I have a kayak I take out to collect plastic on weekends with everyone else. We collect plastic, drink a little, party, and do it again the next day. We've collected something like four-million tons in California. Maybe my numbers are wrong. But it's a lot."

"Do you see a lot of plastic out beyond the surf?"

"Enough to run the Chinese economy for ten years. It's revolting. Especially after it rains. You don't even go in the water for four days after a rain. It's too dangerous."

"What else should I know about my most recent ex-client?"

"I miss my dad. I loved him more than anyone in the world. He was a fantastic dad and a cool guy. He taught me everything I know. College taught me things he didn't, of course. But that's a whole other conversation. Did he deserve to die by jihadists? No one deserves to die for religion. I hate religion. I hate what it does to people. Well...most religions. Some are more honorable than others." He jokingly smacked his own forehead. "There I go again. I'm going to go back and send someone else up. Who do you want?"

"Dr. Sundstrom. Thanks for talking, Johann. I've loved it."

"Thanks for asking me. See you in the morning. I'm going to put on my headphones now and chill. I'm exhausted."

"G'night."

29

Jim Sundstrom came forward next to keep Thaddeus company. He was looking troubled and ready to break down.

"Jim, what's going on?" Thaddeus said when he saw his friend's face.

"It's Louisa. I just talked to her on the phone. The probation officer is saying they're thinking of keeping Becca in juvenile hall until she's twenty-one."

"Oh, shit."

"Exactly. Have you talked to Chris about it?"

"No, but I'll call her. Hang on a minute. Let me get my phone out."

He dialed Christine's number and let it ring.

Then she picked up. "Guess you heard?" she asked.

"Jim was just telling me. What's the big rush to keep her locked up?"

"The DA is taking a hard line. Drug deaths among teens have increased two-hundred-percent in three years. They're making an example of kids like Becca."

"No chance of cutting a deal?"

"Not really. I've presented the whole package—good family, good grades, very sick sister, huge feelings of guilt—her psychiatrist gave me that—and they still won't budge. They want her until she reaches the age of majority."

"Okay, let's talk about the immediate future. Will there be any way of getting a furlough for her to come to Oregon to say goodbye to her sister?"

"That's what I'm working on next. I feel very positive about that. I don't think I'll get any pushback there."

"Good enough. What about the delinquency hearing? Has it been set for trial?"

"In California, a minor's trial is called an 'adjudication hearing.' This is the hearing at which a judge decides whether or not the minor violated a law and should be disciplined. We're not there yet. We're still having the child evaluated by the court. Much will depend on that."

"Thaddeus," Jim whispered, "I think you should be her lawyer on the adjudication hearing. I want you both there."

"Hear that, Chris? Jim's thinking he wants me there to back you up."

"Don't forget about your conflict of interest," she said.

He turned away from Jim and whispered into the phone, "Rachel will be gone by then. There won't be a conflict anymore."

She said, "We'll talk. One day at a time. How's the trip, *kemo sabe*?"

"Good, so far. Everyone's chill. Rachel is doing really well. She was carsick the first day but not today. In fact, she was up here talking to me this morning."

"Oh, bless her baby heart. I'd love to be there and give her a big hug. You and Celena, too. How's our girl?"

"You kidding? She never takes her eyes off her screen. We could be in Anchorage right now and she wouldn't know the difference. What's new? How is the rest of the brood?"

"Everyone's fine. Turquoise says she has a surprise for us?"

Thaddeus' mind immediately jumped ahead. "Pregnant?"

"Would you stop it? Turquoise can take care of herself."

"I know she can. I just hate the term 'surprise' in the same sentence with a daughter's name. That's all. Okay, I'm off of here. Going to talk to Jim for a while. Love and kisses."

"Mwah!"

He ended the call.

"See?" said Jim. "I'm shook, Thaddeus."

They drove another ten minutes in silence. Their mutual confidence in being quiet together was suddenly split when Thaddeus's phone chimed again.

He looked at the screen. "It's Christine, Jim. Gotta take it. Sit still. Hello?"

She took off running. "Well, I haven't been off the phone ten minutes, and I just got the juvenile court order. Adjudication is set seven days from today. I have the Murtagh murder trial starting that day. Murtagh won't continue, and juvenile cases, by law, can't be continued at this point. I'm stuck. I need you back here."

"Which case do you want me to cover?"

"Not Murtagh. It's a ground war in Asia. I'm buried. You'll have to take Becca's case."

"What about my conflict?"

"My staff's preparing a waiver for Jim to sign. He'll waive the conflict on behalf of both girls. That should do it for now."

"All right. I'll fly home from San Francisco. We're two hours out."

"Excellent. See you tonight."

The line went dead.

"You heard?" Thaddeus asked Jim.

"I heard. Not to worry, I've got this end. Celena's fine with us here. We'll make Oregon in a few days. You go get Becca out of trouble and bring her here, Thaddeus. Her mother and I—and Rachel— need her here with us. It can't be any other way."

"I understand. Let me get Sandy up here to take the wheel. He can drop me at SFO. I'll have reservations."

"Hate to see you go, brother, but it's for the best."

"I agree. I'll do everything I can for Becca."

30

Thaddeus grabbed a cab from Lindbergh Field in San Diego to La Jolla and home. After knocking ideas back and forth with Christine about Becca's defense case, he undressed and went to bed just after midnight. Thaddeus tossed and turned until four a.m., when he gave in to the stream of ideas about her case, climbed out of bed, and went to the shower. After dressing for the day, he left the walk-in closet/dressing room and went downstairs. He made coffee and then spread his laptop before him on the kitchen table. He could grab a couple of hours of work before the little guys got up and he helped them dress and dropped them at school.

A couple hours later at his office, Thaddeus wasted no time firing up his computer and reading the law he would have to deal with on Becca's case.

He did his reading on the California jury instruction for attempted murder, then read the instructions for voluntary and involuntary manslaughter. He returned to the idea of attempted murder and the fact that where the abandonment of the plan to kill is free and voluntary, a not guilty verdict can be awarded. Thaddeus considered the area to offer enough gray that he could at least make an argument she had abandoned her plan to kill when she began calling for June to come help.

It wasn't much, to say the least, but it came the closest to offering a point of argument that might work where the judge didn't want to hit someone of such young years with a full-on attempted murder finding. Instead, Thaddeus would suggest lesser included offenses or even argue the state had failed to prove any completed criminal act at all. That would hold only on the sunniest of days under the best of circumstances where the judge had had a nice breakfast and a happy kiss from his wife before he walked out the door that day.

Next up, a call to the prosecuting attorney to discuss Becca's case. First, however, he had to file a substitution of counsel with the court, asking the court to allow him to substitute himself as attorney of record for Christine. Which meant, he would be taking over the case from that moment forward. The judge signed the order within hours, and Thaddeus was then free to call the prosecutor.

Her name was Wendy Frontell, and she worked out of the Kearny Mesa Justice Hall. He dialed her number and then waited while her paralegal tracked her down.

"Hello, Wendy? Thaddeus Murfee calling about Rebecca Sundstrom. She's the attempted murder petition where she obtained heroin for her dying sister in order to hurry up death. She abandoned the idea, however, and called out for her sister's nurse shortly after injecting the heroin into her sister's IV line. I'd like to know your position on a plea to a lesser-included, such as battery. Are you of a mind to reduce this one?"

Wendy could be heard rattling papers then clearing her throat. "Mr. Murfee, welcome aboard. I see you just substituted for Christine Murfee. Your wife or daughter?"

'Wife. She has a first-degree murder trial beginning the same day the judge set Rebecca's hearing. The jury trial won't budge so I got tagged to take over the juvie case."

"Juvie case? We consider our cases much weightier than mere 'juvie' cases, Mr. Murfee. I think you'll find our 'juvie' prosecutors on par with our adult prosecutors. Maybe even better. Regarding your inquiry, no, I'm not inclined to reduce the charge here. I'm looking for a finding of responsibility and a sentence to justice hall until she's reached the age of twenty-one." With barely a breath, she continued on, "Please let me tell you why that is, Mr. Murfee. You see, the use and abuse of the heavier drugs like crack and meth and heroin is skyrocketing all across the US. San Diego hasn't escaped that escalation in numbers of users and abusers. In fact, California is ranked near the top in percent of teenage violators. Our District Attorney has made it clear we're now engaged in a full-on battle with these cases where one of the big three drugs is involved."

"Yes, but my case isn't truly an abuse case. My case is about assisted end of life."

"Doesn't matter. The use of heroin qualifies your case for prosecution as a major crime. By the way, there would be some wiggle room were your client to help us nail the person who provided the drugs to her. We could talk seriously about her spending weekends at home with her family, given Rebecca's circumstances and that her dad is a doctor and so on."

"And what would your plea offer sound like?"

"She would plead to violating the law of attempted voluntary manslaughter, given that heat of passion need not be a sudden overwhelming passion. Your client's kind of brooding emotional state that compelled her to buy heroin would fit her within the definition. It would also serve to treat her as seriously as she deserves to be treated—a person who tried to murder another person. Mr. Murfee, how can I say to you just how serious that is?"

"Please remember, Wendy, that my client committed these acts while trying to help her sister escape from her twenty-four-seven life-altering, unremitting pain that required she be constantly medicated with morphine. But here's the real defense to this case. In our state, in California, if a person is an adult, aged twenty-one or older, they can simply go to their doctor and get the drugs they need to end their lives when they no longer have a life worth living.

"Change the players around and substitute in Rebecca's sister, your so-called victim of the attempted murder, Rachel Sundstrom, who is only seventeen years of age and therefore doesn't qualify under California's end of life law. Because of a four-year requirement in age, she cannot legally end her own life. Although her pain is just the same as the twenty-one-year-old's pain and although she's dying a horrible, slow death, she has nowhere to turn. She's trapped inside a dying body that science and medicine can no longer help."

"Mr. Murfee, you need to take that up with the legislature and get them to change the law. I can't do that for you. I can only prosecute."

"But what you can do is come off your demand that my client spend the rest of her childhood inside a juvenile detention facility when all she did is love her sister too much."

"You have a fine argument to make to the judge. It doesn't move me, Mr. Murfee. Now, what discovery do you still need from me?"

"We seem to have all witness statements and hospital records. What else do you want to admit into evidence that you haven't turned over yet?"

"Nothing."

"Then there's nothing further we need. Thank you."

"Goodbye, Mr. Murfee. Good luck with your case."

"Same to you. Goodbye."

Thaddeus hung up the phone and slammed his fist onto his desktop. How maddening to be seventeen when you can't be helped until you're twenty-one! Didn't that discriminate based on age? Wasn't that a federal case?

31

Becca explained to her mother she needed court clothes consisting of a black dress and low heels. Her mother didn't give it much thought but dropped off the items on her next visit. Becca received the package after it had been opened and searched by the deputies in charge of juvie. Nothing found, the package with the dress and heels was passed along to Becca in her room.

She waited until the next visiting day. She dressed up in her black dress and heels, put on makeup that she'd requested, tied back her hair, and went into the community visiting room. She sat among the crowd. It was one of the busiest days of the week, a Saturday, and whole families were there.

She made sure to chat with most of the other female inmates and their families. She made her way around the room, introducing herself, playing with some of the smaller children. When a three-year-old toddler left his visitor pass on the bench, Becca was right there to swoop it up. Most of the adhesive had worn off, and the ends were curled, but Becca smoothed it out and placed it over her heart.

At the close of visiting hours, she moved with the line to exit the facility. She held the hand of another little girl she'd befriended and who now adored Becca, along with the harried mother who obviously needed help with the large brood—four kids, all under the age of ten.

Becca made it past the first checkout window and continued along with the crowd, making every effort to fit in as the line moved along. Then, at the last minute, at the last window, she was required to show ID, which she didn't have. A supervisor was called after Becca tried to tell the first person that she must have left her ID on the seat of her car.

Becca's likeness was fed into the facial identification software, and she was immediately found to be a resident of the juvenile facility. Guards were called and Becca was returned to her room and told to surrender the outfit she was wearing, which she did. She was then put on a potential flight risk list and told there would be a hearing.

Which was the state Thaddeus Murfee found his client to be in when he visited the following day. First, he learned her visitation rights had been temporarily terminated. So, he identified himself as her lawyer and was, of course, waved on through. Residents and prisoners always had the right to visit with their attorneys.

They met inside a small green-walled room about size of a bedroom. There was a radiator along the far wall and a steel table bolted to the floor with four stools bolted to the floor along with it. A sputtering fluorescent light consisting of two bulbs was over-head and cast a blue tint to faces and lips and hands.

She was now again wearing the customary tan jumpsuit and flip-flops with socks. She looked tired, and he thought maybe she'd been having trouble sleeping, so he inquired.

"Who can sleep with their sister dying?" she immediately responded. "I know I can't."

"I totally understand," he said, "I couldn't sleep either. Would you feel up to answering some questions for me anyway? I really need to discuss your upcoming adjudication hearing."

"All right, Mr. Murfee. Go ahead."

"First of all, where did you get the heroin?"

"At the beach from a guy named Judd something. He rides a black Harley and can get anything you want. I have other friends who use him. That's how I found out. Someone told me he supports himself with sales to students. I don't know if it's true. That's just what someone said."

"Judd supplied the heroin?"

"He did. Five packets of brown."

"If I asked you to, would you tell on Judd?"

"I don't think so. All he did was sell me stuff. He didn't know what I was going to do."

"Selling stuff alone is enough to get him in very serious trouble, Becca. And it could help your case."

"No, I don't want anyone else in trouble. I did this. No one else did it."

"All right. I won't ask you about that again."

"All right. Anyway, he sold me five little packs of brown."

"Where did you get the money?"

"Mr. Murfee, my dad is a doctor. I used my card at the ATM."

"Tell me what you were thinking when you bought the drug."

"I was thinking I wanted to help my sister die. I wasn't thinking I wanted to hurt her or anything like that, so it was funny in a way. I was thinking more about making her pain stop."

"You put the heroin in her IV line?"

"Yes. I melted the heroin in a lid, drew it up into a syringe, and injected into her line."

"Did Rachel help you do this in any way?"

"No, in fact she was asleep."

"So, you injected her without her knowing?"

"I mean, we had talked about it before. She wanted me to do it."

"Had you talked about it that day?"

"Maybe? I can't remember. We talked about it all the time."

"Did she actually ask you go get heroin?"

"Not ask me. More like, if I ever see any for sale, she'd like to buy it. Like that. Like she wanted to buy it."

"But you knew that meant she'd like you to buy it for her?"

"Yes, I understood. So, I got it and melted it and injected it. She was asleep. Your wife went over this with me lots of times."

"I know that. Sometimes it's necessary for us to ask again." Thaddeus folded his hands in front of him. "Now, listen to this question carefully. Why did you call for June?"

"I didn't want my sister to die after all. I realized what I had done, and it scared me shitless."

"So, you were terrified."

"That's right."

"And you didn't want her to die. That was the main reason you called for June?"

"Yes, I wanted her to come help. I didn't want Rachel to die. It wasn't right. My parents didn't even get to say goodbye. I realized it was wrong after I did it."

"You abandoned the whole idea and called for June?"

"I abandoned the idea."

"When you saw June come in, how did you feel?"

"I started crying. I was totally mixed up, Mr. Murfee. I was so sure of myself when I bought the brown. So positive it was the right thing. But then after I did, I realized how wrong it was. When she came in, I started crying. I was relieved."

"You thought June could save her?"

"I knew if anybody could, it would be June."

"What did you tell the police when they first talked to you?"

"At the hospital, they asked me what it was. This was after I woke up. I told them it was brown heroin. But I think they already had her urine test—I don't know, exactly. But I for sure told them what I had done."

"So, you never tried to cover up?"

"No, why would I? I mean, I did it."

"That's right. All right, I think we'll leave it right here for now."

"Is my trial still next Monday?"

"Yes. Just over a week."

"Are you scared?" she asked.

"No, I'm worried for you. But I'm not personally scared, no."

"Good. I need you to be fighting."

"We'll both be fighting. We'll listen carefully to whatever anyone says to you, and we'll give short answers. Don't explain anything when you're questioned. Give yes and no answers only, if possible. Don't elaborate."

"Got it."

"And no more escapes. Let me get you out of here."

"No more escapes. Is my mom ready to kill me?"

"No, she's very sad. But she'll be okay, so don't worry about her."

"I'll try, Mr. Murfee."

"All right. Let's end this now."

32

Turquoise was going to assist Thaddeus with court preparation for Becca's trial. She walked right into his office while he was at his desk.

Surprisingly, Marcel was with her. Thaddeus assumed he would have flown back to Chicago by now, but there was the investigator, big as always. Today, he wore jeans, a T-shirt, and had sunglasses perched on his head.

Turquoise looked as beautiful as always and was wearing a gigantic smile. She seemed to glow with happiness.

Thaddeus got up from his chair and walked to the other side of his desk. After a hug, Turquoise stepped back from him and grasped Marcel's hand. She tugged him forward. "Dad, is your offer for Marcel to stay in the guest room at your house still open?"

Thaddeus was usually quick on the draw, but he couldn't seem to comprehend what he was looking at.

"Dad?" Turquoise asked again.

He snapped out of it. "Of course, he is welcome to stay as long as he'd like. Um..." Thaddeus glanced down at their twined hands.

Turquoise chuckled and held up their hands. "Surprise!"

Thaddeus wasn't sure what she was referring to but was going to take a stab at it. "You and Marcel?"

"Yep. Marcel's going to stick around La Jolla for a bit to see how things go for us."

"Us?" Thaddeus repeated.

"Yeah, we're in love."

Thaddeus had to sit down. So, he did at his desk.

Marcel had been quiet until that point, but now he moved forward, bringing Turquoise with him so that he stood just in front of the desk.

"Thaddeus, I know what you're thinking..."

Thaddeus wasn't sure himself what he was thinking so he doubted greatly if Marcel knew. But he should have said something congratulatory because now she wore a frown on her pretty face. He clapped his hands together. "I'm so glad to hear, guys!"

Turquoise grimaced at him. "Nice try, Dad."

Marcel took a seat at one of Thaddeus's visitor chairs, and after a brief hesitation, so did Turquoise.

"I know I'm about your age, Thaddeus, and that might concern you in regard to your daughter. But I can honestly tell you that Turquoise is a woman beyond her years. Wise, kind, beautiful..." When he said the last word, Marcel turned his face to look at Turquoise. Thaddeus's oldest daughter. A daughter of his own heart.

"So…" Thaddeus cleared his throat and folded his hands on the desk in front of him. Then he relaxed them and leaned back in his chair. He didn't want either of them to feel like they were under an inquisition. Which he was about to start. "What about your investigative work for Michael Gresham then?" he asked Marcel.

Marcel was all relaxed, his one leg crossed over the other. "Well, I have some vacation days I can take to see if I want to settle here with Turquoise, and if that happens, well…Turquoise thought you might need some more help with investigations here in La Jolla."

"She did?" With one glance at his daughter and her furrowed brow, Thaddeus said, "Of course! Yes, I can always use the help."

When Turquoise finally smiled at him, Thaddeus relaxed. Just a little bit.

"Dad, I know it's big news since we've just gotten to know each other…"

Only a few weeks! thought Thaddeus, but he kept that gem to himself.

"But Marcel and I are the type to know…ya know? It happened the first day we were together."

Right. Thaddeus clapped his hands together sharply. "I'm really happy for you guys. It's settled. Marcel will move in with us for a bit. Not you, right, Turquoise?" At her nod, he continued, "And you guys are going to see if you want to continue your relationship? Got it."

She shrugged. "That's about it."

"Well, what say we get to work then? Just get on with the normal?" Thaddeus asked. He needed to redirect himself. He didn't know how much longer he could hold himself together with the two love birds across from him.

Turquoise shared a knowing look with Marcel, and then they both chuckled. "Sure, Dad," she said.

When Marcel rose from the chair so did Turquoise. He said, "I'm just gonna go to the store quick and buy a few things to hold me over." He gave Turquoise a kiss on the lips. "I'll see you later, babe." He nodded at Thaddeus. "Mr. Murfee, will see you in a bit."

As soon as the door closed behind Marcel, Thaddeus asked, "So... Marcel, huh?"

She plopped down in the chair and curled her legs under her. "Yep." She popped the p on "yep."

"Hmm...." Thaddeus didn't know what else to say. Marcel...well, Marcel was much older than Turquoise, yes, but it was more than that. He was ex-Interpol, a very big man, and could probably kick some serious ass. Which Thaddeus realized was right up Turquoise's alley.

"Dad, let's just get going on this. Marcel and I were hoping we could take you and Chris out to eat tonight."

"I think she'd like that, Turquoise. Have you told her yet?"

"She was the first to know."

"Oh." Well, since relationships and romance were more of a mother thing, he could understand that.

Turquoise interrupted his thoughts. "Who do you expect the state to call as witnesses?"

Right. Back to work. The cases wouldn't win themselves. "First off, they'll call Officer McCluskey. He interrogated Becca at the scene after she was awake. He's the one she told about the heroin and told about injecting it into the IV line."

"Which means she's convicted with the testimony of this one witness only."

"If the judge allows it into evidence. That remains to be seen."

"Who else?"

"Then they're going to call June. She can testify about statements made by Becca, the sister's distress when she first saw her after the heroin bolus, and things such as that. She also went to the hospital, so we need to find out what she knows. She's on my list with everyone else, so please call her there and see what you can find out. Again, though, Becca's statements to June are arguably inadmissible hearsay. So, we'll just have to wait and see how the judge rules on that when I object. But I think I lose on that one. Admission against interest."

"What else?

"Then they've got the crime lab to testify that the contents of the baggies found in Rachel's room contained trace amounts of heroin. It had been adulterated several times during its distribution, which is probably what saved Rachel's life."

"It wasn't pure."

"Exactly. It was about five distributors down the line from pure. Which saved her, no doubt." Thaddeus consulted his notes. "Crime scene techs have seized the IV pole, the IV bags, and line and needle. All of the other stuff like the pot lid she cooked in, the fireplace lighter, the syringe, they were all retrieved and will be put into evidence."

"So, they've got a pretty good case of items used to pull it off."

"Yes."

"Then who?"

"Then Detective Jayne Marsh. She took a complete written state-ment from Becca. State's Exhibit 1, no doubt." Thaddeus took off his glasses and rubbed his eyes with his thumb and forefinger. "Last, they'll call the hospital personnel. The ER doc, name of Jackson Black, the nurse, the laboratory analysis people. That's probably three or four witnesses right there. Then they'll rest their case."

"Who do we have?"

"We have Becca and we have Indira Kapur, Rachel's psychiatrist."

"What can Dr. Kapur do?"

"She'll testify that Rachel wanted to die. That she would have jumped at the chance to overdose with heroin if given the chance."

"How can I help?" Turquoise asked.

"You can help by trying to interview Officer McCluskey. See what you can get out of him about any indication Becca had abandoned her plan. Listen to what he says about Becca calling for June. Then go with that and see what else he knows about it. He probably won't talk to you, but you never know until you try. Oh, and you can talk to June again, too. I talked to her briefly in the bus, but see if anything new comes up this time."

Turquoise called June a half-hour later. June said they had arrived in Oregon but were still rumbling down the road. She was drinking a Coke and Rachel had a small cup of ice with some Coke over it as well.

"We're getting ready for Becca's trial, June. My dad asked me to call you and talk to you about the day Becca gave her sister the heroin."

"I don't know how much I know. I basically called 9-1-1 and got the hell out of the way when the troops arrived."

"How well did you know Becca at the time?"

"Oh, just like any other member of the family. Becca and I were great friends."

"She knew you were helping her sister, and she liked you for that?"

"Of course. She would've done anything for her sister. Well, she did, I guess. Look how far that got her."

"Did Becca ever say to you how horrible it was to see her sister in so much pain?"

"Only every day. She'd keep a stiff upper lip when she came in the room. But after she left, she turned into a big baby, crying and swearing in her own room. She was tearing her hair out she was hurting so bad for her sister."

"Did you ever feel she was frustrated that her sister was too young to get help with ending her life by a doctor?"

"Becca's frustration? Like I said, only every day. It was driving her crazy with anger. She read me the law like ten times at least. She said the only thing keeping her sister alive was the fact she was four years too young to die. She just couldn't accept that. Wouldn't accept that, I'd say."

"And that's why she did what she did? Because it wasn't fair?"

"I'd say that's true. Becca doesn't have a mean bone in her body. But she knew the law was ridiculous where older kids like Rachel were concerned. She said once that she'd help her sister die if she were a doctor. Said it would only take one minute to make up her mind. She did what she thought others should be doing that day. She was doing what she thought the doctor should be doing."

"Was she mad at her dad, the doctor?"

"I didn't see that. I saw her madder at the system, the laws, the people that made the laws. That's what I felt from her."

"Are you going to testify in the case? Has anyone contacted you?"

"Yes, they have my cell. They're flying me to San Diego to testify."

"Did you see Becca that night at the hospital?"

"I did."

"Describe her."

"Becca was horrified at what she'd done. She was crying and told me how sorry she was. She begged me to forgive her. I told her it wasn't up to me. But I understood. I held her and patted her back. That's a good kid, Ms. Murfee."

"Turquoise."

"Turquoise, it is."

"All right. Anything I've left out?"

"No, you got it all."

"Thank you, then."

"All right. Goodbye."

33

W hen the RV rolled into Seaside, Oregon, it was five in the
afternoon and Jim Sundstrom was tired. As was everyone
else aboard Thaddeus's bus. So, Jim told Sandy to find a place for
the night. Ten minutes later, Sandy had them pulling into the
KLM campground, about ten minutes from both Seaside and
Astoria.

Dr. Sundstrom went inside the main office. Asking several questions of the smiling desk clerk, he learned the campground had
camping cabins for rent long-term. The clerk took him to see the
unit. It had a living room area with a wood-burning fireplace, two
bedrooms, a bathroom with a very clean shower and toilet and
basin, as well as a kitchen, fully stocked with cooking utensils,
silverware, pots, pans, dishes. He decided that it was the perfect
spot to set up and take care of Rachel.

After visiting the cabin, he registered for the cabin under the
name of Rachel Sundstrom so there would be a written record of
the date she officially began her residency in Oregon. He registered the RV under the name of Thaddeus Murfee as the registra-

tion and license traced back to him. Then he returned to the RV and, with Sandy and Johann's help, they began moving suitcases and medical supplies into the cabin.

Two hours later, they had Rachel set up in her own cabin. The manager of the KLM offered to help rent a hospital bed for the unit and gave the particulars of the rental company in Portland. The next day, the hospital bed arrived with an IV pole and other supplies, and the patient was made as comfortable as possible. It was decided that Rachel and Jim Sundstrom would take the one sleeping room and that Becca and June would take the other. Sandy and Johann would remain with the bus and, when the others arrived, they too would take up residence in the bus. Sandy spent the next day with the bus at a local wash, carefully vacuuming the unit, airing it out, and scrubbing down the interior. He changed all the sheets on the beds and gutted the fridge. When it was sparkling clean, he returned the RV to its camping slot, parked it, and then leveled it with the automatic levelers. He then hooked up the utility connections and all was ready for Thaddeus and Louisa and, hopefully, Becca, if Thaddeus was able to free her.

ON THEIR FIRST NIGHT, JOHANN KNOCKED ON THE DOOR OF THE cabin. He wanted to know whether the cabin needed firewood or kitchen or bathroom supplies. Firewood would be good, said Dr. Sundstrom, as he wanted to bring Rachel into the living area that evening and let her enjoy a wood fire. Johann returned with a dozen logs which he carefully stacked in the wood box off to the side of the stone fireplace. As he was working, he heard Rachel cry out in pain and he looked over at the doctor.

"In my other life, I'm a nurse," he told Dr. Sundstrom. "If you ever need any help with your patient, please let me know. Thaddeus thought I might help. I saw her a couple of times on the bus, we played chess, but she was out of it and doesn't really know me."

"Thank you. That might just be an excellent idea. What kind of experience have you had?"

"After I graduated with my BSN, I worked in a couple different emergency rooms for almost a year. Just lately, until all this happened with the FBI, I worked on the psychiatric floor at Rady Children's Hospital, so I have plenty of experience with emotional support, too. I've done most nursing duties such as medications, patient comfort, PT, and everything else. I can work most pumps and know enough to ask when I need to."

"Yes, Thaddeus mentioned you were coming along to help. Up until now, we haven't had to do too much, and June has been doing most of it. But once she leaves to testify, I'll definitely need your help."

"I'm happy to do it."

"Maybe ease into it a bit with Rachel. Not only does she struggle with her pain, but also depression, a lot of emotional distress. You think you'd be okay with that?"

"Like I said, I'm good. I'm happy to be here to help. When Mr. Murfee suggested it, I was all in. Plus, I'm a heavy-duty surfer, and I wanted to try out some spots up here on the coast."

"Got it. Good for you, while you're still young enough to enjoy. There's a lesson there for all of us. What do you say we start you off doing midnights to six? Is that something you can do?"

"Definitely."

"All right. Starting tonight? I know June would love you for spelling her six hours a night."

"Sounds great. I'll be here tonight."

"Excellent. Thanks so much, Johann."

At 11:45 that night, a knock came on the door. June answered. Jim had moved back out to the bus to sleep in the bus's rear bedroom as Rachel was awake in the cabin bedroom and unable to sleep.

June showed Johann into Rachel's bedroom and officially introduced him to Rachel. Rachel had seen him in the RV, they'd played chess, but they'd barely exchanged words that time. And when Johann had helped to lift, Rachel had been asleep or groggy. She was again all but wiped out with pain, but June did notice she moved to pull her hair away from her face as she met the young man's gaze. He smiled at her and patted her on the shoulder. "Okay if I stay with you tonight? I understand you're having a pretty tough time."

"Fine with me. Just don't—don't look too close."

"I promise I won't. But you should know I'm a nurse by trade and used to all of it. Anyway, I'm Johann and I'm from La Jolla, like you. Small world."

"I was in Surfrider in LJ."

"Me, too! I love to surf, hate plastic. When's the last time you got to go?"

"Couple of years ago, I guess."

"If you like, I can take you down to the beach one of these nights when you can't sleep."

"I'd like that."

"Great. Maybe tomorrow night? Anyway, would it be all right with you if I worked your midnight to six shift? Before you answer, I talk a lot so be warned. What do you say?"

"I think it would help June. I'd like that."

"Then count me onboard. Now, what can I get for you right now to make you feel an inch better?"

"Bedpan."

"One bedpan coming up."

34

Judge Angel Masinelli was a stout, brusque jurist who graduated from Yale law in 2002. He then moved his family to Southern California and went to work at the San Diego District Attorney's Office, Juvenile Division. After four years of outstanding work, he found himself on the bench of the juvenile court at Kearny Mesa following the death of one judge and the resignation of his wife, the second judge, in 2006. He loved his job, loved the kids he got to work with, and was held in high regard by the probation officers and assistant district attorneys. In the space of two years, he had become the chief of the juvenile courts and had enacted sweeping changes in victims' rights and sentencing.

He came to court on Becca's case with his mind focused only on her witnesses and a mindset of seeing justice done. He had no preconceptions, and as he was the sole vote on whether she was guilty or not guilty, she was lucky to have someone of his mindset sitting in judgment of her. He came into the courtroom and had the clerk call the matter of Rebecca Sundstrom. Becca left her mother sitting in the visitors' rows and came forward through the gate. She joined Thaddeus at counsel table.

"I've heard nothing but good things about Judge Masinelli," Thaddeus told his young client after she was seated. "I think we'll find this to be a fair fight."

The assistant DA was Wendy Frontell, a young woman who had given up the nunnery in the midst of the church's problems to go into the field as a DA and work to see justice for the young people of her community. She was tall and possessed an exceptionally low voice; one defendant said she reminded her of God speaking. But her reputation, although tough, had her pegged as fair; it was all anyone could ask.

Judge Masinelli looked up from the file and said, "Counsel, any opening statements?"

"State waives," said ADA Frontell, meaning the state would forego giving any opening statement. Thaddeus did the same.

The state then called Officer Robin McCluskey, the first on the scene at the hospital after the overdose. He testified that he received a call from hospital admissions advising of a heroin overdose. He arrived on the scene and learned the condition of the patient. Then he learned her sister was also in treatment, and it was thought she was the one who administered the heroin to the older sister, so he tracked her down. He found her sitting upright in an examination compartment at the ER. She appeared bewildered and just a little unstable to a non-medical observer, himself, the officer. He read her her Miranda rights, but she only stared at him, so he began asking questions of the in-home nurse, June Cavanaugh, who was in the examination room with the minor.

When he began asking questions, the nurse was forthcoming, relating exactly what had happened at home that afternoon. The officer tried to testify to what the nurse had been told by Becca, but Thaddeus objected as the girl's statements were inadmissible hearsay. The judge agreed, and the nurse's comments to the officer that there had been the purchase of heroin, the preparation of the heroin into liquid form, the injection of the heroin into the older sister's IV, were all barred from coming into evidence. The nurse further related to him that EMT's were called, on-the-scene measures were administered, and both sisters were transported. The older was admitted for heroin OD treatment, the younger for having passed out at the scene after calling for help. The witness finished up with his further observations and statements then was turned over to Thaddeus for cross-examination.

Thaddeus considered what he had seen coming. Becca's statements to the police were inadmissible hearsay. At the scene itself, when June came running in to help, it was an emergent situation and Becca hadn't told June what happened at that point. June knew only that there was an overdose, and whether that was self-administered or administered by Becca, the nurse didn't know, and so there wasn't any testimony how it came to pass the sister OD'd.

Thaddeus spent very little time on cross-examination. The officer was invulnerable, as he had made no estimates and drawn no conclusions and recited only the facts as he discovered them— without Becca's admissions to him.

Next, the state called Detective Jayne Marsh, who had taken a written statement from Becca that night at the juvenile facility. This was before Becca had had the benefit of talking to a lawyer. The state tried to admit the written statement into evidence, but Thaddeus objected. In California, he argued, a child may waive Miranda rights, but only if the waiver is voluntary and, in the case of a child age fifteen or under, the child first consulted with a lawyer. That was definitely not the case here because Becca hadn't first talked to a lawyer before giving her confession, so Judge Masinelli had no course but to rule the written statement inadmissible.

The two officers, Officer McCluskey and Detective Marsh, were the only two witnesses the state could offer who could testify what happened. So far, neither had been able to offer facts into evidence about Becca's actions. Of course, the court was about to learn about heroin in the older sister's urine and the presence of heroin traces in the baggies, so the judge could draw conclusions but, so far, Thaddeus felt quite good about how the case was progressing. He had kept any fact witnesses from connecting his client to the administration of the heroin, and that was huge.

The state next called to the witness stand the supervising crime scene tech, a young man named Edward Tellemaier. He testified about the crime scene, the items found there and seized, such as the IV pole, the IV bags, and line and needle. All of those items, plus the pot lid she cooked in, the fireplace lighter, and the syringe were admitted into evidence without objection. Thaddeus knew the items were damning insofar as what had happened but, still, the state had no testimony about where the baggies came from, who cooked the heroin in the pot lid, who injected it into the IV, and the like. They had all the emblements of a case but without the connector, the line running from Becca to all of those items.

35

June Cavanaugh arrived at the San Diego Airport that morning and was brought to testify by the state. Thaddeus had offered to pick her up from the airport, but the state, because they had paid her airfare to get her to come testify, insisted on picking her up themselves. So, Thaddeus hadn't spoken with her since their time in the RV.

The state next called June. After identifying herself and her job and how long she had worked with Rachel, ADA Frontell asked what Becca had told June about how the overdose happened. June looked at Becca and then looked at Thaddeus. Her lips pursed. She said slowly and at a conversational level, "Becca never told me what happened. There was no time for that."

"Becca being Rebecca?" asked the ADA.

"Yes," confirmed June.

"Did she tell you what she had done?"

"What she had done? No."

"Any other statements that would indicate she had given her sister the overdose?"

"Like I said, Becca and I felt like family. She could've told me any number of things, but I don't remember now. It was all very chaotic that night."

Upon hearing this testimony, Thaddeus relaxed his grip on his ink pen. June could have told the court what Becca had told her since Miranda doesn't apply to civilians. The DA was trying to get from June what she couldn't get from the police officers, a confession or admission against interest. But June had avoided going there, instead claiming she'd heard nothing else in the chaos.

So, the district attorney proceeded in a different direction. "In terms of how this overdose happened, would you be able to tell us whether Rachel had the strength to obtain her father's fireplace lighter, retrieve a pot lid, cook heroin inside the pot, draw the contents up into a syringe, and then inject the mixture into her IV line?"

"I don't know she could do all that. She was very weak during that time. In fact, she had trouble sitting up. As far as getting into the kitchen for a pot lid and being steady enough to boil the heroin, that's highly unlikely."

"What about leaving the house to go into the community and purchase the actual heroin? Could she have accomplished that on her own?"

"Definitely not."

"She had to have help in overdosing herself then?"

"Objection," said Thaddeus, "calls for a conclusion."

"Sustained."

"June, when you heard Rebecca call your name and you came running into Rachel's room, who was in that room?"

"Rachel and Becca."

"Had anyone else been in the house that afternoon other than the three of you?"

"No."

"And it wasn't you who helped Rachel overdose on heroin?"

"Obviously not."

"Then who might have done it?"

"Objection, conclusion," said Thaddeus.

"Sustained," said Judge Masinelli. "The point is taken, counsel. Please move along on that."

"Nothing further, Your Honor."

"June," said Thaddeus, "would it have been possible for Rachel to take the syringe in hand and inject it into her IV line?"

"Maybe."

"Could she have accomplished that by herself?"

"Maybe. Possibly, she could've. It would depend on how long since she'd had her pain medication, too."

"Well, assuming she was as alert during that moment of self-administration of the heroin as she ever was. Could she have done it then?"

"Probably. I can't say for certain, though."

"Let me ask this. Did Rachel want to die?"

"She did. Very much."

"Was she able to get the help she needed from her doctor to die?"

"She wasn't able to get the help, no."

"Why not, if you know?"

"She wasn't twenty-one. You can't get help ending your life in California until you're twenty-one."

"So, knowing as we do that she wanted to die, would it have surprised you that she shot the IV full of the heroin herself?"

"It wouldn't surprise me, no. I expected she wanted to do that."

"Because she wanted to die."

"That's right. She wanted to die."

"Oh, yes, why did she want to die?"

"Pain. It was horrible."

"Your witness," said Thaddeus when he was done.

ADA Frontell wasted no time asking, "June, regarding the other parts of dosing with the heroin, retrieving the pot lid and the fireplace lighter, the heating of the heroin in the lid—Rachel had to have help with these things?"

"Probably."

"And going into the community and scoring the heroin in the first place, not something she was capable of doing?"

"Definitely not."

"So, someone had to bring her the illegal drug?"

"Correct."

The state asked no further questions, and Thaddeus had nothing further, so June was released. She later told Thaddeus she was flying out that night so she could be with Rachel again.

Thaddeus thanked her for all her help.

She understood exactly what he meant.

Then she was gone.

Turquoise and Marcel joined Thaddeus, Becca, and Louisa at lunch, and they went to a Red Robin at Becca's request. It was Becca's trial day so she was in her mother's care just then and could leave for lunch. The judge had allowed it when Thaddeus asked so they could work on their defense case in private. They ordered burgers of various configurations, root beers all around, and put their heads together.

"I think it's looking quite good, Thaddeus," said Louisa. A mother's optimism shall not go unrewarded, thought Thaddeus, so he told her he agreed, and it was going better than he'd hoped.

Turquoise said, "What about the hospital witnesses? Does the ER doctor have any statements by Becca that she did it or she was sorry?"

"Unknown," said Thaddeus. "We couldn't get to him, as little time as we were given to prepare. We'll just have to wait and see."

"Would it be good for me to try to track him down over the noon hour and question him? Maybe try to sandpaper him?"

Thaddeus looked at his daughter with the ever-present Marcel with her again. "It wouldn't hurt. He may not have left the hospital yet."

"Marcel and I will go now," said Turquoise. Without waiting for their food, they jumped up and left the restaurant. Then the burgers came, and the rest of them dug in.

"Finally," Becca said, "some decent food. That place is okay, but it's nothing like home. The good part is I've lost ten pounds already. Most of it from crying myself to sleep at night, I think."

Louisa hugged Becca and rubbed her back.

"You're taking this pretty bad?" asked Thaddeus.

"Oh my God, I can't believe I almost killed my sister. I honestly start crying every time I think about it. I just feel horrible for what I did."

"Well," said Thaddeus, "your sister does need help. She's suffering. Humans can't stand to see suffering. What you did, probably any loving brother or sister would have thought of doing. The only difference was you actually followed through. Don't beat yourself up. That's my advice, Becca."

She tossed the hair out of her eyes. "Am I going to testify?"

"No, you won't be testifying. They can't prove the main case unless you testify or unless the ER doctor remembers you confessing to him. If he remembers, then I might change my mind. But as of right now, no, you won't be testifying."

THE HOSPITAL SAID THE ER DOCTOR, JACKSON BLACK, HAD ALREADY left for court, so Turquoise and Marcel redoubled their path back to the courthouse. She was hoping they might catch him waiting outside the courtroom to testify. She jogged down the hallway to the courtroom, Marcel with her every step.

Sure enough, sitting on a bench outside the courtroom, speaking into his dictating recorder, was a young, pale man with a black beard and tortoise-shell glasses. He was wearing a natty brown sports coat that looked like it might have been with him forever. But when he looked up at Turquoise, she would later say he had the kind blue eyes of a mother dog looking at the world as if her pups were out there somewhere.

"I'm Becca's investigator," said Turquoise, sticking out her hand to shake, "Turquoise Murfee. And this is my partner, Marcel Rainford."

"Jackson Black," he said, "I'm the ER doc who treated Becca Sundstrom. She's Doctor Sundstrom's daughter, so I remember her well."

"Well, listen, doc. The state is having a hard time proving Becca gave her sister the heroin. Unless you come in and say she confessed to you, there's not much they can do to prove she did it. So, what's your memory? Was there a confession?"

"Not per se. She said she was so sorry, but she didn't say for what. I took it to mean she'd helped her sister. But I never asked her what she'd done. That wasn't necessary for me to know in order to treat her."

"So, you'll leave it at she was sorry, generally, but you don't know for what?" Marcel asked.

"That's right. Does that help or hurt?"

Turquoise answered, "I think it helps. Okay, please wait here. We'll be starting back up in just a few minutes. The state will put you on and try for a confession, so please don't let them mislead you."

He laughed. "No chance. I didn't just fall off the turnip wagon."

"Thank you."

"Yes, thank you," repeated Marcel and shook the doctor's hand.

Fifteen minutes later, court was back in session, and Dr. Black was the state's next witness. As he'd told Turquoise, he testified Becca had said she was sorry, but he never asked her for what. He told the judge that wasn't necessary information to her treatment, so he just didn't pursue it.

Then came Thaddeus's opportunity to cross-examine.

"Doctor, when she said she was sorry, did she say anything about giving her sister the heroin in her IV line?"

"No."

"Did she say she'd heated the heroin to make it liquid?"

"No."

"Did she say she'd purchased the heroin and brought it to her sister?"

"No."

"So, she could have been saying she was sorry she didn't watch her sister more closely, correct?"

"Objection, calls for speculation."

"Sustained. The court can imagine other scenarios, too, Mr. Murfee. No need to pursue those."

"Then that's all I have. Thank you, Doctor."

"You may step down," said Judge Masinelli.

The state then put on the hospital laboratory technician who did the fluids workup on Rachel and found the heroin in her system. ADA Frontell also called the nurses and doctors who worked on her that first night and had them talk about what her situation and condition was. But to a man—and to a woman—no one was able to say how the overdose had happened. Rachel had never told any of them that. Not even in the days that followed while Rachel was yet in the hospital. It just didn't come up.

Then the state rested its case.

36

Thaddeus opened his case by calling psychiatrist Indira Kapur to the stand. She came into the court, walking confidently up the aisle and through the swinging gate, to be sworn in as a witness. Today, she was wearing black leggings and a traditional gold and black churidar. She looked graceful and professional.

It was Thaddeus's first time to meet the doctor, so he took his time with introductions, asking questions about her treatment of Rachel Sundstrom and how long she had been her patient. Then he asked, "Doctor what is her mental state when you see her?"

"Which time?"

"General overlay at all times."

The doctor swung her long braid over her right shoulder as she thought. Then, "Well, Rachel is depressed, of course. She's dying a slow, terrible death and has every reason to be depressed. I don't try to talk her out of that. She's entitled to her depression."

"What do you try to do for her?"

"Confirm that her feelings are real and natural. Give her medications to help with the depression."

"Narrowing down, let me ask, is Rachel someone who wants to die?"

"Definitely. She's under twenty-one and can't get end-of-life medical support so she's suffering, just horribly. It's more than I would be able to bear. Probably none of us in this room could go through what Rachel is going through. It's a crime."

"What's a crime?"

"That she can't get end-of-life drugs and medical assistance. The California legislature has got its collective head up its collective ass on this one."

That was unexpected from the woman, but a reminder to Thaddeus to never assume by culture or appearance. "What could be clearer?" Thaddeus commented. Then, "Is Rachel the kind of patient who would ingest end-of-life drugs if given a chance?"

"Objection, speculation," said the ADA.

"Overruled. I want to hear this. I'll give it the weight it deserves and no more."

"She is the kind of patient who would take end-of-life drugs if she had the chance. In a second, she would take them."

"In our case, Rachel's IV line overdosed her with heroin. Would it surprise you to find she had dosed herself?"

"No, it wouldn't surprise me."

"Objection—"

"Too late. Asked and answered. You may cross-examine on the basis for the conjecture."

Thaddeus continued, "In other words, you've told us she would voluntarily ingest the drugs, so shooting up her IV line would just be another way of doing the same thing?"

"Correct."

"Those are all my questions for now."

The ADA wasted no time. "Doctor, in your medical opinion, from having spent as much professional time with the patient as you have, would she have been able to physically give herself a shot?"

"Unknown. I'm not a human factors expert."

"But you as a physician have seen and observed her?"

"Yes."

"Was she able to give herself a shot?"

"Maybe, maybe not. Depends on how recently she's received her morphine."

"Let's say it's at the other end of when she gets her morphine. Let's say it's right before she gets her next shot. Would she be able to inject a syringe into her IV line and push the plunger?"

"Maybe. I really can't say with any certainty."

"But it wouldn't surprise you if she did?"

"No, it wouldn't surprise me."

"Likewise, it wouldn't surprise you if she was unable physically to inject her IV line?"

"No, that wouldn't' surprise me either."

"Doctor, is a terminal patient's wish to die, when suffering terribly, static? Does it ever flip over so all they want is to live?"

"Yes."

"Might Rachel have been wanting to live the day someone injected her IV line with heroin?"

Thaddeus stood. "Objection, speculation, assumes facts."

"Sustained."

ADA Frontell forged ahead. "Might she have wanted to live that day?"

"Maybe. Probably during any day there's a whole succession of feelings. These patients are terribly conflicted between wishing to die and get out of the pain and wishing to live at all costs. It's normal to be that way."

"That's all, Your Honor," said the assistant district attorney.

"Nothing further," said Thaddeus. "At this time, the defense rests."

"Very well, you may be heard in closing arguments, counsel."

ADA Frontell went forward to the lectern. She began with a recitation of what was known: the heroin, the needle, the OD. She then went into what could be concluded: that the patient was very ill and might not have given herself the shot. That there was no one else in the house that afternoon. That the sister, the defendant, Rebecca Sundstrom, was crying at the emergency room, saying she was sorry. That it was reasonable to assume that Rebecca had, at the minimum, obtained the heroin on the outside and brought it into the house. That Rebecca had obtained the pot lid and lighter and liquefied the heroin. That, in doing so, she probably filled the syringe at the same time. That, having the syringe in her hand, it wasn't unreasonable to conclude she also injected the IV line. She spoke about the Rachel's terrible pain and desire to die. She spoke about how difficult it was for us to witness suffering and not want to help. All in all, she did what she could with a case where she had no eyewitness and no confession or admissions against interest. She asked for the court to find the minor had committed the crime of attempted murder. She argued the jury instruction—without a jury—it was still a good guideline. Then she sat down.

Thaddeus stood and thanked the judge and counsel for their courtesies. Then he spoke about the need for legislation that would have made this DIY end-of-life situation unnecessary. He addressed how Rachel was old enough to enlist in the military and put herself in harm's way but couldn't decide that it was time to end her life, even when suffering unremitting and impossible pain. Then he reminded the judge that the burden of proof in minor's cases was the same as for adults—beyond a reasonable doubt. And that the state hadn't met that burden. "Your Honor isn't required, indeed should not, guess at what happened based on physical evidence found at the scene. We really don't know who did what. Most of all, we don't know who injected the IV line, the act of mercy killing. We don't know that, and you, Your Honor, are not allowed to guess at that. If you're uncomfortable right now judging this case, it's because the state hasn't proven the charge to you beyond a reasonable doubt. The state has done what it was required to do in bringing the charges, but it has fallen short. There is no crime proven. The only outcome can be a finding of not guilty, that the minor did not commit a crime."

"Mr. Murfee," the judge began, "while I might agree with you about the older minor's need for end-of-life rights, the court cannot legislate and magically make that happen. Nor would I even if I could because doctors and professionals are needed in making those judgments, not lawyers and judges and police.

"I'm finding your client not guilty. This isn't because I don't believe she didn't do something. I do believe she did something, but—and this is a big one—the state hasn't been able to prove the charges beyond a reasonable doubt. The police forgot you cannot obtain a minor's confession without his or her lawyer present, so those two confessions cannot be in evidence. Whether I would have even given those confessions or statements any weight is another question. We'll never know. But for now, the minor, Rebecca Sundstrom, committed no crime. Young lady, you are free to leave here and go home with your mother. We're in recess."

37

Louisa and Becca joined Thaddeus on his jet for the flight to Portland. They brought enough luggage for a month-long stay, they said, and Thaddeus only nodded. He really had no idea how long the Oregon death project was going to take, but he, too, was ready for the long run. As the plane lifted off the runway at San Diego, he closed his eyes and said a silent prayer for Rachel. She had now been in Oregon two weeks, and the time had arrived to begin establishing residency in earnest.

Once in Portland, Thaddeus rented a red Ford Explorer to get Louisa and Becca to the coast. His Mercedes was still there, but with the number of people they had for the duration, he thought they might need more wheels, for people to come and go, for grocery shopping, for medical supplies, to make small day trips from the campground, any number of things.

They arrived at the campground late afternoon. Thaddeus hadn't seen it before since Jim had booked them in, but he was quite happy with the selection. They found Thaddeus's RV in site 42 as Jim had told him. Rachel was in Cabin 5 down the ways a bit.

Thaddeus and Louisa had both agreed they would surprise everyone in Oregon. They hadn't told them yet the results of the adjudication and that Becca was free. It would be a great surprise. They went to the bus first, and after going inside, there was a loud cry of hurrah from Sandy and Jim and hugs all around. Jim and Louisa cried and embraced. The commotion rousted Johann, who had been sleeping since he was doing night shifts. He came out of the cabin with rumpled hair and wearing shorts and a T-shirt.

June was in the cabin with Rachel. Once Jim led Louisa and Becca over to Number 5, Becca stopped at the door. She asked if it was okay with everyone if she went in on her own first. She needed to see her sister. She needed to tell her how sorry she was. Becca bit her lip, fighting the tears.

Thaddeus and Becca's parents agreed and sat down on the bench outside the cabin facing the sea. They told her to take her time.

For some reason, Becca was nervous. She didn't really understand why, but she didn't want to dwell on it. She just wanted to see her sister. Becca quietly opened the door and slipped inside. June was on the couch in front of the wood-burning stove, reading a magazine.

June gasped when she saw Becca and leapt from the couch, but Becca placed a finger to her lips to tell June to be quiet. June nodded in understanding and whispered, "She's asleep right now."

"That's okay," Becca whispered back. I'll go sit with her and wait until she wakes up. Mom and Dad are just outside if you want to see them."

June said she would and would get the details from them. "Go on," she shooed Becca. "She's going to be so happy to see you." June smiled and walked outside.

Becca drew a deep breath and went into Rachel's room. She was indeed sleeping, so Becca sat at the chair someone had set up on Rachel's left side of the bed. She took her sister's hand and held it. She sat there and watched Rachel sleep as she had done so many times before. But this time Becca really looked at the features of her sister's face to memorize every detail.

Only a few minutes later did Rachel's eyes flutter open. At first, she didn't seem to recognize Becca, her grogginess most likely confusing her. But when Rachel finally did, she squealed and held her arms out to Becca for a hug. She fell into her sister's arms, and they both cried. For minutes, they laid there, no words, just tears of happiness.

Becca was so glad, so very glad, that Mr. Murfee was able to get her released. She was free, and she would spend every minute with her sister until Rachel's end of life.

38

As they gathered that afternoon at the campground after they'd moved Louisa and Becca into the cabins, Thaddeus had a talk with Jim Sundstrom.

"Jim," Thaddeus began, "Oregon recognizes a number of traditional items in establishing residency. One is a driver's license. I know this is coming out of the blue, but can you, as a doctor, think of any steps we might take to present her at the driver's license testing center to obtain an Oregon license?"

Jim Sundstrom nodded, his forehead creased in thought. "I've considered that. The thing is, she can't drive while under the influence of intoxicants or drugs which might affect her driving performance. I'm thinking that rules out morphine, which is her mainstay. So, a weaning off the pain med, followed by a quick run for a driving test, seems the only way. The question is, can she stand that? As her father, I say hell no. I couldn't stand to see her in that much pain. But as her father who wants to help, I can also see her need to get the driving part done. It's a mystery to me, Thaddeus."

"Well, another avenue is the voting age. She's old enough to register to vote, which is also proof of residency. It seems to me that if we gather a month of rental receipts and other items addressed to Rachel locally, plus if we have her registered to vote, we can make an argument she's a resident."

"I should tell you I've also taken her to see an oncologist who's a graduate of the same med school I attended in California. She's started her on a round of radiology. She's given us a sliver of hope. Rachel's also become the patient of Agnes Rosa, an MD in Seaside who is her general practitioner. So, we've done those two things you asked us to do."

"What about a psychiatrist?"

"Dr. Emil Sanchez in Astoria. I really like the guy and Rachel received excellent support and ideas. He also talked to her at length about her ultimate goal and made it clear he supports her in her quest, all else being equal."

"Meaning?"

"Well, if her attending physician and general practitioner also support her application, he will, too."

"What's the oncologist's name?"

"Mindy Raintree. She's a board-certified specialist in oncology with advanced studies in Portland."

"She's the one under the law who will decide residency and who will decide if the drugs are to be prescribed, and when. Have you spoken to her about the need for her advocacy?"

"I asked about her willingness to sign off on the drugs. She said she runs a very tight ship and she only signs when the *I*'s are dotted, and the *T*'s are crossed."

"What about residency? Did you ask her?"

"She wants thirty days beyond voter registration."

"What date was she registered?"

"June twentieth. Which means she'll sign off about July twentieth. After that, there's a fifteen-day waiting period, right?"

"That's right. You've been doing your reading, Jim. So, it looks like Rachel can transition on August fifth. Does she know?"

"She's got August fifth circled on the Wayfarer Shell Station calendar Johann brought her. He's helping her get through this, actually. Together, they cross each day off with black ink at midnight when he comes on duty. It's their ritual."

"That's very brave. I wouldn't have the courage."

Jim gave Thaddeus a hard look. "Yes, you would if you didn't have any other choice, Thaddeus. You'd find the courage, just like Rachel's had to do."

"You're right. How can I help with things?"

"Honestly? I can't very well ask you to spend your summer here. You've got a law practice to look after, and we're talking a month of waiting. Do you need to get back and use that time?"

"It would be good if I did. I've got the little ones at home, plus Christine's got her own practice to worry about. How about if I left Celena here to help Becca through this time?"

"That would be a gift to Becca. Her best friend with her."

"All right, let's do that. I'll fly back down to San Diego, catch up with things, then come back up here on the first of August, just to make sure there are no last-minute legalities I need to help you with. Plus, I'm your support, old friend."

Jim's eyes narrowed. "Believe me, Thaddeus, you have no idea how much that means to me. I'd welcome your support on August first. More than welcome it. I need it."

39

Sandy returned Thaddeus to the Portland airport the next morning and he flew back to San Diego. Thaddeus met with Turquoise later that afternoon. He was drinking a cup of coffee when she came into his office, a big smile on her face. She sat in one of his visitor chairs.

"So, no Marcel with you today?"

"Nope, not today." There was also a twinkle in her eye. Something was definitely up.

Thaddeus hedged, "So, did he return to Chicago?"

"He did." But she was still smiling.

"Everything okay?"

She nodded. "Better than okay."

Turquoise usually didn't play games, so Thaddeus decided to come right out and ask, "What's going on between you two?"

"Like I said, we're in love." The smile again. She placed her left hand on his desk. On her left finger was a small band of diamonds. An engagement ring? Thaddeus asked as much, but she said, "No, a promise ring, but that's just as important. Marcel went back to Chicago to talk to his boss, Michael Gresham, and to pack up his apartment and get everything organized to ship here. Isn't that great news?"

"The ring is beautiful, honey." Thaddeus walked around the desk and hugged his daughter who was still sitting. "Are you sure about Marcel?" he couldn't help but ask.

"Absolutely and completely."

"Well then I'm absolutely and completely happy for you guys."

"Thanks, Dad. So, what's up for today?"

Thaddeus sat back in his chair. "I'm back on Johann Van Giersbergen. Something's troubling me there."

"Like what?"

"I was talking to him on the bus. Did you know he's got a minor in Arabic? Did you know he's sympathetic to radical Islamic causes? Or at least some of them?"

"That's what got his dad killed, the radicals."

"I know that. So, it doesn't add up. Plus, there was the matter of the Semtex in his suitcase. It seems to me that ended very neatly. All tied up and confessed to by a man nobody knew before and just at this time. A man who was a poor Mexican man and definitely not a radical himself. Where did he come from? Why was he confessing to complicity? I think Johann needs more looking at. I'm going to ask you to get me a deep background on him. College, student groups, organizations, protests, work, travels—especially travels to the Middle East and

Europe. That sort of thing. Can you do that in between being engaged?"

"Funny man. When do you want it by?"

"How about Friday?"

"As long as I can make some contacts and follow-ups, no problem."

"Good. We'll talk then."

Turquoise appeared in Thaddeus's office doorway a few days later. "Knock-knock. I have the Van Giersbergen workup. Would you like me to go through it with you?"

"Sure do," Thaddeus answered. "Come right in. Need a water?"

She held up a hand. "I'm good. Let me say, overall, I found his background to be perplexing."

"Why's that?"

"For one thing, we're missing chunks of time."

"Okay. Hit me with it."

"He graduated in nursing with a minor in Arabic. He belonged to the Islamic Student Union for eighteen months. Following graduation from college and after taking and passing the NCLEX, he was off to Germany. A week there, but then he goes missing. However, I did learn he had a visa for Afghanistan when last seen. He surfaced three months later on a flight from Berlin to San Diego. Where was he for those three months? Unknown. It seems that when a U.S. citizen goes to the Middle East, especially countries like Afghanistan, their travel itinerary becomes all but nonexistent. People aren't tracked there like they are here. I called Jack Rasso at the FBI to see what they knew. He gave me a little background on the QT and confirmed the trip to Afghanistan. Where he went from there, he wouldn't tell me. That trip to the Middle East was part of the reason the FBI went after him tooth and tong in the first place."

"My, my, our peripatetic Islamic student. What else?"

"After he came back to the U.S on that trip, he went to Mexico City with his father just a few weeks later. Now get this. He has told everyone he was going around looking for a Spanish language institute? Wrong, he was actually going around looking to make contacts with Arabic language students inside the Spanish language institutes. See, lots of those places don't teach just Spanish. They teach lots of other languages, too, including Arabic. Two of them told me he was looking to teach Arabic. Evidently, he planned on staying on in Mexico if he landed a position. Why would that be? I'm thinking because someone is or was establishing a foothold in Mexico. That's just my wild guess."

"Or maybe someone wanted him planted in Mexico. That's entirely possible, too. Know what? I think I am going to file a FOIA request on Johann and Ned. If the records are clear, so be it, I'll go with that. If not, I'll follow up with a FOIA lawsuit. I need to know more about this guy."

"How can you find out more than the FBI knows?"

"I just want to find out what the FBI knows, no more. They'll drop prosecutions against bad guys if they feel they can't make a case. Or for a jillion other reasons. I need more information. Then I need to act on what I find out. We might not want Johann around the Sundstroms at all. I don't want to wrongly accuse the young man, but I don't want to just blindly take him in, either."

"I agree."

"Put together a FOIA request based on what we know. Make it as fast as possible. I'll call Jack Rasso and see if he'll walk it through for me."

"Consider it done. I'll have that on file today."

"Excellent. Thanks, kiddo."

"You're welcome, Dad."

40

"I'm seeing a very different person developing before my eyes than the young surfer dude he's portraying," Thaddeus said to Turquoise as they discussed the latest on Johann Van Giersbergen. "He is a very sophisticated social media player."

"I'm starting to see why he was wanted by the FBI, even if he isn't guilty of the bombing," Turquoise said.

Thaddeus pursed his lips. "So, we have a heavy-duty Facebook advertiser with a Middle Eastern bent. Neither proves anything in and of themselves. But they do raise one hell of a lot of questions. I think I don't want him around the Sundstroms just yet. I think I'm going to Oregon and have a heart to heart with Jim Sundstrom."

"That'll have to wait a couple of weeks, Dad. You have *State versus David Aguilar* coming to trial next Monday."

"You're right. Two weeks it is."

Thaddeus called Jim Sundstrom that night.

"Jim, Thaddeus. I've got something we need to discuss."

"Fine. Hey, before you get started, most important news of all. Rachel's oncologist has been trying her on a course of radiation. Guess what? It's working. She's gone into remission!"

"What incredibly great news! I'll tell Christine. Is Louisa there and doing all right now? Is Becca?"

"They're as excited as I am. We can't stop talking about it."

"Answered prayers, Jim. Answered prayers."

"I know. We're doing plenty of that, too. It might be only short-term, which sometimes happens and then you move on to maybe chemo. I don't know. It's all so complicated nowadays."

"Well, if we can help, just let us know."

"And listen, this Johann is really something. Rachel just loves the guy. They were together all night, but now he's spending time with her during the days, too. They're really hitting it off."

"Well, he's what I want to talk about. Certain questions have come up about some of his activities in and around politics."

"Really? I've never heard one word of politics out of him. All he talks about is surfing and something called Sea Shepherd. He wants to help Sea Shepherd fight for the whales. Quite a concerned young citizen, Thaddeus. That kind of politics? Animal rights?"

"Not that, no. More along the lines of Middle East ideology."

"Man, you could have fooled me. I've heard nothing like that. Well, as long as he isn't blowing up airplanes, I guess I'm all right with that. But thanks for calling, Thaddeus. Rachel is asking me something. Was that all?"

"Well, for now, okay. I'll be up in a couple of weeks. Just keep your eyes open, Jim. That's all."

"Will do, Thaddeus, good night."

"Good night."

Thaddeus hung up the phone, still feeling unsettled. Something wasn't right about the picture with Johann but, despite his best efforts, he had no proof of anything. He had only unanswered questions and questions weren't enough to impugn someone's motives. Besides, the boy was young. Maybe the jihadist stuff was behind him now. Still...Thaddeus had questions that just wouldn't go away.

On the other hand, there was Rachel's news. It was exciting, and Thaddeus could feel a sense of relief flood his body the more he let it soak in.

Answered prayers, indeed.

41

Doctor and Mrs. Sundstrom were shocked one morning when Rachel asked if she could go on a date with Johann. Actually, she said, it wouldn't be "going" anywhere; it would consist of closing themselves in Rachel's room and watching a movie on Netflix. Jim Sundstrom was stunned. He'd had no idea his daughter was feeling that much better, not even with the new blessed remission she was experiencing.

Louisa Sundstrom was equally stunned, but she also remembered her daughter was seventeen and very sick and, well, she decided she'd set a ground rule: the bedroom door would have to remain open a crack. Rachel laughed and said that would be fine, and they weren't going to wind up in her bed on the first date. She thought it a good laugh; mama wasn't so sure. She'd seen very sick people do some very strange things before.

"What does it matter what she does?" Dr. Sundstrom asked his balking wife. "Maybe it would do her good to get some things out of her system. I say we close her door and leave her alone in the cabin for the date. Let nature take its course."

"Doctors! You would think like that! What if she got pregnant and died? Then the baby would die with her! Or what if she lived? Would the baby be sick, too? Don't try pawning off some answer on me—you don't have the answer and neither does so-called modern medical science. In fact, I'm amazed at how little medicine really does know about Rachel's disease. So, don't even think about going there. Now I might be willing to close it all but one inch, and we stay out. But that's it."

"So, you don't trust Johann?"

"I don't know Johann."

"But you definitely don't trust your own daughter to do the right thing?"

"Wait. This was the same girl who six weeks ago was trying to kill herself with heroin. No, color me odd, but I don't exactly trust her thought processes right now. Funny thing about that."

"Regardless, I say we let her squeeze every last bit of life out of life that she can right now. I say we shut the door, go out to the bus, and mind our own damn business. That's what I'm planning to do."

"You would. We'll see. I'll see for myself how it goes."

On Friday night at six o'clock, Johann arrived with a pizza and two bottles of root beer. The pizza was what Rachel liked—sausage, mushrooms, onions, cheese and black olives, heavy on the black olives. The root beer was old-fashioned with the kind of twist-off caps she'd specified. Johann produced, and she was delighted. Then he pulled out from behind his back a single red rose. He presented it to her as she sat in her bed wearing her Sea Shepherd T-shirt with the trident. Then he closed the door behind him. No one came to object.

"How are we doing tonight?" he asked as he distributed pizza on paper plates with squares of paper towels.

"I can't believe it, but I actually sat up and read this afternoon."

"What are you reading?"

"*The Silent Spring* by Rachael Carlson."

"The seminal work," he said. "That's where I started two years ago. Hey, have you found a movie for tonight?"

He stood, looking down at her, undecided whether he should sit on the bedside chair or on the foot of her bed. She resolved the look on his face by patting the mattress beside her. "C'mon over here and sit next to me. I like to snuggle on the first date."

She could've sworn he blushed. But he did what was asked and took a place beside her on the bed. Then he slipped his loafers off with his toes and lifted his feet up onto the bed. Now they were seated side-by-side, staring at the blank wide-screen TV and chomping pizza.

"What do you want to talk about?" he asked. Actually, during their weeks of long nights together when she'd slept in restless groups of two hours here and an hour or two there, they had exhausted all topics of conversation. By now, they were comfortable just sitting idly together, maybe reading or listening to iTunes. He'd found a new indie artist, Joel Hart, through his youngest sister Adriane. He told Rachel about him.

"I'd like to listen to Joel Hart," she said. "I guess Adriane really likes him?"

"So, she says. Let me dial in his album and let's see what you think."

The music, as it came floating into the room from his iPad, was largely environmental themes with a small mixture of romantic pieces. It was different, but she liked it and told him so.

"Tell me more about Rachel," he said. "Right now, I see a beautiful almost-eighteen-year-old with long blond hair she washed today, blue eyes, an aquiline nose that reminds me of a Gaugin miss from French Polynesia. Her manner is charming, and her brain is forever alert and active and inquisitive. She has, in the past, served her school as a cheerleader and student body secretary and she's planning on attending college and studying marine biology, according to the latest as of last night. News at Ten."

She laughed. "Now let me tell you. I see a charming twenty-two-year-old with a scraggly blondish beard who wishes it was full and lush, blue eyes and light brown hair he wears long on top and very short on the sides and back, a good physique like a serious surfer, spatulate fingers—like that, spatulate? —and feet like a duck. All the better for ocean swimming. He says he's a nurse but, so far, I can tell he's more like a doctor-in-waiting with his extreme knowledge of diseases and treatments and patient care. 'Palliative care,' he called it at first. Now he just calls it plain old patient care. Is there a message in that? I hope so."

She set aside her half-eaten slice of pizza and shrugged. Then her face brightened. "Oh, hey, they just had the Academy Awards. I want to watch the one about the woman who runs the Underground Railroad before the Civil War."

"That would be the movie called *Harriet*. We can watch that, for sure."

He clicked off the iPad sounds and turned on the wide-screen, went to Netflix and found the movie, made the purchase, and the titles and music started right up.

By eight-thirty, she was sleeping, leaned up against her date, softly snoring. He very lightly disengaged, climbed off the bed, pulled his socks and shoes on, and crept to the door. He pulled it open and peeked out. "Oh, hello, Mrs. Sundstrom. She's sleeping soundly."

Louisa Sundstrom smiled a broad smile. "I'm so glad you're doing all right in there. I wondered, when she said she was having a date."

"Well," he whispered, "not exactly a *date* date, but we're doing the best we can, all things considered."

"Can I go out and get her dad now? He's probably ready to come in and join his recliner."

"Be my guest. I'm going to clean up in here and go into my nursing duties early tonight. Tell June for me that I've got it now and she can take off the rest of the night, all right?"

"Will do, that's so nice of you. And Johann, thank you so much. This has meant the world to Rachel, I know."

"Hey, my luck to get a date with a great looking chick," he laughed. "No need to thank me. I thank her."

"Either way, I'm glad it happened."

"I'm going to close her door now and check her medicine drip. Just open it if you need anything or want to check on her."

"Will do. Thank you, honey."

He smiled. "You're so welcome."

He shut the door and checked the morphine drip. Then he sat beside Rachel's bed and fired up his iPad. He went immediately to his Facebook page and began posting stories about the President's primary challenger. The stories were favorable to the challenger, who was known to want to get the U.S. out of the Middle East and bring home all troops. The stories were by and large the stuff of Johann's imagination. It was always the same with his postings— find the friendliest candidate or corporation or group or organization in favor of the U.S. leaving the Middle East and support them. Come down hard against those who wanted to see the U.S. in an active role in the area. It was just what he believed, like he believed foreign fishermen from the Eastern Rim should be banned from killing off ocean species and dumping toxic wastes.

He read and re-read his latest post. Satisfied at last, he hit publish.

Then he picked up *The Silent Spring* on Rachel's Kindle and began reading.

He looked up after ten minutes, sensing a buckle in the rate of breathing of his patient. But it was nothing; she was just turning away. He smiled, thinking of taking her to the beach and then into the surf on his board.

Maybe the sea will claim one of its lovers, he thought.

That would be consistent with her beliefs.

42

Dr. Emil Sanchez practiced adult psychiatry out of his ivy-covered cottage in Astoria, just back from the road and far enough removed from town there was peace in his days and nights. He had formerly served in Iraq and Afghanistan as a Navy doctor and was finished with the clang and clamor, the booms and explosions, of military and industry. Now, all he wanted was to help those who came to him with the kinds of problems found in a more rural America—depressions, bipolars, the occasional psychosis, eating disorders, anxiety, and the like. Then again, occasionally there was the sad case like the one he would be seeing in ten minutes, the case of the girl who wanted only to die. The girl's name was Rachel Sundstrom and she was, when last seen, terminally ill.

At 1:30 she was shown into the office by Emil's husband, Nate, who also served as his administrative assistant. The patient was accompanied by her nurse, Johann Van Giersbergen. Together, they came into the office and took seats on the leather couch facing Emil's office chair. He greeted them warmly as they sat.

"Hello, you must be Rachel?"

"Yes, and this is my nurse, Johann."

"Well, I'm Doctor Sanchez but please call me Emil—everyone does."

"Okay."

"So, last time we met there was talk of end of life planning. Is that still where we are?"

"Actually, the doctors think I'm in remission right now. So...I don't know what to think."

"That's wonderful, Rachel! How do you feel about that?"

"How do I feel? Relieved and scared. Scared that it's too good to be true since everything didn't work when I was in La Jolla. It's like getting out of jail."

"What did your oncologist try, radiation?"

"Yes, radiation plus dietary and vitamins and minerals. The tumors in my back are shrinking, and she thinks they might disappear. It's like God has blessed me in a new way."

The doctor turned his attention to Johann. "What can you report?"

"Oh," he said, "entirely new attitude. And much more sleep and happy times. She's a totally different patient than the one I first saw. I'm so happy for her. We cry together sometimes."

"I'm sure you do. So, we're out of the end-of-life planning, of course, and now we're into the embracing of new hope. This is what, your first remission?"

"No, it happened early on. But this one was unexpected. Thank God she tried me on radiation again."

"What about the meds, the Zoloft? Any changes there?"

"The depression is definitely better. I'm not all gloom and doom. I can actually see some light at the end of the tunnel."

"What are your plans—if I may call them that?"

"Well, if this keeps going on, I'd like to start school in September. Maybe a junior college after I get my GED. I had to drop out of high school my senior year and never did graduate. But the GED should be a skate for me."

"I'm sure," said the psychiatrist. "Any ideas what you'd like to study?"

"Marine biology. I want to work at Scripps."

"The dream of a lifetime," said the doctor. "I'd love to see that for you, then. Well, anything else I should know about?"

"Just one thing," Rachel said. "Johann is more than just my nurse. We've also become like boyfriend and girlfriend."

"How's that work? Can a nurse have a relationship with a patient, Johann?"

"I don't know. I wanted to talk to you about it."

"Well, it's probably inappropriate in most settings. But in a case like this, where it sprang up organically, and given the situation, I think I'd put the rules on the back burner. I can't come right out and say it, but that's what I think I'd do. How did you meet —nursing?"

"I was—am—his patient. We've done a month of night shifts together, and we talked about everything. For me, I liked Johann right off."

"And for me," said Johann, "my feelings were mutual. I'd never seen such a beautiful girl. But she was so sick, I couldn't even think about relationships, you know. That wouldn't have been good. But since she got the good news, we're both kind of coming out of our shells and talking more and telling each other how we really feel. I know from working at Rady's, I could get fired for falling for a patient, but this isn't a children's hospital. Besides, who knows? If something— I don't know how to say it. Let me try again. If the treatments aren't a hundred-percent successful, we want each other to know we have something that's going to last for however long we have. We aren't just two people who are going to someday go our own ways and say goodbye. That isn't what this is about now."

"Well said, Johann," said the doctor. "Wow. This is a lot to think about. My only advice to you both is to take it slow and see where it goes. If this is a new long-term chance for Rachel, wow, then who knows? That's certainly everyone's hope. So, the meds are good, life is good, and you're feeling much better. I'm glad to see this for you. Shall we make another appointment for a month and see where we are?"

"Yes," Rachel said. She was quick to jump at a follow-up. Johann nodded beside her.

The doctor handed Rachel a card with the new meeting date.

The couple left, smiling and leaving behind a doctor who was glad for the girl, cautious about the relationship, and hoping for the best.

The couple drove away in the Ford Explorer Thaddeus had rented, looking for a burger drive-thru. They found an A&W just inside the city limits and pulled in. The waitress came over, took their burger orders, and left.

"My back is hurting," Rachel confessed. "I think I'm not as well as I think sometimes."

"No one said you have to get well all at once. We'll do a day at a time."

"I'm thinking of a trip to the beach before long."

"Tomorrow?"

"Dusk. I want a sunset. It's been so long without a sunset."

"Dusk it is. I'll tell June so she has the night off."

"All right."

She leaned across the front seat and kissed her new boyfriend on the cheek. He turned to her and kissed her long and tenderly on the lips.

43

"The beach is calling," Johann said to Rachel two evenings later. She had been feeling stronger and had been talking about walking on the beach. He knew she wouldn't be walking far, but he was willing to carry her if that's what it took. Who knew, maybe old man ocean, Neptune himself, was calling? Was it her time?

First, he went down the road to the QuikMart and picked up supplies he would need on the beach. Then he loaded her supplies and meds and a fine meal from Colonel Sanders into the Ford. She was wearing a two-piece her mother had picked up in Astoria. Over it she was wearing cutoffs and a sweatshirt that said DUCKS and was green.

He took her hand and steadied her as she walked from the cabin to the SUV. He helped her into the passenger's seat and buckled her in, placing a pillow between her right side and the door so that, in her residual weakness, she didn't slump against the door. Nobody was imagining she was better than she really was. There was still considerable pain and great weakness. She needed help just to stand; she took morphine tablets regularly.

He slid his surfboard onto the roof rack and lashed it down with bungees. "Time to hit the waves!" he called to her from the rear bumper. She smiled gamely in the outside rearview mirror. He bowed and came around to the driver's side. In he climbed, checking her seatbelt once again, then buckling up himself. Off they went, heading for the beach two miles away.

It was about six o'clock. The sun was laying down long planks of golden light across the pacific, the surf was crashing and foaming on the shore, the seagulls were calling and swooping, while offshore, sprawled upon the huge rocks growing up out of the sea, a family of sea lions and a larger family of seals were taking in the lingering sun and eating their fill of top feeders.

Johann helped Rachel down the beach to a secluded spot. They laid out the blanket he brought. Then he produced—purchased an hour ago from the QuikMart—four red netted globes containing four large candles that he now used to pin down the four corners of the blanket. With a yellow lighter, he lit the wicks, and together they watched until the sun was lower in the west and the candle globes were glowing vermilion from the flames inside.

He sat down and put his hands behind him. She slid in between his knees and scooted until her back was against his chest. She dreamily reclined and watched the birds and the seals and the sea lions, thrilled that she was once again at the ocean's front door.

They sat together in this manner until the sun was half-gone below the horizon. As if on cue, his hand snaked around to the front and easily found the bottom seam to her sweatshirt. He crept his hand inside the sweatshirt until, finding her bikini top, he easily pushed it aside and held her taut breast in his hand. Then he repeated with the other hand. When he breathed against her neck, she relaxed into him until their bodies were pressed together at all pressure points and held in place as if glued.

He slowly lowered his legs and stretched them out and she followed suit. He dropped his left hand down from her sweatshirt to the shredded edges of her cutoffs. He skimmed his fingers along the edge of her bikini bottom and then pulled it aside, burying his fingers in the fine felt there, new hair growth from her recent remission. He inched his fingers closer to her center until they penetrated her outer lips. She moaned, turning toward him on the sand and then stretched out on along his body. Exhausted from the effort, she didn't resist as he undressed her. He pulled another beach blanket from his backpack and unfolded it to cover them.

Then he entered her, and they remained together as they had wanted for days now. Ever so slowly, he began moving his hips beneath her and she responded—as much as she was able, still holding herself on top him, determined to satisfy him with her hurting body. At long last, he climaxed, and she almost immediately slipped to the side onto her back, completely helpless on the blanket. She could only grunt out two words, "Pain pill."

He fed the elongated white capsule into her mouth, and she washed it down with bottled water. Lying yet on her back, she felt the warmth of the blanket cover her body and felt him tuck it in along the sides. Then she sensed he was over her; her eyes had closed against the pain that had come roaring back. She felt his lips on her own, nuzzling and hungrily saying to her that she owned him now, that he was hers and he would be with her from then on.

When the sun was completely gone, he stood and pulled the backpack onto his back. Then he bent and scooped her up in his arms, double blankets and all, and walked with her back to his SUV. He again belted her in and pressed the ignition button. The car sprang to life. He switched the thermostat to 76 and punched up the fan several times, up to five bars until it was spinning hard and expelling a warm stream of air onto her to drive away the chill of the night air. He took her hand in his after shifting into drive, and off they went, headed back up the sand-blown road, along a street with surf shops and black light outlets, headed for the highway and home.

He thought to himself, *in such a way, we are reminded that to be one, there must be a giving of oneself times two.*

44

Thaddeus had filed a FOIA request with the FBI, seeking all documents regarding Johann Van Giersbergen. It had taken two weeks to get a return.

He had filed a FOIA—Freedom of Information Act—lawsuit and discovery motion with the court, which he pushed through, getting authority to take the deposition of FBI agents working out of the Mexico City office. He began by setting the deposition of Angelo Andrus on a Monday. He left San Diego Sunday morning, headed for Mexico City.

Monday arrived, and the parties met in the conference room of a temporary office Thaddeus had rented by the week in Mexico City. The U.S. Attorney in San Diego sent Assistant U.S. Attorney Manuel Esposito to cover the depositions. Esposito was a lifer, forty-five years old, a barrel-chested man who was all muscle from working out every morning before going to the office. He was dark with black hair and a full beard. Rimless eyeglasses completed his look, a seldom-smiling face being his key feature. A serious man,

Esposito. Thaddeus knew him from prior cases in San Diego and had a high respect for the prosecutor.

"Manuel," he said, shaking hands as they arranged themselves around the conference room table in the windowless, poorly lighted room. Nice touches such as coffee and pastries were unavailable, but four bottles of water perched in the center of the long table.

"Mr. Murfee," said Manuel Esposito, "I plan on these depositions taking no longer than fifteen minutes each where you will get particulars about the agents and then a short statement about their roles on the case. That's all. I intend to allow you no room to maneuver any farther afield than that. Your attempts to do so will result in me instructing my agents not to answer." He wasn't smiling as he dictated the government's terms.

Not smiling himself, Thaddeus replied, "Interfere with my deposition at your risk, Mr. Esposito. If you do, I will stop the deposition, call the court and ask for a court order. Plus, I'll be asking for attorney's fees against the U.S. Attorney's office. Proceed with your interference at your own risk."

"We'll see, Mr. Murfee, we'll see. Please proceed. I have a plane to catch back to the States."

"Plaintiff calls Angelo Andrus," Thaddeus said, and the court reporter began moving her fingers across the keys of her portable machine.

After Esposito went to the door and summoned him, the agent entered the room. Thaddeus looked him up and down. For some reason, he looked familiar. Caucasian, maybe thirty-six or thirty-seven years old, wearing khaki pants and a long-sleeved blue oxford button-down shirt, tassel loafers, and a suede sports coat, brick in color, and a baseball cap with NY letters. He appeared confident but not cocky and smiled easily at everyone in the room after taking his seat. Thaddeus thought him the typical, sociable FBI agent who knew how to charm a room and work through a cocktail party in style. On his right ring finger was a naval academy ring, unmistakable in the size of its grand stone. "So," he said to no one and smiled because life was great to him.

Thaddeus wasted no time. "Please state your name for the record."

"Angelo T. Andrus."

"Your business or occupation?"

"Special Agent, Federal Bureau of Investigation."

"How long have you worked for the FBI?"

"Fifteen years."

"What department do you work in?"

"Counter-intelligence."

"Explain to me what that means."

"Well, Mr. Murfee, the United States is the most spied-upon country in the world. It is estimated that Washington, DC has more alien spies living there than the lawyers, which we measure by the bushel basket. This gives you some idea."

"Where do these spies hail from? Name the three largest exporters of spies to the U.S."

"China, Russia, United Kingdom."

"Our own ally is spying on us?"

He smiled easily. "Mr. Murfee, I'm told everyone spies on everyone."

"Tell me what you know about spies in Mexico City."

"Well, I don't usually work in Mexico City, so what I would know would be hearsay. I'm not allowed by bureau policy to offer hearsay in official inquiries, so I'll defer that question to the local agents."

"Tell me who are the typical spies?"

"Let me harken back to Washington, DC. It's unprecedented—the threat from our foreign adversaries, specifically China on the economic espionage front. The variety of spies has diversified. Your typical spy is nondescript. A spy is going to be someone that's going to be a student in school, a visiting professor, your neighbor, maybe even your son. It could be a colleague or someone that shares the soccer field with you," Andrus said.

"Even a young surfer dude, perhaps?"

Andrus's eyes narrowed almost imperceptibly. "Yes."

"What about counter-intelligence. Your field. How does that work?"

"Embassies and diplomatic missions for hundreds of years have been used to spy in adversaries' lands. Even when spies are discovered, it's often more fruitful to follow them discreetly than to expel them. The cat-and-mouse game of counterespionage is about understanding who that officer is in touch with. This activity of following and watching is how I pay my mortgage. The films have made it much sexier than it actually is. We follow, we watch, we report."

"And you arrest?"

"Not all that often. More often, counter-intelligence will feed a known agent disinformation—false information—to take back to his handlers. For example, in the month of January, the U.S. might actually be exporting a billion tons of wheat to Japan—we'll fudge it instead and make it two-hundred million tons, that's the rigged number we'll give the spy so that China hears two-hundred and thinks, oh, yes, Japan is becoming more able to meet its own wheat needs than last year. As you can see, what I do is anything but glamorous."

"Special Agent Andrus, I defended Johann Van Giersbergen on a charge of conspiracy to commit murder based on the explosion here in Mexico City. In that explosion, his father died. I have filed and received discovery documents from the U.S. Attorney in the case. Those documents indicate that you were surveilling Johann Van Giersbergen at the time of his father's death. Were you surveilling him?"

"Objection," said Manuel Esposito as calmly as a fish making bubbles. "Don't answer that question, Agent Andrus."

Thaddeus sat upright. "For the record, counsel, you're instructing your client not to answer whether he was surveilling Johann Van Giersbergen at the time of Ned's death?"

"That is correct."

Thaddeus turned back to Andrus. "Tell us why you were surveilling Johann Van Giersbergen."

"Object. National security. Don't answer."

Without addressing the attorney this time, Thaddeus went on. "Was Johann Van Giersbergen a foreign agent?"

"Object. National security. Don't answer."

"Counsel," Thaddeus said to Esposito, "this is going to be your course of action for the rest of such questions?"

"Any and all questions directed to the witness that seek to ascertain his work detail is privileged, a matter of national security of the United States, and protected by law. He will not be allowed to answer."

Thaddeus reached into his pocket and produced his smartphone. Placing it on speakerphone, he dialed the number for Judge Mavis McIntyre in San Diego, the judge assigned to the FOIA case. Six minutes later, he finally had the judge on the line.

"Your Honor, we're sitting here in Mexico City and I'm attempting to obtain the deposition of Angelo Andrus, as per your order allowing me to take depositions here. Mr. Andrus works counter-intelligence for the FBI, and I've attempted several times now to inquire as to his work detail and connection with Johann Van Giersbergen, son of one of the fourteen deceased victims in the Mexico City bombing. Mr. Van Giersbergen was a nurse out of San Diego who, I have reason to believe, was being surveilled by the FBI's counter-intelligence arm. The FBI at one time alleged his activities were tied to the bombing. Counsel for the government, Manuel Esposito, has directed a special agent to refuse to answer my questions in this regard. So, I'm calling you, asking for your order directing Mr. Andrus to answer."

"Counsel," the judge's voice clearly rippled through the still, warm air of Mexico City, "what is the government's position regarding this information? Why shouldn't the FBI give up information allowable under the Freedom of Information Act?"

"The information sought is a matter of national security. It threatens the United States."

"Understand," said the judge, "but here is my dilemma. The FBI wanted me to put this young man in jail for thirty years but now won't tell me what the FBI's role was in the case it was complaining about? Does that sound fair to you?"

"Maybe not fair, judge, but necessary to national security," said Esposito.

"Mr. Murfee?"

"Again, Judge, I'm only asking for case connections and activities. I'm not attempting to divulge national secrets here."

"I think I'm going to allow the questions, gentlemen. Mr. Murfee, please continue. Mr. Esposito, instruct your client to answer those questions. Mr. Murfee, if the obstruction continues, call me right again, don't be shy. Attorney's fees next time around."

"Thank you, Your Honor," said both attorneys in unison.

Thaddeus ended the call on his phone. He looked at Esposito and shook his head before speaking. Then, "I've gotta pee. Get your man ready to answer while I'm gone."

45

Sandwiches had been brought in for lunch and soda pop and coffee since the parties had agreed to an early lunch before continuing. They sat around the conference table, trading tales and barbs as old friends will do before taking up the case again.

At 12:30, following brief walks around the block, restroom breaks, and coffee refreshers, the deposition resumed with everyone in their place.

Thaddeus began where he'd left off. "Mr. Andrus, earlier I asked whether you were surveilling Johann Van Giersbergen. Please answer that now pursuant to the court's order."

"Yes."

"You were surveilling?"

"Yes."

"Why?"

"Because we sometimes run quality assurance checks on our agents' families."

"Seriously?" asked Thaddeus. He might have been amused were the case not so deadly serious. "Quality assurance checks?"

"We're all human, Mr. Murfee. Even FBI agents' families."

"Your surveillance was only about quality assurance?"

His smile never faded. "Now, I didn't say that."

"Then what other reason than quality assurance were you surveilling Johann Van Giersbergen?"

"Ned was playing a very important role when he died. I was working to ensure things went as we wanted."

"As who wanted?"

"The government. The FBI."

"Was Ned acting on behalf of the government at the time he died or against the government?"

"Neither one."

"How's that?"

"His activities were being monitored. That's all I know."

"Good guy or bad guy, Mr. Andrus?"

"He was FBI, so he was a good guy."

"But there were questions?"

"There was surveillance. We were finding out what we could."

"Did the FBI want Ned Van Giersbergen dead?"

"Sir?"

"Did the agency want Ned to die?"

"Sir, the FBI never wants its agents to die."

"Had Ned ever been observed passing secrets to a foreign power?"

"Not observed, no."

"Was Johann observed cooperating with or associating with a foreign power?"

"Object! National security."

"Seriously? Do I need to call the judge again?"

"I would save up and call him on all of them if I were you," said Mr. Esposito.

Thaddeus instead made the call right then. Again, the judge ordered the agent to answer. This time the judge was not nearly as easygoing. His tone said he was getting to the end of the line with the FBI. He awarded a day's legal fees to Thaddeus, as well.

Thaddeus began again. "Was there a suspicion Johann was passing secrets to a foreign power?"

"There is always suspicion in the FBI. We monitor many, many people."

"Please answer. Was Johann suspected?"

"There was—there was an interest in whether Johann was completely on the up and up."

"What's that mean, 'up and up'?"

"Well, when he was surveilled, there were questions about his actions."

"Such as?"

"Such as, was he actually looking for work here? Or was he trying to make contacts?"

Thaddeus sat back, frowning. "Mr. Andrus, we're playing word games here. I keep asking questions and you keep leading me away from any answer with your vague references to suspicion, to interest, to questions. You're phrasing and re-phrasing the same vague responses to keep me guessing. If this continues, I'm going straight back to the judge. Now, I'm going to ask again, what concerns did the FBI have about Johann Van Giersbergen at his father's death?"

"We were looking into the actions of Ned's family member. There was a question whether Johann Van Gierbergen had been aware the bombing was coming."

Bingo. Now he had what he'd come for.

"Aware, or a participant in that bombing?"

"That's what we were surveilling, whether he was involved in transporting explosives."

Again, he finally had his answer.

"So, there was a suspicion Johann was working with the bombmakers?"

"'Working with' is stronger language than I'm using. There was a suggestion he might have been sympathetic to Middle Eastern interference."

"How might have he been showing his sympathy?"

"We—we had evidence that Johann set up a California corporation that was funneling money into Facebook by buying ads there."

"Ads such as?"

"Political ads. I can't say any more than that. Go back to your judge if need be, but that's as much as I can give you, Mr. Murfee, because I don't know any more than that."

"Who else would know more?"

"Unknown."

"Agent Andrus, who do you report to?"

"As in my SAIC?"

"Yes, who is in charge of what you do."

"That would be Robyn Brennan. She's in Los Angeles."

"Los Angeles FBI field office?"

"That's right."

"Mr. Andrus, that's all I'm going to ask you today because you've just told me you won't go further. But I will want to come back to you, sir. Oh, and one last question. What's the name of the California corporation set up by Johann?"

"That would be the National Broadcasting Consortium."

"NBC?"

"NBC, yes."

"Thank you. That concludes my questions."

"Deponent will read and sign," said Manuel Esposito, meaning his witness would read the deposition and then sign off—or not—as to its accuracy.

46

It was a bluestone diamond, 1.5 carats, that found its way from Johann to Rachel's ring finger. She was shocked as she moved from reclining in her hospital bed to a sitting position. Her mouth opened wordlessly, closed, then, "Seriously?"

"Uh-huh," he muttered. "Expressing my love. Will you marry me?"

"Seriously?"

"The sooner the better."

"I haven't even thought about it. Give me awhile." But then she smiled at him. The way he looked at her, she could see the same love she held in her own heart. "Yes, okay, I do. I will!"

"On the sand, foam lapping at our ankles, a friendly preacher."

"Johann!"

"I don't want to wait. I love you, you love me. Why wait?"

"My mother and father—"

"They'll approve. They love me, I'm sure."

"Of course, they do."

The couple approached the parents. Jim Sundstrom welcomed the idea with the caveat that they wait and see how the remission goes with his daughter. Louisa Sundstrom thought it worked "sometime down the road," something to be looked forward to, prepared for, approached cautiously. The young people settled it between themselves: 72 hours.

She wanted the vows exchanged beneath a chuppah so Johann drove to Portland and back all in one day to buy one for her. He also located a Methodist minister to perform the ceremony since he had agreed to both chuppah and surf. He called his mother, the surgeon in Los Angeles, to attend. She was beyond happy and said she wouldn't miss it for anything. She would be there. The two fifteen-year-olds, Becca and Celena, were enlisted as members of the party on the bride's side. The groom had met two surfers who grumbled but said, in the end, yes, they probably had white shirts someplace and they would stand up with their fellow dude.

A rehearsal dinner was planned at the Seaside Golf Club where catering could be provided for as few as a dozen guests and where a house band would provide three hours of tunes for six-hundred dollars. As it happened, there was an engagement announced on Wednesday, rehearsal dinner on Thursday, and wedding on Friday, at noon, in the surf at Seaside.

The couple moved quickly, knowing that time was a precious thing. Neither knew what tomorrow or even the afternoon might bring. They were in love, so why wait?

Dr. Van Giersbergen was the financing arm of Johann's engagement, ring and wedding. There had long been a trust set up for Johann, and it vested upon his marriage. Johann's mother arrived at the campground by air from LA Thursday noon and was told she had a private bedroom waiting in the bus that was just for her.

The rehearsal dinner kicked off at six. Rachel took a morphine tablet before the dinner that did its job, though left her drowsy for most of the forty-five minutes she was actually able to attend. By seven-thirty, the dinner was over for everyone else, so the bus boys were making the rounds of the tables while the band played on, reverting from romantic ballads to hard rock favorites that no one listened to save the bus boys and the janitor.

The band finally finished at eight-thirty, helped the drummer take down his kit, and moved all the equipment to the waiting van. They were off into the evening just as the fireflies blinked to life along the beach. The rehearsal dinner was declared a success, and Rachel was in bed fast asleep before nine. Johann was in the room with her, tending to her, listening to her breathe, shuffling the bedpan in and out at midnight.

47

Thaddeus flew to San Francisco then drove to Facebook's Menlo Park headquarters, following the filing of his FOIA lawsuit against the FBI. This time, the Agency's civil arm would be defending the lawsuit, a woman named Rita Jennings at the helm. She had been in touch with Thaddeus several times, had objected in court to his successful quest to accelerate discovery depositions, and had already warned him there would be no settlement in the case, that the FBI civil arm would fight him to the bitter end—a challenge he gladly accepted, he told her.

They both arrived at Facebook about the same time and were waiting to be shown into the company's deposition Suite H. Thaddeus surveyed the green building. All employee workstations were equipped with manually height-adjustable desks. Herman Miller's classic Aeron chairs provided the majority of seating. Even Mark Zuckerberg, the company's CEO, was located at one of the open plan workstations provided for all employees. He did, however, also have a personal conference room, according to the Welcome to Facebook brochure. Treadmill workstations were also spread throughout the campus, and for those seeking natural light on their workstations, the layout provided a mixture of windows and skylights.

Moving through the first building, Thaddeus was shown into the legal operations area where there were private offices and where deposition rooms abounded.

The depositions were being taken at the company headquarters rather than at Thaddeus's office because he'd wanted proximity to Facebook's records, as the first witness he was after was the custodian of records for the sprawling giant.

Assembled around the giant conference/deposition table were Thaddeus, Rita Jennings from the DOJ representing the FBI, Amity Nobeker from Facebook's legal department, Jimmy Morris from Facebook's records department, and a court reporter and videographer. Thaddeus wanted video just in case the chairs got moved around on down the road and he needed to prove who'd been present by a face count. Oftentimes, custodian deps are handled cavalierly, but not this time; he wasn't taking any chances, given that a recent ex-client's FBI surveillance might still be ongoing.

He began the questioning with the usual admonition and then addressed Jimmy Morris with his first substantive question: "Do you have any record of advertising purchases by a company calling itself National Broadcasting Consortium?"

Jimmy Morris consulted his laptop, evidently tapping into the monstrous company database. "Yes, I have hundreds."

"How many hundreds?"

"Wait while I change the query to request a count. Here we are, four-hundred-and-twelve incidents of advertising buys."

"Covering years 2015 and forward?"

"That would be—again, I'm varying the database query. That narrows it down to three-hundred-seventy-seven, Mr. Murfee."

"How do we get copies of those ads?"

"I'd have to sort them out and establish them in a photo album for ease of use and send them to you."

"Can you do that right now?"

"Sure, it will take about five minutes."

"Please proceed. I can wait."

"Give me your emails, everyone, and you'll all get a copy," said Jimmy, already at work compiling the jpeg catalog of files. "How can you use these, Mr. Murfee? I'm not prepared to answer questions about them."

"Who can I ask about the contents of the ads, Jimmy?"

"That would be up to the advertising department."

"Counsel," said Thaddeus off the record, "who would I talk to about the ads?"

Amity Nobeker raised a finger and ducked her eyes to her laptop screen. "That would be either Norm Blackwell or Mary Esther Cummings. They both handled the account."

"So, there was an account rep?"

"Yes, two over the course of the years you've queried."

"Is there any chance we could get them in here now?"

Facebook was there to please. They had no problem handling Thaddeus's request, even though his request was very unusual:

learning a deponent's name the same day you took the deponent's statement.

Amity dialed her cell phone. She asked Norm Blackwell for help. He was out of the office. So, she dialed up Mary Esther Cummings. She said she'd be right with them.

"You ask, you receive," Amity joked at Thaddeus.

They refreshed their drinks at one of the food courts and returned inside. Mary Esther Cummings had joined them. She was a full-bodied, pretty woman in her early thirties with a wonderful smile and warmly welcomed the visitors to Facebook.

Then Thaddeus began. "Ms. Cummings, I understand you've been an account executive for National Broadcasting Consortium, is that correct?"

"Yes, another gentleman and I rep them now. I have North American sales."

"Regarding their advertising, what is the usual subject matter?"

"They are a socially-conscious company with a political agenda. They're neither Left nor Right but are more of an economic political bent."

"What kind of economics?"

"If I were pushed, I'd say extreme socialism."

"Consider yourself pushed."

"All right."

"Does extreme socialism equate to communism?"

"I wouldn't go that far. And maybe I misspoke. Maybe I'd say their bent is more Eastern."

"As in eastern United States or what we normally call the eastern part of the world."

"Further east."

"As in Middle East."

"Yes, as in Afghanistan."

"The advertisements are pushing Middle Eastern agendas?"

"I wouldn't say that at all. There's nothing wrong or illegal about foreign countries having opinions on American elections, Mr. Murfee."

"I hope you aren't under the impression I'm saying that. I'm only trying to understand their main thrust. I know your ads are largely images with very small amounts of text allowed."

"I'd say their thrust is neither Left nor Right. They seem to want to create a variety of positions and encourage many different political positions among their viewers."

"You're telling me they're trying for chaos?"

"They certainly aren't looking for a reasoned, systematic politic, no."

"In other words," said Thaddeus, "National Broadcasting Consortium is trying to create confusion among its more political viewers?"

"Yes. I must say, that seems to be the case."

"Is there anything illegal about that?"

"Nothing illegal or wrong with it, as far as I'm concerned."

"Let's talk about that phrase, 'as far as I'm concerned.'"

"Okay."

"Do you answer to anyone in terms of which ads you approve?"

"Our ads are approved and disapproved by artificial intelligence. It's only when there's an appeal from a user that a human gets involved."

"Would that appeal be to you?"

"Never. We have teams that handle the appeals. Shift workers."

"Where are they located?"

"Physically?"

"Yes."

"The appeals teams work around the world, Mr. Murfee. They're everywhere and nowhere."

"Do they have political agendas?"

"Never. You couldn't patch together a consortium of one political tendency from among all these workers in your wildest dreams. They are everything and they are nothing. But they do all have one thing in common: they try to implement Facebook policy."

"And that policy is what, where electioneering advertisements are concerned?"

"Only that they cannot be over thirty words of text, they cannot contain profanity, they cannot be insulting to religious beliefs of any ilk, stuff like that."

"So, it's more in the nature of use than substance?"

"I'd say so, yes. Company policy. No profanity. No religion, no sexism, no personal attacks, and so forth. But anything else is open season."

"So, an ad could attack the color blue, for example, but couldn't attack Joe Blow."

"Exactly."

"But it could contain a short story about Joe Blow."

"Yes."

"Even if the story were untrue."

"What is true or untrue, Mr. Murfee? In the end, it's all opinion."

"So, stories can say whatever the advertiser or poster wants them to say?"

"That is correct. As long as there isn't profan—"

"Religious, sexist, personal attacks, and so on."

"Now you're talking."

"So, I could post a story on my page saying Joe Blow is a communist or sympathetic to communism, and Facebook wouldn't ever object to that or try to limit it?"

"Correct."

"All right. Let's leave it right there as far as substance. Who is your supervisor, Ms. Cummings?"

"We don't have supervisors at Facebook. We have team leaders."

"Who might that be?"

"It depends on the topic. It could be any number of people."

"Regarding the substance of Facebook ads, who would you report to?"

"John M. Schell, Jr."

"Thank you. I believe that is all. And thanks so much for coming right in."

"No problem. Thanks for giving me the workout."

"All right, you're excused unless anyone else has questions?"

"No questions," said Amity.

"No questions," said Rita.

"You're excused, Ms. Cummings. Thanks again."

48

The wedding ceremony was short but beautiful. Johann wore khaki linen pants rolled at the ankles and an open white shirt with a collar. He waited at the chuppah that had been placed just at the surf's edge so that the couple would literally marry in the ocean. The waves lapped at his feet, shifting the soft sand around him so that his toes were covered in the first few minutes. Next to him were two of his surfer friends he'd made while staying in Oregon, both wearing white collar shirts and board shorts. The minister wore a clerical collar and shirt but black shorts instead of a cassock.

Dr. Sundstrom had carried Rachel down from the carpark, and she and her two bridesmaids, Becca and Celena, waited in a small line for the music to start. When Jim nodded, Sandy played "Ode to Joy" on his phone, broadcasting the music over a Bluetooth speaker. The song was Rachel's choice, for at this point, she felt she had a second chance at life.

First Celena and then Becca, both in pale rose sundresses, walked slowly to the chuppah. They had a small bouquet of wildflowers each and both turned and stood to the side opposite the surfers.

Rachel took her father's arm. Johann thought she was the most beautiful thing he'd ever seen. She wore a ringlet of wildflowers in her hair, which was down and loose, long blond waves around her shoulders and down her back. Instead of a bouquet, she carried only one single long-stem rose. She smiled at him as she walked, their gazes locked onto one another.

When she reached Johann, the music faded away. Dr. Sundstrom released her arm and handed her over to Johann. In her bare feet, she came up to his chin. She wore a simple white strapless sundress that came mid-calf on her leg. He took both of her hands in his, and the ceremony began.

It was short and sweet. Just perfect. The sun was shining overhead, the seagulls crying out, the waves crashing softly on the shore. After they said their "I dos," everyone came in for hugs and then Johann carried his bride back up the sand to picnic tables set out with food.

There was music and plenty of laughter that afternoon. They had set up a hammock so Rachel could nap when she needed to. June helped her with her medicine as the day wore on and she became more tired. The small group consisted of Johann's mother, Rachel's parents, Celena and Becca, June and Sandy. The two surfers left shortly after they'd stuffed their bellies, but Johann didn't care. All he wanted was Rachel.

And now he had her.

Just after four p.m., Johann announced he was taking his bride back to their cabin. It was time for them to be alone. There were some giggles from Celena and Becca, but the others willingly gave up their Rachel to Johann.

He carried her to the Ford Explorer and belted her in. When she smiled at him and told him how happy she was, he kissed her gently on the lips. By the time they made it back to Cabin 5, Rachel was asleep, so Johann carried her across the threshold, just like they used to do when two young people were married.

He laid her onto the bed, still dressed in her wedding gown. He lay down next to her and rested his hand on her stomach.

She must have read something in his action because she said, "I know what a man and wife are supposed to do at the end of their wedding night...but I'm too tired. I'm so sorry, Johann. Do you mind?"

Like any virile young man, he was always into sex, but he understood. "Not at all. I'm happy just to lay here next to you. We can talk if you like."

"Okay," she said and turned to her side. But her breathing grew deeper, as if she was settling into another sleep.

"I was thinking," said Johann, "that now we are married, you might want to take my religion."

Her eyes popped open. "I didn't even know you were religious, Jay." That was the nickname she called him.

"Yes, very. I converted to Islam when I worked in Afghanistan."

"Really? When you were with Doctors Without Borders?"

"Yep. It's the only religion out there. You'll love it. And you'll be proud to call yourself Muslim."

"Well...I'm not so sure I want to." She cradled his cheek with her hand. "Honestly, my mom and dad are super Christian. You know that. And their religion was what kept me from ending my life when I wanted to. I'm really not sure I want to change to anything right now."

"But don't you see?" asked Johann. "Because they forbade it, you're alive today, right?"

She sighed. "I can see your point. I'm just not ready to jump ship, I suppose. I'm still not sure what I believe." She laid her head down on the pillow and closed her eyes.

Johann pinched her chin and turned her face his way. "You'll believe what I believe."

She frowned, her eyes dull with fatigue and pain. "You're scaring me, Jay."

Yes, he realized he was, and that probably wasn't the way to win her over. He needed her to want it as much as he did. "Let me introduce you to Islam, at least. I can take you to the Mosque when we return to La Jolla. There is even an Islamic high school just down the road from the hospital I worked at where our kids can go when they are older."

Her brows pierced in confusion. "Jay, what are you talking about?"

"Our kids. They will be Muslim like you will be."

"I said I didn't—"

"Shhhh," he said and laid a finger on her lips. "Of course, you will."

She sat up, taking precious energy to do so. "No, Jay, I won't."

"Lay back down." Johann soothed her by running his hand over her hair until her eyes drooped. "Everything will be okay."

Her exhaustion made her sleep, a troubled look on her fine features.

49

J ack Rasso called Thaddeus Friday afternoon. Rachel and Johann had been married three hours at the time of the call. Thaddeus hadn't heard from Jack for a few weeks and was somewhat surprised to see his number come up on his cell.

"Jack, Thaddeus here. What's up with you?"

"Thaddeus, I know you're still knocking around with the FOIA lawsuit and the discovery efforts you've undertaken."

"Yes."

"I'm referring to the Johann Van Giersbergen boy, Ned's son."

"Yes. I still have my questions. See, Jack, I've introduced him into the family of my long-time friends, Jim and Louisa Sundstrom. In fact, their eldest daughter just today married Johann. The girl is quite ill, so it's kind of a long story I won't take up your time with."

"Well, here's the thing I wanted to tell you. Can we talk off the record here?"

"Consider us off the record, Jack. What do you have?"

"Your Johann has been at times very active in the Surfriders Foundation group."

"I don't know about Surfriders Foundation," said Thaddeus. "What or who are they?"

"It's a foundation composed mainly of young people along the Pacific coast. Their chief activity, and it's a great one, no doubt, is taking to the ocean in kayaks and fishing plastic bottles out of the water. They collect it together beyond the surf, bring it to shore, and recycle it, as I understand. Anyway, I've been handed an incident report about Johann that I wanted to make you aware of."

"Can you send me a copy?"

"Can't do that, but I can summarize it."

"Good enough. Go ahead."

"In the summer of 2018, Johann was in his kayak with another worker by the name of Sue Ellen Wainwright. Sue Ellen was the daughter of a Coca-Cola bottler out of Oceanside. She was a student at SDSU and very active in Surfrider. In fact, she was a local officer and weekend warrior. They were in the kayak when, according to Johann, they hit a strong rip current. The kayak collapsed, and Sue Ellen couldn't make it to shore. Johann did make it in, swimming with the rip current as surfers will do, and he came out of it pretty much okay. Sue Ellen drowned. The police investigated as standard procedure, and there was a huge question mark in everyone's mind."

"Why was that?"

"Because Sue Ellen won the California Surfing Championship for Women in 2017 and was one of the strongest swimmers in the state. It couldn't have happened the way Johann said. But here's the kicker. He and Sue Ellen were engaged, and she had broken up with him two nights before, calling off the engagement. Nobody knows why, really, but they were slated to attend the Saturday cleanup together, so they went ahead with that anyway. It was part of the Foundation's work, and Sue Ellen lived and breathed the Foundation. According to the other kids there that day, the rip was always there. The surfers in the area all knew about it, and everyone pretty much dealt with it every time they went surfing. I don't know much about those things, but it evidently was a common enough occurrence that Sue Ellen should have had very little trouble coming ashore. Despite hours of questions by different investigators, Johann stuck to his story of kayak collapse due to a strong rip. This is what I wanted you to know. And now you tell me this same guy just married the daughter of your best friends? I'm a day late and a dollar short, as they say."

"I don't know. I've got to take this to Rachel's father. This sounds alarms all around, Jack. Could I have Jim Sundstrom call you and hear this from you?"

"I don't think that's such a good idea, Thaddeus. I'm bringing this to you under the table. I can't go on the record with it."

"Understood. Can I at least quote you?"

"Sure. Just keep my name out of it. 'An unnamed source,' kind of reference is fine."

"All right. Well, I don't know if I should thank you—yes, thank you. Really appreciate you taking the time, Jack."

"It's just this kid, Thaddeus. I know he was Ned's boy and all, but after the Mexico connection that we let go of, and now this with the drowned girl, my own alarms are going off and red lights are flashing. I know you know. I for damn sure wouldn't want my daughter around the guy."

"Nor I. So, thanks again. Let me talk to Jim, and we'll go from there. Thanks again, Jack."

"No problem. Adios, amigo."

"Goodbye."

THADDEUS'S GULFSTREAM LANDED IN PORTLAND. PASSENGERS aboard were Thaddeus, Turquoise, and Marcel. Sandy picked them up in the Mercedes. Before they hit the interstate, they stopped at a 7-Eleven and bought large coffees; Thaddeus dumped in a slug of half and half while Sandy took his black, as did the investigators. It was about three o'clock.

Driving on toward Seaside and the campground, Thaddeus's thoughts came back to the present. It still wasn't adding up: the FBI, the Semtex, the suitcase, the surveillance of Johann, the fact the only off-site trace of Semtex after the explosion was Johann's suitcase, the death of Johann's ex-fiancé.

He was troubled more and more by the juxtaposition of the young man described by the FBI and the reports he was now hearing from Jim Sundstrom about the wonderful Johann Van Giersbergen who Thaddeus had introduced as one of Rachel's nurses. They couldn't thank Thaddeus enough, they'd said.

Could it be that Johann wasn't all one way or the other? Could Johann still be a decent young man but still have passionate views on religion and the environment?

Perhaps, some people were both, but you never knew which, and that was how good people got hurt. Especially good FBI agents like Ned Van Giersbergen who just might've perished at his son's hands.

He shook his head hard as they were driving into the sun.

It was time to see for himself since he was back.

They drove into the campground, and Thaddeus located Jim inside the cabin, watching TV in the living area with Louisa. They were delighted to see him, and he expressed his apologies for not being able to attend the wedding in person. The door to Rachel's room was closed; Thaddeus assumed she was inside, in her bed, medicated.

"Jim and Louisa, can I talk to you about something that's come up?"

Jim pressed the mute button on the TV. "We're all ears."

"Let's go outside for this. It's private."

"Sure."

They went out on the front porch and sat themselves in the webbed porch chairs. The late afternoon was cool, and the air was breezy from the ocean two miles west.

"Sweater weather," said Louisa, who went back inside and then reappeared moments later in a blue sweater pullover.

"How's Rachel doing after her big day?" Thaddeus asked, motioning back inside toward the girl's door.

"We were just talking. She and Johann took off hours ago. Frankly, we're worried. It's really late, she's never been out this long without a much stronger IV than what the capsules provide for pain. We can't imagine," said Louisa.

Said Jim, "I did and didn't like this from the get-go. But what can you say? That you got between your sick daughter and the man she swears she loves? That you prevented her from marrying and then something bad happened to her? We're not those parents, Thaddeus, as you know. We politely butted out, but now we're quite worried for her. She should've been home by now."

"Were they in the red Explorer?"

"Yes, Sandy had the Mercedes to collect you from the Portland airport."

Thaddeus said. "What time was the ceremony yesterday?"

"Well, they didn't get around to doing it until one o'clock finally. It was late."

"Had they made plans for after? Like they had a party or a short trip? Anything?"

"Not yesterday. For today we arranged a BBQ at the beach. It didn't last for very long, just a couple of hours. We didn't want Rachel to overdo it," Jim said. "They didn't plan a honeymoon—how could have they? She's sick, too sick to travel anywhere but to the beach and home. But they're still not home. Damn it!"

"I'm thinking of driving around," Thaddeus said. "I have no idea where, but I'll start with the motels in Seaside."

"I'll go with you," Jim said.

"So will I," said Marcel.

"Why don't you all stay here?" said Thaddeus. "Just in case they show up here. If they do, perhaps keep Johann in line of sight until I can get back to you."

"Please hurry!" said Louisa.

50

He knew her weakening cries would wake up other campers along the beach if he rolled the window down to smoke. So, he left it rolled up while he enjoyed his Marlboros and she leaned her head against the window and existed somewhere between consciousness and sleep. The meds had run out hours ago and she was hurting, but he didn't want to go back, not just yet. First, they had to surf. She had expressed her love of the sport, and he wanted to take her in just once and let her feel the water again.

He regretted not having wet suits. The Oregon surf was meant to be encountered only from inside wetsuits.

There, she stirred again, moaning now, whispering.

"Yes, love?" he said.

"Home...please...hurts."

"We'll be going home very soon. But first, you get to surf. I brought my board, and you get to use it with me. We'll just wait for the sun to come out. Sunshine can mean five degrees warmer air."

"Home. Why won't you...? Why don't we...? Home..."

"I know, I know. We're out of those damn morphine tablets. I wish we had more, but we don't. Just bear with me, Rachel. We're on our way home just as soon as we ride a wave."

He reached across and pulled the blanket covering her. Then he raised her arms and removed the sweatshirt she was wearing. He decided to leave her shorts on—they were too damn hard to remove and not worth it. She'd still feel the ocean on her skin even with those. Then he climbed out and went around to her side of the car.

He opened the door, and it was all he could do to stop her from spilling out onto the sand. He looked around. It was too late for anyone else to be out and about as the sea was dark and surly. So, he reached across her body, grasped her far arm, and lifted her into a fireman's carry. He struggled beneath her weight down to the water's edge where the high tide was pounding the rocks.

Then he returned to the SUV and slid his surfboard off the roof. He quickly carried it back down. He lifted her by the arm, getting her partway to her feet and partway leaning on him, and struggled into the surf with her and the board. He placed the board in the knee-deep water and laid her down on her stomach on the surfboard. It looked like it was going to work just fine.

He began walking alongside the board, nosing it out toward the open sea now, moving into deeper and deeper water, now chest deep.

≈

CHIEF WYNN—SO NAMED BECAUSE OF HIS HONORARY TITLE AS THE chief of a local Indian tribe—and his wife and five-year-old daughter, parked in the lot above the surfing couple they saw out in the icy water. "They've got balls," said Chief. "Too damn cold for my blood."

"C'mon daddy," his daughter cried, "let's go down by the water!"

"Marilyn, I'll get the ice chest," said Chief. "Take Denisse and go on down."

The woman named Marilyn took the little girl's hand, and together they skipped over the sand, down to the water's edge. There, the mother unfurled a large red and yellow beach towel and then a large green beach towel. They both plunked down onto them, facing the incoming waves. "See the man and girl?" said Denisse. "Going swimming."

"Too damn cold for me," called Chief, holding the ice chest by the handles on either end. He trudged through the sand, a backpack hanging off one shoulder. As Chief Wynn and his family watched the man and girl with the surfboard, the man in the water turned the nose of the board and began walking laterally along the shore-line. When the Wynns had arrived, it had looked as if the couple were heading out to sea, bucking the waves, fighting to get beyond the breakers.

JOHANN SPOTTED THE FAMILY EXITING THEIR VAN. A MAN AND HIS wife and a kid. They began unloading an ice chest, umbrella, and it looked like a backpack. At just that moment, Johann decided against crashing through the first wave with Rachel on the board. The family might be watching. So, he turned the board ninety degrees and began crossing the water parallel to the breakers, parallel to the shoreline. He stood at the tail-end of the surfboard with his hands holding the tail-piece.

She lay stretched out on the board, her arms hanging off the sides, her hands trailing in the water. Her head was turned to the side, her mouth ajar, and from where he was positioned, it appeared her eyes were closed. He pushed very slowly through the water, bobbing on his feet where it was deep, the water threatening to turn the board over at any moment and spill its human cargo into the freezing boil of surf on the starboard side.

Rising and falling with the waves, the water depth was at his waist, then at his chin, while the girl floated ahead of him. She wasn't moving, wasn't moving her head when the waves came, and it looked like she was taking water down her throat, but Johann wasn't concerned. He knew she would cough up the water as she needed and keep her airway clear. It was a natural choking response, nothing serious, just the body's defense mechanism.

BACK ON THE SHORE, THE MAN AND THE GIRL HAD THE FULL attention of Chief Wynn. "Hey," he called to Johann, "did you need help out there?" But Johann didn't hear him. Or maybe he was ignoring him; Chief Wynn wasn't sure which.

"Goodness, she isn't even moving," Marilyn exclaimed to her husband. She had climbed to her feet and now stood facing the surfboard, her hands on her hips, her eyes squinting in the direction of the man and his human cargo. "Hey!" she called. "Are you all right out there?"

Ignoring or not hearing their calls, the man turned and began moving farther away, heading around a rock outcropping. At various times and places, the man had to hold onto the board and swim and kick as the water deepened. Then they were around the rocks and hidden from view of the man and his wife.

JOHANN TURNED THE NOSE OF THE BOARD TOWARD THE WAVES AND, lying half-sprawled atop Rachel, swam with her and the board through the first breaker, rising and now falling as the wave came in and then rolled away, leaving them in its trough as the sea arranged the next wave they would encounter. Johann was swimming now, holding the end of the board, pushing toward the second line of breakers. Suddenly, he felt a tug at his elbow. He turned in the water. The man from the beach had joined him. "Hey," the man said through a mouthful of water, "your wife isn't moving. Let's get her out of here."

Johann forced a look of surprise on his face. "You're right!" cried Johann. "That last wave must have caught her wrong!"

Together, the two men turned the board in the water and let the waves take them back to the shore. They waded from a dozen yards out, Johann carrying Rachel around her mid-section. The surfboard went ahead and crashed against the sand, where it lay, moving out then in as the waves came and retreated.

"Where's your car?" said Chief Wynn. His worried look told Johann that his surfing was over for now. He would have to take all steps to help his bride.

"It's the red Explorer up in the lot."

"Let me help carry her. Hell, this girl is freezing!" said the man

when he grasped Rachel's legs and began marching ahead of
Johann toward the SUV. They made it beyond the large rocks
ringing the parking lot. Johann's pocketed key sufficed to unlock
the doors when he pulled the handle. The man swung open the
passenger door and planted Rachel's feet and legs in the compartment. He then helped Johann arrange the rest of her body into the
vehicle. Chief Wynn reached across the seat and pulled the
blanket up and over the girl. He took her hand and rubbed. "Hey!
Miss! Can you wake up?"

"She really must've swallowed some water," said Johann.

"You know what, buddy? I'm signaling the lifeguards. Don't move."

The lifeguard tower was just off to the side of the parking lot.
Chief Wynn whistled a piercing whistle, and a guard looked down.
"She won't wake up!" he cried toward heaven.

The guards came running. One carried a backboard and one
carried a unit with an oxygen hose. They pulled Rachel out of the
vehicle onto the backboard and began applying CPR. Rachel
didn't respond. She remained unconscious.

"She's been very sick," Johann stuttered. "I think I just need to take
her home."

"Bullshit," said the lifeguard, a young blond man twice the size of
Johann. "You're not taking her anywhere."

Then they summoned an ambulance, and Rachel was loaded
inside. Johann climbed in back with her and off they went to the
hospital.

"Whoa," said the attending EMT as the vehicle roared along, "this
girl has an IV in her hand. Hey, buddy, what's up with all this?"

"It's a long story."

"You're pissing me off, man."

"It's a long story. I'm her nurse and her husband. She wanted to surf again."

"Not like this, asshole. This ain't right."

51

The hospital got the full story. The girl came around, her morphine drip was re-hung on a pole per her local doctor's orders, and she was returned home by ambulance that evening. She had managed to tell the attending physician and nurses her story of the hellacious day she'd just spent with her new husband after he left with her following their barbecue.

She told them how they had driven around, found a motel, and he'd made love to her, then they had gone down to the beach and parked. She guessed she had blacked out from then on because the next thing she remembered was regaining consciousness in the hospital. After arriving home, she told her mother and father and Thaddeus the same story.

"You were kidnapped," her father said. "That's the last you will see of Johann."

"What in the world?" said her mother. "He almost let you die!"

"Where is he now?" Thaddeus asked grimly.

"I saw him at the hospital. He said he was going back to the beach to get the car," Rachel said.

"Where's Marcel, he isn't around either?"

"He ordered a rental car. He left an hour ago. He was looking for you. Turquoise went with him."

"I'll go find Johann," said Thaddeus. "He and I need to talk. I brought him here, and I feel responsible. You all take care of Rachel. I won't be gone a half hour."

Thaddeus went into his bus and unlocked the top drawer in his bedroom. He removed a semi-automatic pistol and stuck it in the waistband of his jeans. He then jumped into his Mercedes and tore off in the direction of the beach.

When Thaddeus arrived, the red Explorer was empty of Johann, so Thaddeus pulled in alongside, doused his lights, and killed his engine. He could wait. He looked around. His Mercedes and the Explorer were the only vehicles in the lot. The lifeguard station was dark since they'd gone home hours ago.

Fifteen minutes later, a taxi pulled up on the other side of the Explorer and the door opened. Johann climbed out, still wearing his swimming trunks. He moved toward the driver's door of the Ford Explorer and then opened the door and climbed in.

A knock on the window. Thaddeus. Johann rolled down his window and smiled. "Hey, Thaddeus. Just headed back home. We had an accident out surfing today."

"You were surfing with Rachel? You knew she shouldn't be in that freezing water."

Johann laughed a forced laugh. "Oh, man, was it cold! It was too much for Rachel, so I took her to the hospital. I told her it was too cold, but she insisted on going."

"A guy told me you drowned a girl in La Jolla. Girl named Sue Ellen. Ring a bell?"

Johann's face paled in the dash lights. "Purely an accident. She drowned in a rip current."

"The same guy told me she was a better swimmer than you. How come she drowned, and you made it into shore?"

"She was unlucky. I was lucky."

"You know, Johann, I brought you into this family. Now I regret that. I need to clean up my mistake."

"We're married. I'm going to grab my wife and head back to California just as soon as I get back to the cabin and change my clothes. We'll be leaving tonight."

"Wrong answer."

Thaddeus whipped out the pistol and placed the muzzle between Johann's eyes. "I brought you into this family, and I can take you out."

"You wouldn't dare. I'm the new son-in-law."

"Oh, wouldn't I?" When Thaddeus cocked the gun, Johann's eyes widened. "Put your hands on the wheel."

"What?"

"Do it now, and slowly."

Johann placed his hands on the steering wheel at the nine and two positions.

"Good. Now, you want to tell me what happened in Mexico?"

"My dad died—that's what happened!"

"But how did he die, Johann? That's the question. There was no one for six square blocks around the scene that had any marking of Semtex in their luggage except you. So, I'll ask you again, how do you think it got there?"

"I have no—"

Thaddeus pressed the nuzzle of the silver gun to Johann's temple. "Think carefully on your response."

Johann snorted out his nose. "Maybe he deserved it!"

"Who are you to decide who does or doesn't deserve life and death?"

"The Americans do!"

"So, you think you have the right? Like with Sue Ellen? Like with the FBI agents, including your father?"

At first, Johann didn't say anything but stared straight ahead. A muscle in his jaw jumped when he ground his teeth together. "Sue Ellen deserved it, just like my dad. Yes, I did them and I'd do it again! You'll never understand, Mr. Murfee."

"What about Rachel? Did she deserve it too?" Thaddeus prompted.

Johann turned to face Thaddeus, lights from the dashboard betraying his rage. "Go ahead! Pull the trigger!" he shouted.

"Dad?" came a voice. It was Turquoise, but Thaddeus didn't move. He hadn't heard the second car arrive.

"Thaddeus?" This time Marcel. "How about I take care of things from here?"

Thaddeus kept his gaze on Johann, the gun leveled on his head. Turquoise and Marcel walked up to him. Turquoise took his gun from him and engaged the safety while Marcel opened the Explorer door.

"He confessed to me," Thaddeus drily whispered to Marcel. Marcel motioned for Johann to get out and then pinned him with his chest to the rear door. Marcel easily cuffed him with his belt and calmly asked Turquoise to call the police.

"Dad?" Turquoise repeated. "Are you okay?"

He didn't answer.

He had come close. So damn close.

52

Thaddeus went into Rachel's room and closed the door.

"Some men aren't who they seem," he said.

She was still exhausted from the beach and had caught a cold. "I know. They told me what happened."

"Johann has a long dark night ahead with the police and the FBI. We'll work to get the marriage annulled."

Tears came into her eyes. "I understand. When he was good, he was very, very good. But when he was bad—wow."

RACHEL'S ATTENDING PHYSICIAN WANTED TO SEE HER FOR A FOLLOW-up after treating her at the hospital. She appeared in his office with her father and mother. She was doing much better now and had been. Up and around, talking, making coffee in the cabin kitchen.

"Jimmy, our girl's getting her chatty back," said Louisa with tears in her eyes.

They arrived at the doctor's office five minutes early. Then she was taken into the examination room while her parents waited outside. The doctor did her vitals, listened to her heart and lungs, and asked her questions for ten minutes. She described the entire ordeal and, when Dr. Agnes Rosa was satisfied that all was well in her life once again, she sent Rachel on her way.

Jim and Louisa then took her to see her oncologist, Dr. Mindy Raintree. This time, the parents went with Rachel into the exam room. Dr. Raintree came in, smiling ear-to-ear, and wasted no time giving them the news. "She's in complete remission. The tumors in her back are gone. Her bloodwork is normal. I think we're looking quite good, folks."

Rachel's eyes clouded with tears. "Oh, God, thank you, Dr. Raintree. Thank you!"

"So, what does this mean for your life?" asked the doctor.

"School. Marine biology. Then Scripps in La Jolla. All I want to do is spend my life on the ocean."

"You might very well have a very long life to do that," said the doctor.

"One thing," Rachel said. "This is hard with my mom and dad here."

"Do you want us to leave?" asked her father.

"No, you should hear this. I still want Dr. Raintree to prescribe the end-of-life drugs. I want that prescription."

"Just in case," said the doctor. "I understand, and I will do that."

"So, if it happens again, I don't have to die a long, painful death. I can just take the medicine and fly away."

"Yes, fly away."

"Or go out with the tide."

The doctor took less than a minute to write the prescription.

"Less than a minute," Rachel said.

"Less than a minute," said her doctor. "May you never have to use them. But you have them if you do."

"Doesn't she have to have a life-threatening illness with a life expectancy of less than six months to get these medicines?" asked Louisa. "I don't see how you can just give her this."

"Oh, but she does. It's in remission, but she does have a life-threatening illness. If anyone asks, I'll add to that and say her life expectancy was six months when I wrote the prescription. I'm covered. She's covered. You—well, it's really only between her and her doctor." Dr. Rosa gave the mother a stern look.

Louisa backed away. "That's right. I was forgetting."

"Well," Rachel said, "Mr. Murfee's RV is waiting outside. I'm ready if everyone else is ready."

Thaddeus was driving the bus. Jim took the passenger seat while Rachel and her mother joined the others at the back around the table and on the couch. They pulled away from the curb and headed back south.

"What happened that night?" the doctor asked Thaddeus. "You came back looking like you'd seen a ghost. I've never seen you so upset."

"I don't know what you're talking about."

"Johann. What happened to him?"

Thaddeus stared ahead at the road. "Him? He had the wrong lawyer."

"The wrong lawyer?"

"We can make the border by nightfall."

"All right, then. Away we go."

THE END

UP NEXT: THE LAWYER

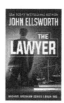

"The Lawyer is the very first book in the Michael Gresham Series, and the perfect place to start after the Thaddeus Murfee Series."

"Mr. Ellsworth is an excellent writer, as I would expect of a lawyer of so many years. This is a keep up late in the night to see what he comes up with next. Criminals are nothing if not crafty - at least in their own minds."

"The twist and turns in this legal thriller will have your head spinning. "

"I started to read this book with the intention of stopping for frequent breaks. That could not happen. Immediately I became addicted."

Read The Lawyer: CLICK HERE

ALSO BY JOHN ELLSWORTH

THADDEUS MURFEE PREQUEL

A Young Lawyer's Story

THADDEUS MURFEE SERIES

The Defendants

Beyond a Reasonable Death

Attorney at Large

Chase, the Bad Baby

Defending Turquoise

The Mental Case

The Girl Who Wrote The New York Times Bestseller

The Trial Lawyer

The Near Death Experience

Flagstaff Station

The Crime

La Jolla Law

The Post office

SISTERS IN LAW SERIES

Frat Party: Sisters In Law

Hellfire: Sisters In Law

MICHAEL GRESHAM PREQUEL

LIES SHE NEVER TOLD ME

MICHAEL GRESHAM SERIES

THE LAWYER

SECRETS GIRLS KEEP

THE LAW PARTNERS

CARLOS THE ANT

SAKHAROV THE BEAR

ANNIE'S VERDICT

DEAD LAWYER ON AISLE 11

30 DAYS OF JUSTIS

THE FIFTH JUSTICE

PSYCHOLOGICAL THRILLERS

THE EMPTY PLACE AT THE TABLE

HISTORICAL THRILLERS

THE POINT OF LIGHT

LIES SHE NEVER TOLD ME

UNSPEAKABLE PRAYERS

HARLEY STURGIS

NO TRIVIAL PURSUIT

LETTIE PORTMAN SERIES

THE DISTRICT ATTORNEY

JUSTICE IN TIME

EMAIL SIGNUP

Can't get enough John Ellsworth?

Sign up for our weekly newsletter to stay in touch!

You will have exclusive access to new releases, special deals, and insider news! Join today!

Click here to subscribe to my newsletter: https://www.subscribepage.com/b5c8a0

ABOUT THE AUTHOR

For thirty years John defended criminal clients across the United States. He defended cases ranging from shoplifting to First Degree Murder to RICO to Tax Evasion, and has gone to jury trial on hundreds. His first book, *The Defendants*, was published in January, 2014. John is presently at work on his 31st thriller.

Reception to John's books have been phenomenal; more than 4,000,000 have been downloaded in 6 years! Every one of them are Amazon best-sellers. He is an Amazon All-Star every month and is a *U.S.A Today* bestseller.

John Ellsworth lives in the Arizona region with three dogs that ignore him but worship his wife, and bark day and night until another home must be abandoned in yet another move.

johnellsworthbooks.com

johnellsworthbooks@gmail.com

Made in the USA
Columbia, SC
15 June 2020